PRAISE FOR

ALTERNATE SIDE

"Exquisitely rendered . . . [Quindlen] is one of our most astute chroniclers of modern life. . . . [*Alternate Side*] has an almost documentary feel, a verisimilitude that's awfully hard to achieve."

—*The New York Times Book Review*

"With her signature wisdom and wit . . . Quindlen once again proves she's the doyenne of hyper-local drama, this time with a dark and dangerous eye."

—*People* (Book of the Week)

"Anna Quindlen captures the angst and anxiety of modern life with . . . astute observations about interactions between the haves and have-nots, and the realities of life among the long-married. . . . Quindlen's book reads like a metaphor for our divisive times."

—*USA Today*

"[Quindlen] once again digs into the often-precarious nature of family life."

—*Parade.com*

"*Alternate Side* is not only about the ripple effects of one violent act in one desirable block but also endings and tentative new beginnings. It's the mature work of someone who knows marriages can be 'happy, miserable, and somewhere in between,' and the path from one to the other can be as unpredictable as a mudslide and just as irreversible."

—*Pittsburgh Post-Gazette*

"Quindlen's quietly precise evaluation of intertwined lives evinces a keen understanding of and appreciation for universal human frailties."

—*Booklist* (starred review)

"[In *Alternate Side*] Quindlen shows what a master she is."

—*NJ.com*

"Provocative . . . Quindlen's novel is an exceptional depiction of complex characters—particularly their weaknesses and uncertainties—and the intricacies of close relationships."

—*Publishers Weekly*

"A complex story of family, marriage, and alternating sides, this novel will leave you with a lot to think about after you've turned the final page."

—*PopSugar.com*

"If you're big on novels about seemingly perfect marriages between seemingly perfect people that get turned upside down by a big neighborhood incident, then you're going to want to pick up *Alternate Side*. Even if you're not a wealthy New Yorker and you've never fought over a parking space, you'll still love this story about a tight-knit community that's forced to take sides."

—*HelloGiggles.com*

BY ANNA QUINDLEN

FICTION

Alternate Side

Miller's Valley

Still Life with Bread Crumbs

Every Last One

Rise and Shine

Blessings

Black and Blue

One True Thing

Object Lessons

NONFICTION

Lots of Candles, Plenty of Cake

Good Dog. Stay.

Being Perfect

Loud and Clear

A Short Guide to a Happy Life

How Reading Changed My Life

Thinking Out Loud

Living Out Loud

BOOKS FOR CHILDREN

Happily Ever After

The Tree That Came to Stay

ALTERNATE SIDE

ALTERNATE SIDE

· *A Novel* ·

ANNA QUINDLEN

RANDOM HOUSE

NEW YORK

2018 Random House Trade Paperback Edition

Copyright © 2018 by Anna Quindlen
Reading group guide copyright © 2018 by Penguin Random House LLC

Published in the United States by Random House, an imprint and division of Penguin Random House LLC, New York.

Random House and the House colophon are registered trademarks of Penguin Random House LLC.

RANDOM HOUSE READER'S CIRCLE & DESIGN is a registered trademark of Penguin Random House LLC.

Originally published in hardcover in the United States by Random House, an imprint and division of Penguin Random House LLC, in 2018.

LIBRARY OF CONGRESS CATALOGING-IN-PUBLICATION DATA
Names: Quindlen, Anna, author.
Title: Alternate side: a novel / Anna Quindlen.
Description: New York: Random House [2018]
Identifiers: LCCN 2017047079 | ISBN 9780525509875 |
ISBN 9780812996074 (ebook)
Classification: LCC PS3567.U336 A79 2019 | DDC 813/.54—dc23
LC record available at https://lccn.loc.gov/2017047079

Printed in the United States of America on acid-free paper

randomhousebooks.com
randomhousereaderscircle.com

2 4 6 8 9 7 5 3 1

Book design by Caroline Cunningham

For Lynn Shi Feng

Exceptional mother, wife, and attorney

Beloved daughter (in-law)

The secret of a happy marriage remains a secret.

—HENNY YOUNGMAN

ALTERNATE
SIDE

"Just look at that," Charlie Nolan said, his arm extended like that of a maître d' indicating a particularly good table.

"Oh, my God, stop," said Nora Nolan, looking through the narrow opening of the parking lot, at the end of which she could just glimpse the front bumper of their car.

"It's beautiful, Bun," Charlie said. "Come on, you have to admit, it's beautiful. Look. At. That." That's what Charlie did when he wanted to make sure you got his point, turned words into sentences, full stop.

Some. Sweet. Deal.

Big. Brass. Balls.

The first night they'd met, almost twenty-five years ago, in that crowded bar in the Village that was a vegan restaurant now: You. Are. Great.

Really. Really. Great.

Nora could not recall exactly when she'd first begun to think, if not to say: Just. So. Annoying.

In the line of narrow townhouses that made up their side of the block, standing shoulder to shoulder like slender soldiers of flawless posture and unvarying appearance, there was one conspicuous break, a man down, a house-width opening to a stretch of macadam turned into an outdoor parking lot. It held only six cars, and since nearly everyone on the block wanted a space, it had become a hot commodity, a peculiar status symbol.

A book about the city's history, in the archives of a museum at which she had once interviewed for a job, had told Nora that a house in that space had been gutted in a fire, and the family that owned it had never bothered to rebuild. It had happened in the early 1930s, when the country, the city, and the west side of Manhattan had no money, which of course had happened again in the 1970s, and would doubtless happen again sometime in the future, because that was how the world worked.

At the moment, however, it seemed scarcely possible. A house on the next block had just sold for $10 million in a bidding war. The couple who sold it had bought it for $600,000 when their children were young. Nora knew this because she and her neighbors talked about real estate incessantly. Their children, their dogs, and housing prices: the holy trinity of conversation for New Yorkers of a certain sort. For the men, there were also golf courses and wine lists to be discussed; for the women, dermatologists. Remembering the playground conversations when her children were small, Nora realized that the name of the very best pediatrician had given way to the name of the very best plastic surgeon.

A single block in the middle of what seemed like the most populous island on earth—although it was not, a professor of geography had once told Nora; it was not even in the top ten—and it was like a small town. The people who owned houses on the block had watched one another's children grow up, seen one another's dogs go from puppy to infirmity to the crematorium at Hartsdale Pet Cemetery. They knew who redecorated when, and who couldn't afford to. They all used the same handyman.

"You live on that dead-end block?" someone had asked Nora at an art opening several years before. "One of my friends rented a place there for a year. He said it was like a cult."

None of those who owned on the block cared about the renters. They came and they went, with their sofa beds and midcentury-modern knockoffs, their Ikea boxes at the curb. They were young, unmoored. They didn't hang Christmas wreaths or plant window boxes.

The owners all did, and they stuck.

From time to time a real estate agent would troll the block, pushing his card through mail slots and scribbling notes about that odd empty parcel on the north side, to see who owned it and whether a new townhouse could be built there. For now it was a narrow, ill-kept parking lot, oddly shaped, like one of those geometry problems designed to foil students on the SATs: determine the area of this rhomboid. In the worst of the parking spaces, the one wedged into a cut-in behind the back of the neighboring house, Charlie Nolan's Volvo wagon, in a color called Sherwood Green, now sat. It had been there only for five hours, by Nora's reckoning, and already the windshield was pocked with the chalky white confetti of pigeon droppings.

That morning, just after sunrise, Charlie had flipped on the overhead light in their bedroom, his face lit up the way it was when he was part of a big deal, had underestimated his bonus, or paid less for a bottle of wine than he decided it was worth.

"I got a space!" he crowed.

Nora heaved herself up onto her elbows. "Have you lost your mind?" she said.

"Sorry sorry sorry," Charlie said, turning the light off but not moving from the doorway. There was a marital rule of long standing: Nora was to be allowed to sleep as long as she liked on weekends unless there was an emergency. She thought of herself as a person who had few basic requirements, but sleep was one of them. The six months during which her children had wanted to be fed, or were at least awake, in the middle of the night were among the most difficult months of her life. If she had not given birth to twins she might have had only one child, the sleep deprivation was so terrible.

Charlie knew this. He got up and went to work earlier than Nora, and the top of his dresser, the bathroom, his closet were all equipped with small flashlights by which he would dress, and dress again after he had taken the dog to the dog run, come home, and showered. Usually by the time he was in a suit and tie and eating his All-Bran, Nora was at the kitchen table in her nightgown, although it was her preference that they talk as little as possible in the morning.

Yet here was her husband, waking her on a Saturday, with the light full in her eyes.

"I got a space," he said again, but less maniacally, as though he was setting his emotional temperature closer to hers.

And now she could see their car in the space, already moved from the enclosed garage two blocks away to the dogleg in the lot. Charlie was humming to himself. When they had first moved to the block, Charlie asked around among the other parkers to see if he could inherit the space vacated by the people they were buying the house from. It was communicated in no uncertain terms, and in that osmotic way in which things became known on the block, that a space in the lot was a privilege, not a right, and Charlie somewhat truculently signed up for the indoor garage nearby, privately adding the failure to his list of Things That Were Not Going the Way They Should for Charlie Nolan, a list that in the last year Nora suspected had become a book, perhaps even an encyclopedia.

While Charlie often complained to Nora that the fee for the enclosed garage was only slightly less than the rent on their first apartment, there had never even been a question of parking on the street. Paying for parking relieved one of those petty aggravations that was like dripping water on the stone of self, until one day you discovered it had left a hole the size of a fist in your head. Nora knew that for Charlie, living in the city meant more drips, with harder water. He reminded her of it often enough. New York was not Charlie's natural habitat.

Nora hoped that this morning's triumph, small but seemingly monumental to her husband, would make up for that in some fashion. It had rankled for years, when Charlie passed the opening to the lot, and now he had finally scored a space. On the dining room table lay the typed notice, slipped through their mail slot, informing Charlie that the spot formerly allotted to the Dicksons was his if he wanted it; in the spot now was their Volvo. It was a car like their life, prosperous, understated, orderly—no food wrappers, no baby seats, no coins or crumbs on the floor. When the lease on the car was up it would barely need to be detailed before they got another just like it. Charlie always wondered aloud about other manufacturers, models, colors. Nora didn't care. She was scarcely ever in the car.

A white plastic bag eddied around Nora's bare ankles for a moment in a breathless summer breeze, touching her, tickling her, circling her painted pink toes. She kicked it aside and it moved down the block, rising and falling like a tiny ghost, disappearing between two parked cars. The street smelled like dank river low tide, melting tar, and, as always in warm weather, the vinegar tang of garbage. Nora had had to yank their dog away from a cardboard container of moo shu something, pulled from a hole in a bag by some other dog and upended near the dead end.

It was crazy, but there was a small, secret part of Nora that was comfortable with trash on the street. It reminded her of her youth, when she'd first arrived in a nastier, scarier, dirtier New York City and moved into a shabby apartment with her best friend, Jenny. A better New York, she sometimes thought to herself now, but never, ever said, one of the many things none of them ever admitted to themselves, at least aloud: that it was better when it was worse.

Homer teased the air at the entrance to the lot with his muzzle and then sat. Their dog knew their block, their house, even their car, and he tolerated riding in it, wedging himself into the foot well alongside Oliver's enormous sneakers. Rachel complained that Homer was not as affectionate with her as he was with her brother, which Nora thought was probably true. But ten minutes of Homer on Rachel's insteps and she would be whining that her feet had fallen asleep and there was no reason their dog couldn't ride in the way back like other dogs. Nora worried that her daughter had difficulty discerning the difference between what she really wanted and what other people made seem desirable. Now that Rachel was out of her teens and in college, Nora hoped she was outgrowing this, although in New York it made her merely typical.

"I don't know what you're talking about," Charlie had said when Nora mentioned it to him. Which had become a bit of a theme in their house on every subject.

"Listening to you people," said Jenny, the only one in their women's lunch group who had never been married, "marriage sounds sort of like the den. It's a good place to chill out, but it's not the most important room in the house. Which makes me wonder why you're all so anxious for me to have one."

"I think the den *is* the most important room in the house," Suzanne, who was a decorator, replied.

"The kitchen is the most important room in the house," Elena said.

"If you cook," Suzanne replied.

"Who still cooks?" said Jean-Ann.

Jenny turned to Nora. "Did everyone miss the entire point of what I said?" she asked.

"Absolutely," Nora said.

"Absolutely," Nora had said when Charlie asked if she wanted to walk down the block to the lot once he'd moved the car in, knowing that staying at the breakfast table to finish her bagel and read the newspapers was not conducive to a day of amity. But she balked at going any farther into the lot than that. "Come take a look," Charlie said now, as though the lot contained infinite vistas, gardens, and statuary instead of just three brick walls, several other cars, a center drain, and two of those squat, black plastic boxes that were everywhere in the parks and backyards of New York City, sheltering blocks of flavored rat poison from passing dogs.

"I'm not going back there," Nora said. "Charity says that's where all the rats live."

"So are the subway tracks, and you take the subway."

She didn't take it much. Nora liked to walk, and when she did take the train she made certain not to look down at the tracks. She'd tried to analyze the depth of her rat phobia, but she'd given it up as pointless. Why were squirrels fine, anodyne, and rats insupportable, provoking a chemical reaction so profound that her breathing didn't return to normal for minutes at a time? Everyone had something; when they were growing up her sister had wakened her at least a dozen times because there was a spider in her room. Charlie hated snakes.

"Everybody hates snakes," Rachel had said, dismissive even as a small child.

"I don't," Nora had replied.

And why had she chosen what seemed to be the rat capital of the world in which to make a life? She remembered her friend Becky from college, who was terrified of water—no need for deep analysis; her younger brother had nearly drowned on the Vineyard when they were children, pulled from the surf and given CPR by a lifeguard. Still, Becky had gotten a job managing a spa with an enormous saltwater pool. She'd insisted she didn't mind, but as soon as she could she'd moved on to a sprawling country inn. There was a river at the bottom of the hill on which the inn sat, but she was never required to go near it. Nora understood that, unlike Becky's phobia, most of these aversions were chemical and intuitive, the way some people immediately fell in love with New York, and other people said that they could never live there. ("I don't get it," Nora had said once to her sister, Christine, on the phone. "If I went to Greenwich and said, 'I don't understand how anyone can stand to live here,' people would think I was rude.")

Charlie walked to the back of the parking lot and out again, as though he were surveying his property. It wasn't a long walk. "No rats," he said.

"Just because you can't see them doesn't mean they're not there," said Nora.

Halfway down the block one of the guys who worked for

Ricky taking care of their houses was hosing down the side-walk. Ricky's guys tended to be small, dark, and stocky, former residents of some Central American country who were willing to do almost any kind of work to earn money. This one had just washed out all their garbage cans, but the effort was fruitless. The greasy sheen on both the pavement and in the cans would reassert itself, summer's urban perspiration. It was one of the reasons people who could afford to do so fled New York, for Nantucket, the Hamptons, somewhere cleaner, greener. Some-where more boring, Nora often thought to herself.

Two young people dressed for exercise approached them, both with that peeled-grape skin of youth that was hypnotic and hateful when its moment had passed you by. "The park's that way, right?" said he, pointing toward the end of the block.

"That's a dead end," Charlie said. "This is a dead-end block. There's a sign at the corner."

"A sign?" said she.

"It's a dead-end block," repeated Nora, for what felt like the thousandth time. They'd petitioned the city to put up two signs, one on each side of the street. DEAD END. It made no difference. "Go back, go left, go left again. You'll hit the park." This, too, was a sentence Nora had uttered many times.

"It's a dead end," said he to her. Nora stared at the girl's face. Her eyebrows were like sparrow feathers dividing her high, smooth brow in two. Nora sighed. She supposed she had looked like that once, and hadn't appreciated it a bit. When she looked in the mirror nowadays, which she mainly did to see if she had anything in her teeth, the clean edges of her jaw seemed to have blurred, the corners of her mouth sliding south.

The young woman put her hand out toward Homer. Sitting

on his haunches, he leaned forward and smelled it, then looked her in the eye. Homer had very pale blue eyes, the color of eucalyptus mints, which made him look demonic, although as he had aged he had become a calm and businesslike dog, too intelligent to waste time on aggression. Sherry and Jack Fisk, who lived halfway up the block, said that when someone reached toward their dog they could feel a faint buzzing through the leash, an interior growl that meant they should hold tight and step back. But the Fisks' dog was an enormous Rottweiler who looked as though he should be patrolling the fence at a maximum-security prison. Brutus was, as Charlie once said, a lawsuit waiting to happen. Sherry Fisk complained that their house was far too big, but that there wasn't a co-op in Manhattan that would have accepted her and Jack as residents with Brutus in tow.

"The minute that dog dies, I downsize," she had said.

"We're not going anywhere," Jack said. "Maybe she's moving, but if she is, she's going alone."

"I might," Sherry said.

"Yeah, you do that," Jack had said. Nora hated bickering, but with Sherry and Jack she scarcely even noticed it anymore. As long as Jack was not actually shouting, things were tenable. Nora always had knots in her shoulders after talking to Jack Fisk. It was as though her body sent messages that her mind didn't recognize until afterward.

The basic layout of the Fisk house was almost exactly like the Nolans', which was almost exactly like the Lessmans' and the Fenstermachers' and the Rizzolis': a kitchen and dining room on the lower level, a double living room above, and two or three bedrooms on each of the floors above that, although some of the bedrooms had been turned into dens or offices. The Fisks had done a gut renovation, so their rooms were high and white and unornamented; the Nolans had some period detail, walls of oak wainscoting, ornamented mantelpieces.

"It is a big house for only two people," Nora had said to Sherry. "When the twins are away there could be somebody on the top floor and I wouldn't even know it."

"If I lived with her in a two-bedroom apartment, I might kill her," Jack Fisk said. Nora laughed nervously. Jack rarely laughed at all.

The Fisk house was bracketed by that of the Fenstermachers, who were perfect and hosted the holiday party every year, and a house that had been owned for ages by people who lived in London and rented it out. The renters never had enough stature on the block to gossip with their more durable neighbors, and Alma Fenstermacher never gossiped at all. But Nora suspected that while Charlie sometimes complained about TV noises rumbling through the common wall from the Rizzoli house next door, the occasional child screaming at a sibling or toy dog yipping at nothing, the Fisk neighbors heard more than that, and more often.

Nora looked at her husband. He was not even admiring the rear of the young woman as she turned and went back the way she had come, hand in hand with the young man. Charlie was too mesmerized by his good fortune, staring through the narrow opening at his car in its space, a faint smile on his face. With his thin, sandy hair, round blue eyes, and pink cheeks, he looked like a small boy. He was one of those people whose baby pictures looked more or less like his driver's license photo. He even looked boyish when he was unhappy, his full lower lip protruding a bit when he talked of someone at work who was being unfairly elevated, one of the guys he had come up with who had just gotten a big promotion.

"Congrats, party people," Nora heard from behind her, and she clenched her molars as she turned.

"Major league congrats," repeated George, the most irritating person on the block.

Another of Nora and Charlie's marital agreements was that social intercourse with George Smythe must be avoided at all cost, but this morning Charlie shook George's hand warmly, as though they were concluding a particularly lucrative business deal. Nora supposed they were, since George seemed in some peculiar and unstated way to be the keeper of the parking lot as well as the majordomo of the block, slipping printed notices through their mail slots about everything from street trees to trash disposal. George-o-Grams, Rachel called them when they appeared on the floor of their foyer. Nora thought that Charlie didn't mind George because he reminded him of the sort of guy who was the social chairman at a fraternity house. Nora couldn't bear George for precisely the same reason.

George sensed her dislike, and was galvanized by it. Soon after Charlie and Nora had moved to the block, when it became clear that she was unlikely to meet George's practiced (and often early-morning) bonhomie with more of the same, George had fastened on her as his project, the way men fasten on a woman who will not sleep with them, or a client who proves elusive, or a marathon, or Everest.

"Ms. Twinkletoes," he would say as she sped by on her run to the park on Saturday mornings. "Madame Miler." "The Harrier."

"*Harrier*," he had said to his son, Jonathan, one morning years before, the boy curved into a question mark beneath the burden of his backpack. "There's a word that might be on the SATs. You know what a harrier is, son?"

Nora had never once heard Jonathan respond. George's only child gave off an aura of unwashed T-shirt and contempt. His silence made no difference; George was the kind of man who could carry on both sides of a conversation. In fact he seemed to prefer it. Jonathan had left for college in Colorado three years ago and, as far as Nora knew, had never been seen on the block again.

"Living the dream," George said when someone asked him about Jonathan. "Mountain air, hiking. None of this Ivy League slog. He's living the dream."

"He got rejected at most of the places he applied," said Oliver.

"He works in a pot dispensary," Rachel said.

"Cool job," said Oliver.

"We're not sending you to MIT so you can wind up selling sinsemilla in Denver," Nora said.

"Okay, Mom, but how come you even know what sinsemilla is?"

Charlie waggled his eyebrows and grinned. "Don't encourage them," Nora said when the twins went upstairs.

"Relax, Bun," Charlie said. "You're always so uptight about stuff like that." They had quarreled about whether the twins should be given wine at dinner now that they were away at college and doubtless drinking, but not yet of drinking age. It was notable because they rarely quarreled anymore. Their marriage had become like the AA prayer: "God, grant me the serenity to accept the things I cannot change." Or at least to move into a zone in which I so don't care anymore and scarcely notice. Nora had thought this was their problem alone until she realized that it was what had happened to almost everyone she knew who was still married, even some of those who were on their second husbands. At her women's lunches they talked about the most intimate things, about errant chin hairs and persistent bladder infections and who had a short haircut because she just couldn't be bothered and who had a short haircut because she'd just finished chemo. But while they were willing to talk about marriage generally, they tended not to talk about their own husbands specifically. Marriage vows, Nora had long felt, constituted a loyalty oath.

"As long as he doesn't set anything on fire, I'm satisfied," Elena had said one day, and all the other women chuckled drily, since Elena's husband had in fact once set their screened porch in the country on fire when he brought the barbecue grill inside during a thunderstorm. There had been a prolonged fight with the insurance company, which didn't consider saving the spareribs enough of a reason to use hot charcoal in a confined space. The dispute was ongoing, Elena said, because Henry enjoyed telling people about it, mainly other guys who cheered him on.

"So, Miss Fleet Feet, how do you feel about the parking situation?" George said now, one hand on Charlie's shoulder. "Nothing says you've arrived on the block like a space in the lot." George had a space, the Fisks had a space, the Fentermachers had a space, the Lessmans had a space, and the Rizzolis had a space, although the Rizzolis' had been handed down to their elder son and his wife, who lived in their triplex and rented out the bottom floors. The senior Rizzolis now lived in their house in Naples. Florida, not Italy. "I'm too old for the city now, Nora," Mike Rizzoli said when he and his wife came by to visit. "It's a young person's game, all the nuttiness."

One of the men who lived in the SRO that backed onto the parking lot came down the street with a battered wheeled suitcase. "We're all dying we're all dying we're all dying inside," he said as he went past, smelling of old sweat and fried food. Homer woofed slightly, at the suitcase, not the man. Nora had never figured out exactly why Homer distrusted things with wheels. He reacted suspiciously to both strollers and bicycles.

"I hear they're going to convert the SRO to condos," George said as the man disappeared down the block.

Nora felt forced into the conversation despite her better judgment. That's how George got to her, by saying things she knew to be untrue: the mayor is not going to run for reelection, the Fenstermachers are selling their house, small dogs are more intelligent than large ones. "It's never going to happen," Nora said. "So many single-room-occupancy buildings were converted in the eighties and there were so few beds left for homeless men that the city put a moratorium on all conversions. All the SROs have to stay SROs." And Nora preferred the SRO residents to George anyway. Before they had made an offer for the house, she had visited the precinct, worried by the presence of a building full of ramshackle men. "That place?" the desk sergeant said. "They're basically down-on-their-luck guys working minimum wage and some old men on disability. There's a few schizos, but they're not dangerous. You know the type, the guys who talk to themselves about Jesus and the president and whatever. You'll be fine." Then he asked how much they were paying for the house. Even the police, who all lived on Long Island or in Orange County, were mesmerized by the absurdity of Manhattan real estate values.

George ignored her comment. "That'll make a huge difference, if they get those guys out," he said. "They really dirty up the lot." Nora knew this was not the case, but she wasn't going to engage with George again if she could help it. The men in the SRO did not so much throw trash into the lot as leave things on their windowsills that fell down into it. It was just like college, old-fashioned outdoor refrigeration. Nora herself had once had a string bag that she hung from a nail outside her dorm window, full of containers of yogurt and the odd banana. In winter the sills on the back side of the SRO, which looked down on the parked cars, were dotted with pints of milk, tubs of pudding, packages of hot dogs, just as her dorm sills had been. Sometimes a high wind ripped through all their yards and down to the river, and the food on the sills fell to the ground below. Nora had once seen an enormous rat run across the entrance to the lot with a plastic envelope of what appeared to be salami in its mouth. At least she thought the rat was enormous. They all seemed enormous to her, even when, after having been lured by the poison in the bait traps, they lay curled into stiff, furry commas on the sidewalk.

Nora looked down the street, which was no cleaner than the parking lot. The gutter was edged with leavings: the pointillistic wisps from a home paper shredder, the poop from someone who wouldn't pick up after his dog, a tangle of some unidentifiable vegetable matter, brown and sad as a corsage three days after the prom. It was much grubbier on the West Side than the East Side. It was why Charlie had wanted to move to the East Side before they moved into their house. Now they got a lot of mileage out of living on a dead-end block, which had mollified Charlie somewhat.

"Let's go to the park and get this dog some exercise," said Nora, who wanted to get away from George. Rachel had said once that George reminded her of the kid who glommed on to you at a new school until you started making real friends and found out why the kid had been available for glomming. Nora had been amazed at her daughter's powers of perception, although when she said that to Rachel, she replied dismissively, "Oh, duh, Mommy." George was exactly that kid, circling the cafeteria of life, looking for the yet-unmoored, blind to his own unpopularity.

"I don't know why you dislike him so much," Charlie said when they got far enough away.

"Because he's a self-important jerk," Nora said. "Homer! Drop it!" Homer dropped the twist of waxed paper with a pizza crust inside and sighed. It was his cross to bear, obedience, and a diet of kibble.

Behind them they heard shouting, and turned to look as George sprinted from his front stoop to the entrance to the parking lot, where a white panel van was backing in.

"Ricky! *Amigo!* What did I tell you the last time?" he yelled.

"*Amigo?* Really? Every time he tries to speak Spanish to Ricky, I can see by the look on Ricky's face that he can't understand a word George says. That's leaving aside the fact that Ricky's English is as good as his. *Amigo?* Oh, my God."

"Come on, smile, Bun," Charlie said, putting his arm around her shoulder. "We got a space! Wait till I tell the kids!"

Under NO CIRCUMSTANCES is Ricky permitted to park his van in the lot. He has been REPEATEDLY told this. Any suggestion that he has permission from Mr. Stoller to do so is INCORRECT.

Inform me IMMEDIATELY if you see him parked there or at the entrance to the lot.

George

During the week between the end of their summer internships and their return to college, Rachel and Oliver came home, to see their friends from high school and to spend money, she on clothing, he on computer gear. Nora was both delighted to have her children around and a little weary of being awakened in the middle of the night by footfalls on the stairs. She sometimes thought that if she had envisioned the twins as young adults she would have put the master bedroom on the top floor and Oliver and Rachel below rather than the other way around. But when she felt mildly disgruntled as someone stomped by her bedroom door at 3 A.M., she would consider the future, with Rachel living in her own place somewhere, with Oliver living in his own place somewhere else, with she and Charlie living in a quiet house, just the two of them. Some of their friends had started to complain about college graduates who circled around and, because of high rents and low-paying jobs, wound up back in their childhood bedrooms. Nora always thought she wouldn't mind that one bit.

When the twins came home the house was always full of people, although none of them stayed long, except for one or two of the girls, who would tumble into Rachel's bed at night and appear again in the late morning, tousled, in boxer shorts and T-shirts. The others just passed through: Hello, Nick; Hello, Bronson; Hello, Grace; Hello, Elise. Charlie's mantra was "What is her name again?" He was even flummoxed sometimes by Rachel's two oldest friends; their names were Bethany and Elizabeth, and Charlie still sometimes confused the two. Luckily the girls thought this was hilarious, except for Rachel when she was in a mood, when she would say what kind of father can't be bothered to figure out his daughter's best friends' names. Then she would flounce, although the more time she spent at college, the more she had traded flouncing for tromping.

Because no one used the doorbell anymore, preferring to text one another *OMG I'm outside let me in* instead, there was no telling who was down in the kitchen while Nora and Charlie were asleep two floors up and the faint smell of smoke, cigarette or pot, drifted up from the backyard to their bedroom window. When they awoke, the counter was usually littered with the remains of food eaten long after they had retired, and the garbage can was full of takeout containers.

"Who drinks beer with a peanut butter and jelly sandwich?" Charlie muttered to himself.

Dad so weird park lot wtf, Rachel texted Nora in the middle of the night, when the twins and all their friends were wide awake. It was as though they lived in different time zones, as though the parents were in China to their children's America. Nora couldn't get used to the notion that when she was asleep, her children were awake, and vice versa. "Mom, please," Rachel had said. "Don't text me at eight in the morning. Just . . . no."

"You don't have to read it then."

"My phone is under my pillow. It wakes me up."

"I will never understand why you sleep with the phone under your pillow."

"Never mind. Just. Never mind. If I block you, you'll know why."

"I thought people only blocked stalkers."

"You are my stalker," Rachel said, going upstairs with her phone in hand.

"You walked right into that one, Bun," Charlie said.

"Can I text you at eight?" Nora asked Oliver.

"I guess?" he said.

Oliver's internship had been with the Massachusetts River Consortium. He was testing the Charles River for contaminants. Rachel had been on the Cape, working for The Nature Conservancy. Neither had ever shown much interest in wildlife before, except for the early years, when Rachel had begged for a puppy and Ollie had kept a tortoise under his bed who ate whatever lettuce in the fridge was too limp to serve and who was so sedentary that Nora would regularly check that he was still alive.

Go, dad! Oliver had texted when Charlie sent a photo of his car in the lot.

Car pic omg wtf ice, Rachel texted Nora.

"Ice?" Nora said to Oliver.

"I can't even," Oliver said. "Get with the program, lady."

Nora was not surprised that Charlie had texted the twins pictures of his car in its new space. Nothing had pleased him so much since Parents' Weekend at the twins' respective colleges, where he had participated in a rugby game with Rachel (Williams) and a sculling competition with Oliver (MIT). Nora knew only in the vaguest way that her husband had had a spate of recent disappointments at work: a former classmate who had promised to send something his way and hadn't, a headhunter who had come after him hard for a big job and then disappeared. "Nora," he called her on those nights, instead of "Bunny" or "Bun," the term of endearment he had come up with so many years ago and had become the substitute for her actual name. They were more commonplace now, those evenings when he arrived home with a face like a fist and went straight for the vodka.

"What's the matter?"

"Nothing."

"How was your day?"

"Fine."

"Are you okay?"

"Why wouldn't I be okay?"

Rachel, too, was dolorous about the impending end of her college years. "So, so tired of being asked what comes next," she'd said between gritted teeth when she and her mother had run into Sherry Fisk on the block. There was so much Nora could have said, knowing that when Rachel graduated what came next would be so fluid and various: maybe this job, maybe that guy, maybe one city or another. Nora remembered drawing in the sand of her future with a stick. What she couldn't recall was when the sand had become cement, the who-I-want-to-be turned for once and for all into who-I-am. She remembered a lunch the year before, when Suzanne had seemed unusually glum. "I don't know—sometimes I feel as though I should reinvent myself," Suzanne said, poking at her asparagus. "I mean, how many sideboards can you have distressed, and then distressed again because the client didn't think they looked distressed enough?" She sighed and added, "Don't you ever wonder how we all wound up here?" And before Nora could say, Yes, I do, I think about it all the time, I'm so relieved I'm not the only one, Elena said drily, "What is this, existential Thursday?" Leaving the restaurant, Elena turned to Nora and Jenny and mouthed the word "Menopause," and Nora had almost hated her at that moment, even though she and Elena had known each other since a childbirth class more than twenty years before and had been having lunch together almost that long.

Nora wondered where Rachel was now. The plan had been for the four of them to go to an outdoor classical music concert in Central Park after dinner at the Greek restaurant nearby, but the plans had gone awry. Nora had forgotten that she had a business meeting with a potential donor who was in from the Hamptons for one day only to check the paint colors in her apartment renovation. Rachel had gotten a text, made a yelping sound, said, "I'm sorry, guys, but I absolutely have to take care of something," and blown out the door. So Charlie and Oliver had trudged off together and had wound up having wings and a pitcher of beer at a bar Oliver recommended.

"He didn't get carded?" Nora said.

"He's got a fake ID," Charlie said.

"Oh, great."

Charlie shrugged. "Where did our daughter get to?" he asked.

This time Nora shrugged. Changes of plans were more common in their household than sticking to them. After the twins were born, Nora had learned at a Mommy and Me class that the most important thing she could do to keep her marriage intact, other than practicing her kegels and installing double sinks in the bathroom, was institute a date night. Their first date night Oliver spiked a fever and they spent the evening walking the floor with a mewling baby. Their second date night they talked about how crazy their first one had been, and whether Rachel was meeting her developmental milestones before Oliver, and whether Charity, their nanny, was as good as she seemed. Their third was canceled because of a business meeting Charlie had, the fourth canceled because Charity had to take her sister to the emergency room. Nora couldn't remember when they'd dropped date night, but the routine of cancellation continued now in almost every arrangement they made. A dinner party Nora had to attend alone after the state commissioner of banking wanted to have a drink with a group at Charlie's firm and Charlie was afraid to miss it. A professional conference Nora couldn't go to as Charlie's plus one because of a new press preview she needed to handle personally at work. Once they tried to factor the twins in, the possibilities for cancellation became infinite.

They had miraculously all managed brunch the day before, and had walked home through the shimmering August air of Central Park together. Rachel had stopped to look at the memorial plaques on the park benches, and to read them aloud. For Robert A. Davidson, Who Loved the Park. Joan and John, Fifty Years and Counting. Happy Birthday, Janet—Have a Seat!

"'Maisie, sorely missed, 1999 to 2012,'" Rachel read. "Oh, Mommy, look. That would make her only thirteen years old."

"It's probably a dog," Nora said.

"What?"

"Lots of people do this for their dogs. I bet Maisie was a dog."

"Because a teenage girl is too threatening?" Rachel said. Nora sighed and shook her head as her daughter trudged along next to Charlie. Oliver dropped back to Nora's side. Coming toward them was first one double stroller, then another, both inhabited by toddlers of the same age. "My peeps," said Oliver, smiling.

"You have twins," people had said when they first met Nora and Charlie, with that knowing look. New York City was lousy with twins, twins that meant you and your husband had had sex like normal people for a year or two, then like people charting ovulation on a graph in the bathroom, then like people whose relationship consisted mainly of one giving herself shots of nuclear hormones while yelling at the other. Twins meant a doctor's office with your eggs in a dish and your husband's sperm in the little vial they'd given him to fill in a closet, along with some fairly tame porn. When the Nolans' pharmacy put Nora on hold, the recorded message said it was the number-one purveyor of fertility medications in the New York City area, as though that were an achievement.

When she'd first pushed a double stroller Nora had wanted to hang a sign on the front: THEY ARE <u>NOT</u> THAT KIND OF TWINS.

"I don't know why you care," Charlie had said.

Oliver had always liked the idea of being one of two. Rachel, not so much. "It's a good thing we're not identicals," she said more than once.

"A boy and a girl, identical twins," Oliver said. "That would be one for the bio books." Rachel's singularity was her national flag, her official seal.

"I saw some people on campus—they had triplets," Oliver said to Nora now.

"God bless them," Nora said.

A group of Japanese tourists wearing surgical masks went by, taking pictures of one another without bothering to lower the masks. Nora sighed again. "I wish your sister would stop pushing my buttons," Nora said.

"She's fine, Mom," Oliver said. "I know you feel like she unloads on you, but sometimes she just goes down a rabbit hole. She'll be fine. Don't worry."

"Okay, now I'm worried."

"No, don't be, it's just—be cool. Senior year is hard on people. Not me so much, but a lot of people. She's just a lot more breakable than she seems sometimes."

"Ollie, if you're trying to make me feel better, you're not doing such a great job."

"Mom," said Oliver. "Everything's fine. Just cut her some slack."

Nora watched Charlie put his arm around Rachel's shoulder. She had spent some of the best years of her life worrying about Rachel, staring at the bedroom ceiling as Charlie snored beside her, thinking mainly about terrible things she'd read about in magazines. If Rachel lost weight, Nora worried that she was anorexic. If she was distracted, Nora worried that she was taking drugs. The sound of vomiting echoing through the stairwell during high school first thing in the morning—that one didn't even bear thinking about. Alma Fenstermacher, who was twenty years older than Nora, once said there was a fine line between worrying about your daughter getting pregnant accidentally, and obsessing about when she would finally give you grandchildren. Luckily Rachel threw up in the morning only twice, once because of tequila, once because of bad sushi. Nora worried about her no less now that she was out of the house much of the time, and she didn't suppose she would worry about her any less even when she was gone for good. Which Nora thought was a horrible turn of phrase.

Nora rarely worried about Oliver. That worried her.

"Ollie, want to check out the parking space when we get home?" Charlie called as Rachel leaned into him.

"Wait until the first time he has to dig the car out after a snowstorm," Sherry Fisk had said.

"Charlie says he finally feels like he's part of the block," Nora said, as Sherry rolled her eyes.

Nora had felt as though they were part of the block long before, when the twins had been invited to babysit for the Rizzoli grandchildren (which had sometimes consisted of Nora helping to sit for the Rizzoli grandchildren), when they'd received their first invitation to the holiday party on Alma Fenstermacher's beautiful thick note cards with the engraved border of holly, but especially when Ricky first rang their bell. For Nora, Ricky was one of the two linchpins of a daily existence that, between the house, the twins, the dog, and the job, was always in danger of tumbling out of control in some minor but annoying way, like a persistent itch. They had lived on the block for almost six months when the doorbell rang on a Saturday morning. The twins, who had spent their first nine years in an apartment, were still agog at the idea of answering their own door, and ran down the stairs, shoving each other aside.

"It's some man who wants to talk to you or Daddy," Rachel said. "I said Daddy was at work. Like always."

The man at the door was someone Nora had already seen dozens of times on the block, wearing a uniform of drab green pants and matching shirt, often with two or three others trailing behind him. "Missus," he said, removing a baseball cap that said

METROPOLITAN LUMBER, "my name is Ricky. I do fixing, paint-ing, putting out the recycle, you name it. I am reasonable and reliable." There was no doubt that it was a carefully rehearsed speech.

He handed her a slightly grubby business card. ENRIQUE RAMOS, it said, with a phone number.

Satisfaction guaranteed.

No job too small.

Reasonable rates.

References available.

He'd crammed every cliché from every small business onto the card, so that the type was almost unreadable, it was so tiny. George had been his patron then, telling everyone he met that Ricky had done a great job rebuilding the brick wall in his backyard. "Rock-bottom prices," he said.

Nora insisted that the twins address him as Mr. Ramos, and she never called him Ricky when she spoke to him directly. "Enrique," she would say when she ran into him on the street, "there's a short in that backyard light again." Or there was a problem with Oliver's toilet, or a clogged sink in the basement, or a tap in Rachel's bathroom that dripped, and, according to Rachel, kept her from sleeping for even a *single minute* during the night. Ricky would ring the bell and stand just inside the front door slipping paper covers over his shoes, the kind that surgeons wore when they were operating. If it was a bigger job, he would have one of his guys with him, but Nora had never learned any of their names and they rarely spoke. Once there had been a young one with gelled hair ridged into rows like a cornfield and a shabby little soul patch flaring beneath his lower lip. He had arrived with Ricky and another guy to reattach a section of the furnace duct work that had come loose. Rachel had gotten home from school as the young guy was pulling off his shoe covers, and he had said, *"Hola, chica,"* and Ricky had let loose a string of Spanish that Rachel said she had not understood despite an immersive summer program. What Nora understood was that she never saw the young guy again. "He's gone," Charity said darkly.

"Without Ricky and Charity, this whole house falls apart," Nora said to Charlie, tapping the message from George, whose patronage had later given way to some minor dispute with Ricky, probably over a bill. "We can do without your car. We can't do without them."

"It's your car, too," Charlie said.

Nora didn't think of it as her car, but she said nothing. She hoped that the acquisition of the space in the lot would make Charlie stop talking about selling the house. This, too, was George's fault, and had increased her antipathy toward him to the point that she barely acknowledged his pugs when they trundled, bow-legged, across her path, breathing asthmatically. George was a person of serial allegiances: to the writer who was researching the block and would give all of them free copies of his book if he could just take a quick look around their houses; to the roofer who was willing to repair flashing and gutters cheaply; to the salvage yard that had period doors that could be made to fit the jambs with only a bit of tweaking. He would send out missives vouching for the writer, the roofer, the manager of the salvage yard. "Mom, there's a new George-o-Gram on the floor by the door," Rachel would say.

This always ended in disaster, and disavowals. The writer never found a publisher. The roofer did half the job and then disappeared. The tweaking meant the doors looked dreadful. But his latest had sucked them all in, or at least all the men. An appraiser had estimated the market value of all their houses. He'd expected to be paid afterward, as people often did, and George had stiffed him. But before that George had gotten him to cough up some numbers. Charlie had come home from his morning walk with Homer, and said, "We should put this place on the market as soon as we can get it into shape."

"What? What are you talking about? It is in shape. And it's our home. Why would we sell it?"

Sherry Fisk told the same story, and Linda Lessman, who lived across the street, and George's wife, Betsy, had probably heard the same sales pitch, too, although the other women never saw her much, nor, it seemed, did George. The houses on the block, like most of Manhattan, had appreciated so much they constituted a lottery prize. The women saw them as homes, the men as real estate. Charlie would be reading the *Times* on the weekend, and he would suddenly look up thoughtfully and say, "If we sold this place, we could buy a great old house in Savannah and bank the rest."

"I don't want to live in Savannah," Nora said.

"You've never even been to Savannah, Bun," Charlie said.

"You've never been to Savannah. I went there for work. It's a beautiful place. I don't want to live there. I live in New York. I have a job here, remember?"

"There must be museums in Savannah." Or Charleston. Or Santa Fe. It depended on which town with reasonably priced housing was featured in the paper that week.

Nora hoped the parking lot would insulate her from Charlie's sense that they could no longer afford to live in their house because it was too valuable for them to do so. Of course there was really no earthly reason to have a car in New York City, but Nora knew enough not to mention it. Their children did not even have driver's licenses, although they were twenty years old. Rachel had driven up over a curb her second time out in the car, turned to her mother, and said, "See," and had never, as far as they knew, driven again. Oliver had let his learner's permit expire. He came home from college on the train. Rachel hitched a ride with whichever suburban kid was willing to pass through Manhattan in exchange for gas money.

Still, Charlie insisted on having the car. It was used to transport his clubs to golf courses on Long Island and in Westchester County. There was a small stone house upstate they had owned when the kids were small, although they had sold it when Rachel and Ollie were in middle school. Charlie complained that they'd gotten to the point that they never used it, but the truth was they'd never used it much anyhow, mainly for Thanksgiving dinner and as a base from which to cut down a tree at a tree farm and bring it back to New York for Christmas. And Nora remembered how much Charlie had actually hated the drive, the kids wailing in the backseat—*I have to pee I'm so hungry she's touching me with her foot he smells so bad he's farting am not are so.* "If you don't stop that I'm going to leave you by the side of the road," Charlie had yelled at the end of one Thanksgiving weekend, and both children had started to sob. "I'm never going in the car with Daddy again," Rachel said that night as Nora tucked her in. "Me neither," yelled Oliver from his room next door. "Copycat," Rachel yelled back.

"Daddy didn't mean it," Nora said.

"He sounded like he did," Rachel said.

Nora remembered that before George had gotten a space in the lot, he had insisted loudly to anyone who would listen (after a while no one would listen) that it was absolutely unnecessary to pay for parking. George had been one of those New Yorkers who had a second job—or, as far as any of them could tell in George's case, a first one—gaming the alternate-side parking rules of the City of New York. Like some odd circus act, the cars wove around, away from the dirty curb, over to double-park across the street, then in behind the traffic cop and the street cleaner to pull back to the curb, often into the very same spot they'd occupied just minutes before.

"Let me give you a tutorial," she had heard George say one morning to a young man who had just moved onto the block. "See the sign? No parking, nine to eleven, Monday and Thursday. So what you do is, you sit in your car and you check for the agent. Don't jump the gun! Wait until she's coming up on you or ticketing the guy behind you who forgot or overslept. Then you move out and up. It's easier than it sounds because you'll probably be following the guy who was parked right in front of you. You sit tight on the other side of the street, the Tuesday-Friday side, and wait for her to get to the end of the block, wait for the street cleaner, boom! You finish the circle and you're good to go."

"What about the double-parking? Won't I get a ticket for double-parking while I wait?"

George shook his head. "I've never seen it happen."

There were many measures of the insanity of living in New York City: private school recommendations for four-year-olds; co-op boards that asked the question "What do you think you will bring to the gestalt of this building?" But those cars circling the block behind the mechanized, rotating whisk brooms and spray of the street-cleaning truck, wagon trains on a pitiless paved frontier, were one of the most ubiquitous and conspicuous. The drivers were mainly men, cultlike in their understanding of the underpinnings of their work. The high, grubby walls of cindered, hardpacked snow that foiled those who parked in the lot, the municipal plows leaving a huge berm atop the curb cut, were a boon to the hardcore alternate-side parkers. Alternate-side parking was suspended when snow accumulated. This being New York, it was also suspended not only for Memorial Day and Christmas but for Chinese New Year, Purim, the Hindu festival of lights called Diwali, and the Feast of the Ascension.

"That's just ridiculous," Linda Lessman, who had grown up Catholic, had said one year at the block barbecue. "Ascension Thursday is a minor holiday."

"More minor than Shavuot?" Jack Fisk said.

"You've got me there," Linda said.

Of course once George had gotten a space in the lot, he had forsaken all others. "Suckers," he said when he saw someone sitting at the curb at 8:45, sipping coffee from a go-cup and checking his mirrors for the street cleaner. Almost overnight he had gone from being the alternate-side aficionado to the parking lot overseer, so that people sometimes made the mistake of thinking that he owned it. One of the things Nora hated about Charlie's new space was that it had made him friendlier with George. The trade-off was that it had made Charlie friendlier in general.

"Which is a good thing," she said to Jenny, their conversation punctuated, as usual, by the occasional click of their wineglasses against their respective phones. Nora found it the ideal way to end the day: a little Chardonnay, her comfortable club chair, Jenny at the other end of the line.

"I've never really understood the car-in-the-city thing," said

Jenny, who was a professor at Columbia and lived in university housing a block from campus. "It's so male. But whatever. How are my godchildren?"

"Much the same."

"Which means Rachel is making you totally crazy, and Oliver is completely chill. But don't ignore the fact that the newest research shows your best chance of being well cared for when you're aged is having a daughter."

"I feel aged already. This is going to be a big house for just two people. Although complaining about something like that makes me feel like a terrible person. I should count my blessings."

"Oh, honey. If you can't complain to me, who can you complain to? And blessings are all relative."

"My first-world problems. That's what they call them. 'First-world problems.'"

"Who does?"

"Rachel and her friends. One of them will start complaining about how she needs a manicure, or she has salt stains on her boots, and somebody will say, 'First-world problems,' meaning, 'There are real problems in the world and your nails don't qualify.'"

"I don't think being worried about your kids leaving home and your husband's moods is commensurate with salt-stained boots. Although I'm surprised that none of my students has used that turn of phrase. *First-world problems.* That's actually a good phrase. Not to be pedantic, but it reminds me of the research showing that societies that eschew material possessions are happier overall."

"God bless you."

"What?"

"*Eschew.* God bless you. Ollie did that with my father once, and he thought it was so clever. Although my father thinks everything Oliver does is clever. And has anyone told poor people that they should be happier overall?"

"Ah, that's the thing. The entire society has to eschew—don't say it; now I'll never be able to use that word again without cracking up—the entire society has to eschew material wealth."

"Do those societies exist?"

"Hard to believe, isn't it?" Jenny said. "They're all matriarchal, too."

"You're just saying that to make me feel better," Nora said.

"It's true, but if it makes you feel better, I don't even care that it's true. Hold on." Without Jenny saying a thing Nora knew she was opening the refrigerator to take out the bottle of wine and pour some more into her glass.

"I'm back," Jenny said. Always.

"My children are almost exactly the same age I was when I came to New York," Nora said. "They're almost exactly the age we were when you and I moved in together. Doesn't that seem like a long time ago?"

"It does," Jenny said. "It seems like a million years ago, and it seems like it was just last week."

"Oh, Mrs. Nolan, Mr. Harris just called you," said Nora's assistant, Madison. "He'd like you to call him back as soon as you can."

"Who?" Nora said, standing in the doorway of her office.

"Mr. Harris? He said you knew him?"

"Did he give a first name?"

"Bob?" Madison said. She handed a message slip to Nora. "He said to use this number."

"Close the door, Madison," Nora said. "Please."

Nora looked down at the message slip in front of her, the request to call Bob Harris, founder and chairman of the investment firm where Charlie worked. For just a moment she had a nonsensical thought: that work was like school, and that just as the head of the middle school had called to tell her that Rachel would suffer an in-school suspension for hiding in the girls' room during an obligatory morning meeting, his boss was calling to give her bad news about Charlie's continued employment. Nora knew this was ridiculous, but she could think of no other reason that Bob Harris, a man who had become legendary for his cornpone demeanor and uncanny ability to make money, would call her. That was how he was almost always described: the legendary Bob Harris.

"Well, hey now," he said when she dialed the number, which was clearly his private line, no secretary, no intermediary, no screening. "I wonder if you and me could have a little meeting."

"About what?" Nora said.

"See, that's one of the things I always liked about you. You're a straight shooter. None of this, Sure, Mr. Harris, when, Mr. Harris, whatever you say, Mr. Harris. About what? That's what I like."

"Thank you," Nora said. "About what?" There was something about Bob Harris that always brought out the peremptory headmistress in her.

"I've got a business proposition for you, but I want to have a sit-down to talk more about it. How about if my girl calls your girl and they sync our schedules? What's your girl's name again? She told me but I don't think I heard her right."

"It's Madison."

"Well, hell, I did hear her right. Whatta ya know? Tell Madison to call Eileen. I want to get together real soon."

"About what?" Nora said.

"There you go. Like I said, straight shooter. Nothing better. I hate the telephone. Let's get down to brass tacks when I see you."

Nora put down the phone and looked at the clock on her desk. Jenny was in class, teaching, so she couldn't call her. Her sister, Christine, would be barely awake in Seattle. And she certainly couldn't ask Charlie why Bob Harris would want to speak to her. Nora was completely baffled, but there was no mystery in how her husband would react to a personal call from the man he felt insufficiently valued his talents. Unless he already knew. She had to hope Bob Harris didn't run into Charlie in the elevator anytime soon, that assistant Eileen didn't pass along the word to Charlie's assistant, Maryanne, while they were picking up sandwiches for lunch.

Nora wondered if Madison had recognized Bob Harris's name. She wouldn't put it past her. Madison had grown up in New York City, and she was as hungry a twenty-four-year-old as Nora had ever encountered. "This is my dream job," she had said during her interview, following up with "I want to be you when I grow up," which Nora told Jenny made her feel a million years old, and Jenny said would have caused her to shred Madison's résumé. "Plus, I'm sorry, but how do you take seriously a person who is named after an avenue?" Jenny said.

"You must have had at least one Madison as a student," Nora said.

"Of course I have," said Jenny. "Right now I have a student named Celestial, and another named Otto, who insists on spelling his name with a lowercase *o* at the beginning. But I didn't choose to hire them. They were thrust upon me."

Madison was a heat-seeking missile; Nora, by contrast, felt as though she'd fallen into nearly every job she'd had, although Jenny always insisted she was selling herself short. During the summer between sophomore and junior year at Williams she had wanted to stay on campus because the man with whom she was topsy-turvy in love was working on a historic restoration project nearby. There had been an opening for an assistant in the development office, which was fine with her, although she had had no idea what a development office actually did. Two weeks in, the assistant director was put on bed rest with a dicey pregnancy, and Nora found herself showing more rich alums around the campus than anyone had expected, and taking several trips to the enormous shingled houses of Nantucket and Naragansett while the director asked for what Nora quickly learned to call a significant multiyear gift. At the end of summer the director had asked her if she would continue part-time during the school year, and when the director left to go to the Folk Art Museum in New York City, she had taken Nora with her.

Even before college Nora had understood that there was a kind of desire expected of smart and capable people that she had never really had, that wanting fever that so clearly ran through Madison's veins. Nora's ambition was a simmer, not a boil. Her best friend in high school had wanted to be an actress with a ferocity that was like a mental illness; it shaped the way Amanda looked at everything. Nora was certain that because of this she would succeed, that it was this inflammatory ambition, not talent, that made a difference. But in the back of her mind was the understanding that having that kind of hunger was a razor blade hidden at the bottom of the bag; that it meant that not getting what you wanted would be crippling. Nora had to admit that she was slightly relieved not to have it, to be content to move from one responsible position to another in a business that, after all, was all for a good cause. Raising money first for the folk art museum, then for the law school. The fashion institute job seemed a bit less like giving back to humanity, but it was the first time she'd been asked to head the office rather than sit second seat, and the money was good. There had been private-school tuitions, and the economy had hit one of those speed bumps that made Charlie ask if Rachel really needed to spend the summer at drama camp.

The job she had now was some steps up from a development job, and it had literally fallen into her lap. The fashion institute had had a lunch to launch its exhibit of a collection of women's clothes of the Jazz Age, the waitstaff weaving carefully among mannequins wearing beaded shifts, fur neckpieces, cloche hats. The Cobb salads and glasses of iced tea were already on the tables when they sat down.

"When did the Cobb salad become the official lunch food of New York City women?" said the woman on her left, who had given them a modest gift although she could have afforded to give them something larger, and who was seated next to Nora so Nora could pry something larger out of her.

"And why is a Cobb salad called a Cobb salad?" Nora said.

From her other side came a loud, nasal voice: "It's named for the owner of the Brown Derby in Hollywood, who invented it. Out of leftovers."

Nora swiveled. "Well, thank you for that," Nora said, in her best development-officer voice, trying to read the woman's place card without obviously squinting. (She would really have to talk to the staff about making the names larger on the place cards.) "And I'm so pleased that you're interested in the institute. May I call you Bebe?"

"You can call me Queen Elizabeth if you'd like," the woman said, pulling the soft center out of the popover on her bread plate. "I'm not interested in the fashion institute. I'm interested in you. I want to offer you a job."

As soon as she got home that evening she called Christine and told her about the meeting she had had after lunch, which had taken place in the backseat of a Mercedes SUV. "She's insane," Nora said. "She wants to start her own museum, from scratch, and she wants me to run it."

"What kind of a museum?"

"Jewelry. She wants to start a museum of jewelry with her

own collection, which apparently is pretty large, and the collections of her friends after they die. She says she has two friends who are already willing to kick in."

There was a long silence. "Crazy, right?" Nora said.

"It's a fantastic idea," Christine said. "It'll be a huge success, Nonnie. Women will beat down the door."

Nora was the one who was silent this time. Her sister and her husband had started a business in Seattle making yoga clothes with inspirational sayings written in tiny, almost imperceptible letters at the nape of the neck or the edge of the cuff, which Nora had thought was a waste of two good college educations. Each time Nora read a piece about the company—and there were many pieces about the company now—the number of millions it was said to be worth rose. Nora had once made the mistake of saying at a business lunch that her sister was the Christine of Small Sayings—"Shouting Is So Over" was their slogan—and she'd had to listen to fifteen minutes about the cotton, the fit, the durability, even the sayings, which Nora had once compared to those found in fortune cookies. "I know it sounds silly, but every time I put on that shirt that says 'Today might just be the best day of my life' on the hem, I feel good," the director of development at Hunter College had said.

"I have that shirt!" her assistant had chimed in.

"Oh, come on, who's going to beat down the doors to look at jewelry?" Nora said to Christine. "If you want to look at jewelry you can just walk into Harry Winston."

"Ordinary people aren't going to walk into Harry Winston. They made me feel like a shoplifter the one time I was in there. Even Tiffany's makes you feel uncomfortable. But with a museum you're inviting them in and not even asking them to buy. Although the gift shop opportunities here are major. Major.

You'll get all those women who want to own some big honking opal but could never afford it and are thrilled to have a facsimile. Your whole crazy city is aspirational now, people spending more than they can afford, trying to live a big life that's beyond them. This is perfect. It will be huge, I'm telling you."

And her sister had been right. Despite condescending comments in the art magazines and a few digs in the newspapers, the Museum of Jewelry took off almost from the day its heavy steel-and-smoked-glass double doors opened. There wasn't much of the sort of work Nora had done before, raising money from people who were constantly being asked to write a check, the ones who were tired of being asked and the ones who just loved the attention. The museum had a decent endowment; Bebe sold three Impressionist oil paintings she said she had always found depressing, and supplemented that with a chunk of her late husband's massive investment portfolio. And they had a large, rather handsome space that Bebe owned outright. Her husband had been a real estate developer, who, she said, saw Chelsea as an up-and-coming area before anyone else did. He had built a square Brutalist building close to the river that he intended to market as a mall for galleries, "one-stop shopping for the discerning collector." (One of the things her husband loved about her, Bebe liked to say, was that she wrote his slogans.) But significant galleries were not charmed by the mall idea, and less significant ones couldn't afford the rent, and then Bebe's husband had died, went, according to Bebe, "out like a light in the car on the way home from Le Cirque." Bebe took a tour of the empty building while the estate was being settled and, as she liked to tell reporters, she had a brainstorm while looking down at her cuff bracelet: the museum was born.

Bebe's own jewelry had been the bulwark, still was, but over time they had added a collection of black pearls here, a tiara that could be turned into a necklace there, some really spectacular rubies, a group of brooches that had been smuggled out of Czsarist Russia sewn into somebody's skirt, and so on and so forth.

Sitting at her desk now, looking out her office window, Nora couldn't imagine a place that would have less appeal for a man like Bob Harris, who wore a Timex watch that looked as though it had been purchased in a drugstore many years before. They had certainly hosted corporate events at the museum, but they tended to be for cosmetic companies or women's magazines. One of the law firms had had a dinner in one of their galleries, but it was for trust-and-estates clients, mainly the kind of older women who were most likely to appreciate the museum and perhaps become benefactors. Nora had realized that there was a certain sort of woman in New York who wouldn't think of leaving her jewelry to anyone but her daughters and her granddaughters. But there was another sort—not as many, but enough—who loved the idea of having her name in a display case beneath an emerald parure, a word Nora had not even known until recently. They tended to be much like Bebe, a rich second wife, no children and no interest in those of her husband. And the law firm had been the one that represented Bebe, which went a long way to explaining why they had had a dinner there. Nora could imagine no possible nexus between Bob Harris and the Museum of Jewelry.

Nora had been at the museum from the beginning, when they were choosing staff, fonts, names for the place itself. They decided against Bebe's name since her last name was Pearl.

"People are just dumb enough to think there's nothing but pearls in the place," Bebe said, wearing what would become part of the collection, a huge cuff bracelet inlaid with rubies and a matching brooch shaped like a dragon. "What was your last name before you were married?" Bebe had once asked Nora, and when Nora told her, she rolled it around in her crimsoned mouth like a piece of hard candy: "Benson. Nora Benson. What a nice Protestant American name. But so is your married name. Benson to Nolan. You hardly went anywhere."

The suggestion was that Bebe herself had traveled some distance, and so she had. Her name had once been Edna Wisniewski. She had gone to a high school in Brooklyn famous for graduating nearly every one-hit wonder in the pre-Beatles pop era; on its wall of fame the two Nobel laureates in medicine were at the far end, back by the boys' bathroom. The first year the museum was open the school added Bebe to the wall. There was a photograph of a portrait her husband had commissioned right after their marriage. The portrait itself hung inside the museum. It made Bebe look like Elizabeth Taylor, whose jewelry collection she had attempted to emulate. Bebe always dressed in bright Chanel suits with at least two or three stupendous pieces of jewelry, a brooch nestled over her breast, a bracelet that seemed in danger of decommissioning her arm, spectacular earrings. She told Nora that they were copies of the originals, but Nora couldn't tell the difference.

Nora never wore any jewelry to work except her wedding ring and a pair of diamond stud earrings. She had scarcely any good stuff, and it seemed somehow improper to wear costume jewelry to the museum. She wore a work uniform: black pants, black shirt in the summer, black sweater in the winter, black jacket, black wool coat, black suit jacket, all of it of good fabric and cuts. When she had a business lunch she wore a black skirt. "Someday, babe," Jenny had said once, "you are going to cut loose and wear navy blue."

Bebe approved. She had decided that Nora had made a conscious decision to fade into the background of the museum, not that Nora was accustomed to fading into the background wherever she went. Nora's concession to variety and color was a scarf. She had dozens, maybe hundreds, of scarves. It had made her birthday and Christmas easy for Charlie, who was the kind of terrible gift giver who, when they were first married, had given her craft-show jewelry made of papier-mâché and small appliances that had limited use. Bebe always referred to Nora's scarves as "schmattes," which was as close as she ever came to acknowledging her own origins as a fit model in a low-end sportswear house, whose showroom, ironically, had been just a few blocks from the museum.

"Do you know Bob Harris?" Nora asked when she passed Bebe's office on the day that Bob called her.

"That super-rich guy? I don't think I've ever met him. Don't get me wrong, I'd love to, but I'm pretty sure I would remember if I had. Why?"

"Just wondering," Nora said.

"Here's what I keep wondering about, cookie," Bebe said. "How come we can't get rid of that hobo outside?"

"*Hobo.* Now there's a word I haven't heard in a long time."

"Why can't we get someone to move him along?"

"The Constitution? The right of the people to assemble? Free speech? The sidewalk?"

Bebe made a sound of dismissal and disapproval not unlike

the ones Charity sometimes favored. The man who sat on the sidewalk near the museum entrance said his name was Phil, but who knew? When Nora had contacted the city about him after the museum first opened, when he was out on the street with a lugubrious mutt of some indeterminate kind, she'd been handed from office to office until finally she gave up and called the local church shelter and got someone smart, with a sense of humor, who recognized the sign he had then, which read PLEASE HELP WITH DOG FOOD HE'S HUNGRY. "Not to worry," the woman said with a throaty chuckle. "He's not really what we classify as homeless. Call the ASPCA about the dog. They'll make him leave it home." Nora had had one of their security people work overtime to keep an eye out. As it turned out, Phil picked up his blanket, his sign, and his dog as darkness began to fall and took everything to a battered Subaru Outback parked in a spot reserved for vehicles with commercial plates, which the car actually had. The security guy had friends who were cops, and one of them did a computer search and found out the Outback was registered to a P. J. Moynes, who lived in a two-family house in Queens that had been carved up into apartments.

"You are a complete fraud," Nora said the following week when Phil appeared in his usual spot.

Phil laughed. "You, too," he said. His sign now read A SAND-WICH IS ONLY THREE BUCKS. Two women stopped and dropped a dollar bill into his big red cup. Phil put his finger to his lips as the women moved away. "If you don't tell on me, I won't tell on you," he said. "How's the jewelry biz?"

"It's a museum," Nora said.

"Tomato, tomahto," Phil said. "I hope you're happy now. My poor dog is cooped up in the house all day instead of getting fresh air."

"Where can you get a sandwich for only three bucks?" Nora said.

"You need to relax more," said Phil. "You're too literal-minded."

"That's what my daughter says," Nora said.

"Smart girl," said Phil.

It is necessary to raise the monthly charge for parking from $325 to $350. Please remit on November 1 accordingly.

Sincerely,

Sidney Stoller

As the weather grew colder and the days shorter, as Nora moved the sweaters from basement closets to bedroom bureaus, the atmosphere on the block seemed to darken. One evening, taking Homer out for the last walk, she had stumbled on something on her front steps, and, as she righted herself, Homer stepped forward gingerly to sniff at a small bag with a knot at the top. Someone had left discarded dog poop on her stoop. With two fingers Nora put it in the trash can. She looked up and down the street, but there was no one in sight. "Yuck," she said aloud, and Homer looked up solemnly.

It had also begun to feel as though the parking lot was more of a curse than a blessing, as though the men on the block had sold their souls to some devil of convenience. "We let Nolan in and everything went to hell," George said jovially one morning. It was another reason Nora couldn't bear him; there was no one like George for saying something lacerating in a hail-fellow voice.

First the Lessmans had come out to find the windshield of their car shattered. There was a good deal of speculation about what had happened, although George had immediately said, "Let's not fool ourselves, folks," and gestured toward the windows of the SRO. Linda Lessman said that their insurance company had refused to pay until the adjuster had determined whether it was a "spontaneous event."

"Like spontaneous combustion?" Linda said, her fists on her narrow hips. "Are there numerous instances of windshields just shattering into a thousand pieces?"

After that, there was the junker of a car with stickers for Carlsbad Caverns, the Sierra Club, and Ralph Nader that had been abandoned in front of the curb cut leading into the lot, so that all the cars within were trapped and effectively held hostage. That was bad enough, but Jack Fisk, who had once had what he habitually called "juice" with city government, now no longer seemed to wield the same power. When the junker had first appeared Jack had snapped his fingers at the others as he stood in his blue chalk-striped suit on the sidewalk: gone, like that, he'd promised. But it wasn't until three days later that a tow truck had snagged the car's dinged front bumper with the hook. "I hate working this block," the tow operator said to Nora as Homer sniffed at his front tire and then lifted his leg in a casual arabesque. "It's a nightmare getting in and out of here."

"It's about goddamn time," Jack Fisk had shouted when he saw that the junker was gone.

Sherry had told Nora that Jack's firm had a mandatory retirement age of sixty-five; after that, your name moved from the equity-partner column on the left of the letterhead to a column on the right for what were called "senior counselors" but were understood to be the over-the-hill guys. "They call it the obituary column," Sherry said.

"Yikes," Nora said. It was early on a Sunday, just past nine, and Nora was still in her running clothes. Sherry was carrying a bag of bagels.

"Oh, it gets worse. Guess who dreamed up the idea for mandatory retirement when he was a Young Turk?" Sherry nodded down the block toward her husband's back.

"Yikes," Nora repeated.

There wasn't even anyone to complain to about the problems with the parking lot. It was owned by a ghost, a man none of them had ever actually met. Sidney Stoller: that was how they made out their checks, sent to a post office box and due the first of the month. Every time she ran into an old man on the block, Nora imagined it might be Sidney Stoller, finally come to call, but as far as she knew, it never was.

"Please can we go back to the old garage?" Nora had said the week before as she and Charlie read the inside sections of the Sunday *New York Times,* the ones that were printed early.

"Why? Because the lot is twenty-five dollars more now? I know you weren't a math major, but even you can figure out that that's still a net savings."

Nora lowered the book review. "There's no need to get nasty," she said. "The parking situation on the block is causing a lot of bad feeling. Not to mention that now all of you are being ordered around by that idiot George."

"What is it Rachel always says about you? You're so judgy. All I know is I've got a lunch in two hours in Stamford," said Charlie, pushing back his chair and not looking at her, "and if Ricky has me blocked in, there's going to be more than bad feeling."

"It's Saturday, Charlie. Ricky doesn't work on Saturdays." But of course that wasn't true. Ricky worked whenever anyone needed him. Sherry Fisk had once called him at home on a

Sunday night when a pipe in her basement was spewing water all over the floor, and a half hour later he was downstairs, his toolbox and a Shop-Vac on the steps, taking care of business.

Obviously Jack Fisk had forgotten all about that. He'd come out one morning to take his car from the lot and found Ricky's van blocking him in. Or at least that's what he said. It was only a day after the junker had finally been towed, and Jack was still in a bit of a rage, which was more or less his natural condition. When he finally tracked Ricky down at the Rizzolis', where he was fixing a garbage disposal in which a teaspoon was thoroughly jammed, Ricky tried to argue that Jack had room to get around his van, which made Jack only angrier. "Don't tell me I can get around you," Jack screamed while Ricky stood with rounded shoulders on the stoop. "It's not my goddamn job to get around you. It's your job to stay out of my goddamn way."

Sherry had apologized to Nora for her husband. "Predictably, of our two sons, one has a volcanic temper, and the other is so conflict-avoidant that if you ran him over with a tank he'd say, Oh, sorry, I was in your way," she said sadly. "Andrew and his wife want to have kids, and I suggested that before they do, he try anger management classes."

"What did he say?" Nora asked.

"What always happens when you suggest a man take anger management classes?"

"He gets angry?"

"See, and you're not even a therapist," said Sherry, who was.

Linda Lessman, who always saw the world in black and white, which Nora imagined must be a useful quality in a criminal-court judge, unless you were a defendant, had once said she didn't understand why anyone who was a therapist would put up with a man like Jack. But Nora had always tended to see most things in shades of gray, and she had noticed that logic and marital relations often seemed at odds with each other.

Nora also understood the genesis of Jack's immediate rage: in her experience, nothing made a man angrier than being told that he couldn't drive like NASCAR. She remembered one terrible day when Charlie had been trying to get the car into a tiny street space on the way to an open house for a co-op apartment. It had taken so long that Oliver, whose toilet training was a bit dicey well into kindergarten, had wet his pants. When Charlie zoomed away—because the space was far too small, Nora had been sure that if you'd used a tape measure you would have discovered their car was a good foot longer than the space was—Rachel had made the mistake of saying, "Aren't you going to try again, Daddy?"

That had been one to remember.

And so it went on the block, mishap by misadventure. After the broken windshield, the junker, and Jack's tantrum, a transformer blew in a Con Edison grate and the entrance to the lot was temporarily blocked while it was repaired. Charlie, Jack, George, Harold Lessman, the oldest Rizzoli son, and two of the guys who lived in the SRO were standing that Sunday morning at the edge of the hole the utility workers had made. Nora had stopped to look into it when she was out with Homer. The improbable guts of New York lay exposed below her in the kind of filthy trench she imagined you could find anywhere from Lexington Avenue to Wall Street. Peering into the hole made by the Con Ed guys, Nora thought it was amazing that anything held together at all, that water came out of their taps, that power went into their outlets, that their houses didn't all tumble to the ground. The dirty little secret of the city was that while it was being constantly created, glittering glass and steel towers rising everywhere where once there had been parking lots, gas stations, and four-story tenements, it was simultaneously falling apart. The streets were filled with excavations and repair crews, the older buildings sheathed in scaffolding cages.

"Scaffolding," Charlie had muttered one day not long ago. "That's the business I should have gone into. If I owned a scaffolding firm I'd be a rich man today."

"A lot of salt damage," she heard the older of the SRO guys say now as the men clustered around the hole. Despite what they had all believed when they moved onto the block, most of the SRO guys worked, the kind of journeyman jobs that once used to allow for a small apartment in Hell's Kitchen and now only provided for a room with a hotplate in a single-room-occupancy hotel. Rumor had it that Sidney Stoller owned the SRO, too, but no one had ever been able to determine if that was true. There was no point in looking at the deed; there would surely be some corporate title obscuring the name of the true owner. All real estate in Manhattan now seemed to change hands under the cover of an LLC. No millionaire ever sold his duplex on East End Avenue to another millionaire. It was always Blair Holdings LLC to Sadieland LLC, or such like, the names of children being popular covers for the true identities of their parents.

Down the block the men were squatting at the edge of the hole, desk guys pretending they knew what it took to work with their hands. Nora remembered how contemptuous she had once been of couples who drove in the car with the two men in the front and the two women in the back. The men and women on the block now did the same when they got together to talk. The women were talking about people, the men talking about things. It was why so many of the men prospered on Wall

Street and in the big law firms, where things could be turned into money and people were interchangeable and even insignificant, and there were hardly any women running the show. The night before, she and Charlie had gone to have dinner with Jenny and the man with whom she was currently sleeping, and Nora and Jenny had decided that they were giving boy-girl seating up because Charlie and Jasper spent the entire evening talking to each other, and Nora and Jenny the same, which was fine with everyone involved.

"What does Jasper do?" Nora had asked Jenny in the kitchen.

"He's a cabinetmaker. Also a voice-over actor and a dialect coach."

"Promise me he's not also a mime. Anything but a mime."

Jenny put cheese and grapes on a platter. "Would I sleep with a mime?" she said.

"You slept with that circus clown."

"That was a long time ago. And I was really drunk."

In the car on the way home Nora said to Charlie, "You seemed to get on with him."

"He's a smart guy," Charlie said. "He's kind of wasted making kitchen cabinets but, hey, who am I to talk. Jenny'll have a nice kitchen, and he'll get whatever. I wonder if he charges less if you're sleeping with him while he's doing your kitchen."

"Wait, I knew she was redoing her kitchen, but I didn't know the guy she was dating was the contractor."

"She's your best friend. How come you don't already know this? And is 'dating' a term that ever applies to Jenny?" Charlie had always found Jenny's promiscuity threatening, as though it were a communicable disease, as though Nora were going to have breakfast with Jenny and then give a man she met in the coffee shop line a blow job in the restroom.

"My best friend is seeing the man who is redoing her kitchen," Nora said to Sherry Fisk now, not meaning to say it aloud until she'd already done so. "Seeing. Sleeping with. What do we call it now?"

"I bet it will be a great kitchen," Sherry said.

"You have to do something to make a kitchen renovation bearable," said Alma Fenstermacher, who had stopped to join them. She stared for a moment at the scrum at the end of the street, then walked on, perhaps, Nora thought, to attend church. Alma seemed like the sort of person to attend church on Sunday.

"Why do I like her?" Sherry said. "I shouldn't like her. She's so—"

"Perfect," Nora said. "You can tell her closets are always tidy. See, *tidy*—that's a word I've probably never used before to describe anyone, but it's perfect for Alma. She's a throwback to another era, before we wore workout clothes all the time and used profanity. She's perfect and yet she's perfectly nice. It's impossible not to like her."

The Con Ed truck rumbled down the street, and the men at the lot entrance began to disperse. "I have to tell you, I'm grateful for this," Sherry said, gesturing down the street. "At least it gives my husband something else to obsess about. This whole thing with the parking lot is a metaphor for his entire life right now. These guys have no life except for their jobs. So without their jobs they have no life. Jack gets out of bed mad and goes to bed mad. I think he's mad in his dreams."

"Yikes," said Nora again, but she couldn't help nodding.

Nora thought Charlie's dissatisfaction with his work and therefore his life had begun to grow with his fiftieth birthday two years before. She had hosted a dinner for twenty at an expensive restaurant they both liked, but her husband had so much to drink that he started to sob during Oliver's toast ("And it wasn't even that good," Rachel said the next day) and fell asleep with his mouth open in the back of the car on the way home.

Charlie was an investment banker. It had become enough to say that, at parties, in conversation. No one really knew what that meant except other finance guys, and they liked the fact that they spoke a secret language that others, especially women, couldn't understand. Nora had made it her business to listen carefully to the long, discursive stories he told at dinner about deals, firms, personalities, possibilities, but it was all too boring. At a certain point simply pretending to listen, looking attentive, nodding and umming from time to time, seemed like enough of a sacrifice. So Charlie would say, "You're not going to believe this one . . ." and Nora would go elsewhere in her mind: replacement of the living room drapes, bong in Oliver's bedroom drawer, press for the upcoming exhibit. She'd gotten good at it: Charlie would say in the dark at night, "Remember that deal I told you Jim and I were working on?" And Nora would say, "Yes, of course," and start umming again, and he'd be content.

Rachel had begged Charlie to be one of the parents at career day at her school when she was in third grade, one of the phases of Oedipal transference in which she thought her father was handsome and brilliant and her mother was nobody and had stupid hair. The two of them had come home at the end of the day, each wearing the expression of someone sorely disappointed.

"Apparently I am a bad explainer," Charlie said, filling a glass with ice cubes and vodka and yanking Rachel's favorite pink-patterned tie, the one with wolves in sheep's clothing, through the lariat of his collar. Rachel had already started upstairs to her bedroom. "A horrible explainer," she yelled, before slamming the door. "Even I can't really explain what Daddy does," Nora said later, when she was tucking her in, but Rachel said, turning to the wall, "Then he shouldn't have come to school to talk about it."

Increasingly what Charlie talked about was what he called "the short-pants boys," by which he meant the young associates, some of whom prospered to what Charlie insisted was a laughable degree by means ranging from nepotism to ass-kissing to dirty-dealing. Charlie had once been one of those young men, and while he had done his share of ass-kissing, he had at first prospered because he shone with simple decency, which was still the case and owed more to fair hair and skin than anyone ever realized. Over the years his colleagues had waited for the shark to emerge from behind the nice guy, the wolf in sheep's clothing to make an appearance, the open-faced mask to drop. Nora suspected that when they realized it was not a mask at all, they had begun to value Charlie less. She never mentioned those early years, when, as he liked to say, the sky was the limit.

Nor did she intend to mention that the legendary Bob Harris had been so very anxious to meet with her. When she had finally agreed to sit down with him, she had insisted on meeting on an evening when she knew her husband had a client dinner across town. When Nora arrived at the office she slunk onto the executive floor as though she were there for an assignation, and indeed Bob Harris had attempted to corner her in the past at at least two office functions. "Can't blame a guy for trying, now can you?" he'd said. Unlike many of the New York transplants Nora met, Bob Harris did not pretend to be to the manor born, but instead went the opposite way, milked his origins preposterously. He twanged like a banjo, called soda "pop," and liked to say things like "when pigs fly." His firm was called Parsons Ridge, after the town in West Virginia where he'd been born. "That sounds picturesque," the PR-assistant wife of one of the short-pants boys had said at a cocktail party.

"It's a shit hole," Harris had said.

"You look fine," he said now, Nora sitting opposite him in his office.

"And you, Mr. Harris."

He sighed, reached for his bourbon. He always took it with a maraschino cherry for some reason, and Nora had noticed that the level in his glass stayed more or less the same through any event or evening. Nora had passed on a drink. She'd worn a black fluted skirt not conducive to giving the person sitting opposite a peek at her panties. Some of the men she had to do business with would drop their pens so their eyes were level with her knees and any gap between them. Bob wouldn't see the point of that.

"No matter what I do, you're never gonna call me Bob," he said. "Even if I get you to come work for me."

"Hard to figure how that would happen," Nora said, "since I know next to nothing about your business." She'd noticed that when people were around Bob Harris they tended to lapse into his syntax and vocabulary. She'd once heard a partner who had attended prep school and Yale unthinkingly use the verb "reckon." As in Bob saying:

"I don't reckon it's much of a secret that I'm putting a pile of money into a foundation. A pile of money."

"How much is a pile?" Nora asked.

"You are a pisser," Bob Harris said, shaking his head. "Anybody else sits there all quiet and mealy-mouthed, butter wouldn't melt in it. Thinking what you're thinking but not saying it. For now, let's keep the exact number on the QT. Let's just say it will make all these folks sit up and take notice. What do you think about education?"

"Do you care about education?"

"Hell, woman, everybody cares about education. Not that I did much with mine. Just—" He chuckled and gestured to the enormous plate-glass window as though it were a trophy case, assorted skyscrapers just beyond the sill. Bob Harris liked to make much of the fact that he had gone to a third-tier state school and gotten thrown out for making a chain of women's undergarments that stretched around the entire administration building. Twice. "In every color under the sun, boys, not just your white ones, either. A lot of black and red. A lot." He had a mysterious wife whom various profiles said he'd married while he was still in school, who was never seen and was said to live nearly all the time at their farm, which was in Virginia. There were no photographs of her in his office, nor of their son, who was said to be a geologist in New Mexico.

Nora refused to fill the silence. "So what about it?" Bob continued. "Come run this foundation for me. People I know think you're good at what you do. You got to have better things to do than shepherd a lot of housewives around looking at bracelets."

"It's a museum. We offer historical and educational programs."

"There you go. You're already in the education business. You got no learning curve, and a nice manner." He leaned forward, and Nora pressed her knees together and smoothed her skirt, she thought surreptitiously, until he grinned. "You know why you're really here? One time I asked you about that museum, which I have to say I don't get the point of one bit, and you said to me, All jobs sound silly unless you're a pediatric oncologist, or a plumber. You remember saying that?"

Nora shook her head, although it was certainly possible. Somehow she always found herself more outspoken with Bob Harris than she was with almost anyone else.

"I'd need to know a lot more about how you plan to proceed to even think about this, Mr. Harris. The regulations governing foundations are pretty stringent. And the foundations that do good work do it because they're focused, certain of their mission, with a clear sense of where and how to spend their money."

Bob Harris waved his hand in the air, picked up his bourbon glass, looked at it as though he were admiring the brown velvet color, which Nora had to admit was pretty, put it down again. She couldn't help herself; she said, "Do you ever actually drink one of those?"

Bob Harris raised the glass to her. "Smart. Smart girl. 'Scuse me, woman, smart woman. That'd be good, too, have the foundation run by a woman. Whatever needs to be done, we'll do it. Whatever you need, we'll get it for you. Just have a little think on it, all right? Just a little think."

On her way out Nora turned and said, "May I ask a small favor?"

"God bless you, girl, I love the way you put words together."

Nora couldn't help herself. She started to laugh. "Oh, can the hayseed act, Bob," she said.

To her surprise and admiration he started to laugh as well.

"What's the favor?" he said in an almost accentless voice, as though he were an actor who had heard the director cry, "Cut!" and had gone back to his everyday way of talking.

"I already think one problem with your plan is the nepotism issue," she said. "My husband works for you. So in the meantime, would you not mention to him that we've discussed this?"

Bob Harris shrugged. "Darlin', I mentioned to him just this morning that we had a little meeting scheduled. Swear on my mama, I was amazed that he didn't seem to know anything about it." And before her opened a vista of the evening, and probably the week, to come: silent treatment, recriminations, questions, recriminations, silent treatment.

Which was precisely the way it went, Charlie at the dining room table with a drink and the greasy paper plate that meant he'd picked up a slice of pizza instead of heating up something Charity had left in the refrigerator. The bottle of vodka was on the table, too. That was the signal that Charlie Nolan was headed for blind drunk, when the bottle was on the table. Drunk. As. Hell.

Nora had stepped out of her heels in the foyer and walked barefoot into the kitchen, wondering how far down that road he'd traveled.

"I thought you had a business dinner," she said.

"Canceled," he said. "When were you going to mention your meeting with Bob Harris?"

"It just happened," Nora said, pouring some white wine and reaching for a container of leftover Chinese. "So I was going to tell you about it once I got home. And now I'm home."

"So you're going to go to work for him," said Charlie, declaratively, savagely.

"No, I'm not," Nora said. "He doesn't have a clear plan, and I already have a good job."

"He won't like that. He doesn't like people who say no to him." Nora sat down and looked at Charlie. She was thinking that Bob Harris struck her as exactly the kind of man who liked people who said no to him. Instead she said, "Too bad for him."

"You don't even know him," Charlie said. The word *don't* was a shapeless, slippery thing in the very back of his throat, and Nora knew that Charlie had gone way down the vodka road before she'd arrived.

"I've met him many times at your events."

"Did he say why he came to you in the first place?" Charlie said, and while Nora had asked herself the same question, she shot back, "That's insulting."

"Come on, Nora. If you're as big as Bob Harris and you're starting a foundation, there are a hundred people you could pick to run it."

"I repeat—that's insulting. I'm insulted. Maybe you want to stop insulting me now." Homer put his head in Nora's lap and whined. "Did you walk him?" she asked. "Of course not. Come on, good boy."

"At least one of us is a winner with that asshole," Charlie said as he stumbled upstairs and Nora went down to the foyer. "Kiss. My. Ass," she thought she heard as she snapped on Homer's leash. His boss? His wife? The universe? Who could tell? On the stoop sat another tightly knotted plastic bag. "What next?" Nora asked loudly. "I mean, really—what next?"

There was no way Nora would speak to Charity about any of this, about the parking situation or the bags on the stoop or Charlie's black moods. It was important that Charity be kept as contented as possible, or as contented as Charity ever got, which was not so much when the twins were not around. The Monday after Thanksgiving she came up from the basement, where she always changed into her work clothes, sweat pants and a T-shirt, and said to Nora dolefully, "My babies back at college now." Rachel and Oliver had arrived toting enormous duffels filled with dirty clothes, knowing Charity would be happy to see, and launder, and iron them, even the boxer shorts. Charity had done just that, repacked them, and sent them back to school refreshed, as she always did. She was habitually downcast after the hubbub was over.

Charity had always been their nanny, arriving at their apartment only an hour after they had gotten home from the hospital, making clucking noises as the two handfuls of swaddle, one dark, the other fair, squirmed and whined. "Peace peace peace," Charity had whispered, and Nora was all in.

Aside from the fact that Charity passionately believed Nora needed to drink Guinness in order to breastfeed successfully, and was sure that the twins were starving and so tried to sneak them bottles of formula larded with rice cereal, she had been a very satisfactory nanny. She was always on time, she never refused to stay late, and she adored the twins without indulging them. She taught Ollie the rules of cricket, arranged Rachel's unruly hair, had muffins on the counter after school when they were young and then fruit juices when they both started playing after-school sports. There was no hint of equivocation or dispassion in her devotion. You couldn't mention the word *Harvard* around Charity because Rachel had been denied admission, and Nora suspected she had found and destroyed all photographs of the girl who had broken up with Oliver senior year of high school.

Nora had only had to have a sit-down with Charity once, years before, when Charity had decided to let the kids know what a friend they had in Jesus. Charlie was a lapsed Catholic, Nora had grown up vaguely Presbyterian, but Charity belonged to the Church of the Living Risen Son of God, a mainly Jamaican congregation, which met in what had formerly been a movie theater. Nora knew this because Rachel had given her a full report after Charity had agreed to stay for a weekend when Nora and Charlie were obliged to go on one of those three-day golf and spa trips that a director Charlie worked with considered essential for team-building. The blood of the lamb seemed to have figured prominently in the service, as did the notion that everyone was a poor sinner.

"I need to be cleansed in the waters, Mommy," Rachel had said. "In the River Jordan."

When Nora confronted Charity about this, she seemed not the least contrite. "Children be needing the Lord in their lives," Charity said.

"I know you believe that," Nora said. "But Charlie and I have different ideas about religion."

"Some things are just believing," Charity had said, lifting her chin. "Some things just the truth."

"Guess that shut you right up," Christine had said on the phone.

Charity was the source of most intelligence about the block, which she got from the other housekeepers and nannies. As they walked the dogs and swept the sidewalks, they gossiped about movie stars, popular singers, and the people they worked for. Three months before the Levinsons put their house on the market—two months before Dori Levinson had given her husband's clothes, tennis rackets, and chess set to a charity shop and had the locks changed while he was at work—Charity had said, "Mr. and Mrs. Levinson, no good." Nora had been able to call Alma Fenstermacher and bring over a tin of cookies in a timely fashion because Charity said, "Mr. Fenstermacher, no more bladder." It was Edward Fenstermacher's gallbladder, of course, not his bladder, but Nora had still been glad of the intelligence. It was important not to cross Charity unnecessarily. Early on Nora had said jocularly, having heard an exchange on the playground between two nannies, "Do all Caribbean women yell at each other all the time?"

"What?" Charity had shouted, and Nora just shut up.

She had had to clear Ricky with Charity before he started working in the house. "Puerto Rico," Charity had said, adding a sound like air going out of a tire under pressure. It had taken two years of his meticulous service for her to acknowledge that

Ricky was not lazy and to stop checking Nora's jewelry box for theft after he left, although how he could possibly steal anything when Charity hung over his shoulder like a shawl Nora could not imagine. Charity eventually acknowledged that he was hardworking and trustworthy, but said this was because he was actually from South America, which was not true, although he was not Puerto Rican, either. She had also let Nora know when Ricky and his wife had had first one child, then another. Nora had passed clothes and sports equipment that had once belonged to the twins along to Ricky's boys, who were now eight and ten and whose photographs, posed in front of a spectacularly phony mountain backdrop, were taped to the dash of the van.

There was a shadow government on the block, a shadow government that knew where all the bodies were buried, a system of mutual dependence, one group needing services, the other employment. Nora was never certain where the balance of power fell. Charity knew when Nora bought new underpants, when Rachel was menstruating. She changed the sheets, so she knew when Nora and Charlie had had sex, which was not so often now. She picked up their prescriptions. She knew their secrets.

Nora would never forget the two of them sitting side by side on the couch in the den of their old apartment staring at the television screen the September morning of the terrorist attacks downtown, the sound the two of them made together as the first of the World Trade Center towers distintegrated in slow motion. That day was the first time she had ever seen Charity sit down while at work. It was the first time Charity had stayed overnight when Nora and Charlie were there as well. At dawn Nora had found her in the kitchen, listening to the radio, making sandwiches for the firefighters at the fire station nearby, Charity wiping the tears from her face with the back of the hand that held the bread knife. Wordlessly Nora had joined her.

The only other time Nora had seen Charity weep was at the twins' high school graduation. She had worn a pink hat with silk flowers and a pink suit. Oliver had gone out and gotten Charity an orchid corsage. Nora would bet anything that that corsage was pressed somewhere, perhaps in the pages of Charity's Bible.

When Nora passed Ricky Monday morning she called, "Good morning, Enrique," in as cheery a voice as possible, given the atmosphere around the parking lot.

"You need me, Mrs. Nolan?" Ricky said.

"Charity says the dryer isn't working properly."

"That vent," Ricky said, shaking his head. "I'll take care of it. We don't want to get on Charity's bad side."

"No, we do not," Nora said.

Linda Lessman was waiting for a cab on the corner to go to work at the criminal courts building. Her fair hair was always damp in the mornings since, having been the captain of her college swimming team, with the square shoulders and narrow hips to prove it, she tried to do laps each day before work. Nora had been a little afraid of her when the Nolans first arrived on the block—of Linda's blunt, declarative sentences and direct gaze—but over time she had come to like her.

Legend had it that residents of the block had once caught up with one another in the supermarket and the drugstore, but the supermarket had been replaced by a twenty-story condo building, the drugstore by a bank branch, and everything was delivered now: the groceries, the dry cleaning, the takeout. When the twins were home they had breakfast delivered, coffee in go-cups and pancakes in foam containers. At 2 A.M. they would often order tikka masala and cheese fries, sushi and baklava.

"You ladies seen Ricky?" George called from halfway down the block. Linda and Nora both stared at him as he approached. He was wearing what appeared to be a baby carrier, the kind of front pack in which Nora and Charlie had once carried the twins, switching their respective burdens back and forth because carrying Oliver was like carrying a sack of flour and carrying Rachel like carrying a bag of ferrets.

In the baby carrier was George's newest rescue pug, who stared balefully at Nora with its bug eyes. Nora thought all pugs looked baleful.

"She's got an issue with anxiety," George said, looking down at the dog "The vet thought this might help."

"Really?" said Linda. One word, and Linda could effortlessly communicate skepticism and contempt. She must be hell on feckless lawyers.

"If George upsets Ricky, I will snatch him bald-headed," Linda muttered as he walked away.

"That is an expression I haven't heard in years."

"I've always thought it was a good one. I wish there was a way I could use it in court," Linda said, a cab pulling up next to her. "Share?"

"I'm walking," Nora said.

Nora walked to work nearly every morning, and had for years. People always acted as though it had to do with staying fit, but the fact was she found it an almost spiritual exercise. When Nora was nine her mother had brought her in on the train for lunch and the Christmas show at Radio City. They had stepped out of Grand Central onto the street and Nora had turned to look up at the façade, and the statue of Mercury perched at the center of the roofline seemed to be looking back toward her. When they got home her mother had slipped off her black pumps in the living room, an angry red line encircling her narrow insteps, and breathed, "I am exhausted," before she went upstairs. Nora had never felt more alive in her life.

She'd never been entirely sure of what to do with herself. She had had a poem in the high school literary magazine, but then she had submitted two short stories and the poem to a legendary seminar at college and gotten them back with "NA" on the front. Not accepted, not good enough. She had taken a prep course for the law boards but her mind kept wandering, and she felt as though graduate school would take forever. The one thing she had always been certain of was that she wanted to move to New York after college, and she had.

That had been a different New York, different from the one she had visited that first time with her mother. Nearly all of the people on the block had come to the city just as it was digging itself out of a deep hole of insolvency and crime. Yet they had wanted desperately to come there nonetheless, despite the need to hold keys thrust between their fingers as makeshift weapons, the need to have a blood test after a night of so-so sex. Then, slowly over the last two decades, New York had become safe, cleaner, and then impossible for anyone who didn't have a lot of money. Times Square, once a tattered circus sideshow of women in hot pants and plastic heels selling themselves cheap, of hunched, half-crazy homeless guys pushing leaflets for peep shows, of all-hours coffee shops that served pancakes to junkies at three in the morning, was now a fever dream of neon and virtual-reality billboards, so thick with tourists that New Yorkers avoided it at all costs. The city had become like that edgy girl in college, all wild hacked hair and leather, who showed up at reunion with a blow-dried bob and a little black dress, her nose-piercing closed up as though it had never existed.

All this had made the future seem impossibly out of reach for the young. During the summer she and Rachel had driven to a spa in Massachusetts for massages and nature hikes, and that night she had let Rachel have a glass of wine with dinner. It had loosened the floodgates of late adolescence. "Sometimes I'm really afraid," her daughter said, her cheeks pink from either the rejuvenating facial or the Chardonnay.

"Oh, honey, of what?" Nora asked.

"Of not succeeding and not making you and Daddy proud of me," she said, her eyes filling.

"We're proud of you no matter what you do."

"Mom, honestly, I hate it when you say that. It's like those trophies everybody used to get at day camp for just showing up. You don't want someone to be proud of you for nothing. You want them to be proud of you for actually doing something to be proud of."

Next morning Rachel had been her usual self, making faces all through barre class and insisting that having her armpits waxed had to be more painful than natural childbirth. "If I have kids I'm taking the drugs," Rachel said.

"It's a labor of love," Nora said.

"Spare me," said Rachel, but she leaned in and kissed her mother as she said it.

Nora's walk to work was a kind of labor of love, too, of that love for the city that occasionally wavered or dimmed but had never gone away. She tended to see always the same people, the Sikh bicyclist with his two small children in a seat on the back, the man who ran while nonchalantly juggling three fluorescent green tennis balls. It was as though they all knew one another without knowing anything about one another, so that if for a week or two Tennis Ball Man did not appear Nora would find herself wondering if he was on vacation, or had moved to another neighborhood, or something worse, a broken hip, a heart attack.

Change was the leitmotif of New York, and yet there was an unvarying fabric for most New Yorkers. At the halfway point of her walk Nora almost always passed the old woman who threw pieces of baguette into the water for the geese and the gulls. Sometimes she wondered about the genesis of those baguettes, perhaps delivered too late for the restaurant's dinner rush because of traffic, cannibalized in part for croutons and bread pudding, the rest junked in the dumpster and rescued by the old woman and loaded into the wire cart she always pushed. Or maybe, Nora thought, the woman was someone with a nice pension and no relations who spent all her disposable income on bread for birds. Nora said good morning to her every day. The woman always ignored her.

She loved this part of her day, even in the worst weather, when the wind, abetted by the open runway of the river, ripped at the spokes of her umbrella and rattled the nylon overhead. Even with the pale scrim of snowfall or fog, she could see the skyline of the New Jersey towns, what always seemed like a halfhearted attempt to echo their triumphant cousin across the Hudson. Charlie tolerated New York City, but was prone to spreading his arms and crooning, "Ah, smell that air," when he found himself anywhere from her father's house in Connecticut to an inn in the Tuscan countryside. Nora liked those places, but her relationship to the city was primal and chemical. There was a great immutability to the Hudson River, broad and gray and dappled like moiré taffeta, and a certain democracy to those she passed going to and fro, who, in workout clothes or the coat thrown on to walk the schnauzer, could be schoolteacher or CEO.

Occasionally she passed the walk-up building where she had lived for two years after college, sharing a one-bedroom. She and Jenny had flipped a coin to see who would sleep on the living room futon, and Nora had lost. Actually, Jenny scarcely needed the bedroom since there were many nights when she did not come home, and Nora lay awake wondering how long she should wait before calling the police. Then just after dawn, with mascara-ed raccoon eyes and pantyhose in her purse, Jenny would tiptoe through to the kitchen, and coffee.

She was getting her doctorate at Columbia then and stayed on to teach there, although when the time came she was almost denied tenure. She had expanded her thesis on matriarchal societies into a popular book that had gotten a lot of attention and landed Jenny on several television interview shows, which worked perfectly because she looked like an actress playing a young and beautiful anthropologist, all curly hair and big eyes and bohemian clothing. This led the chair of the department to refer to her as a "popular" academic, with the word *popular* used as a perjorative. But two weeks later the chair of the department had died of a stroke, and the week after that the provost's wife invited Jenny to speak to her book club, which was convenient because all its members were the wives of administrators or professors. There were no other women in the anthropology department, and the university was being investigated for gender bias, and Jenny got tenure and then, later, an endowed chair.

"Just a series of lucky breaks," she always said with a grin. "Especially that stroke."

Every once in a while, when she had a meeting, Nora would pass the narrow windows of the bar at which she'd met Charlie. Fourteen Carrots, it was called now, with its vegan menu, but then it had been The Tattooed Lady. Nora hadn't wanted to go that night, she remembered. She'd had an unremarkable romantic life in the city compared to that of her other girlfriends, which was to say it hovered between pathetic and disastrous. She had arrived in the city still deeply in love with her ex-boyfriend from college and had had the bad fortune, on an early date with a broker who had been attractive and not at all obviously psycho, to see James at a table across the room, laughing, combing back his wavy, dark hair with one hand in a gesture she knew as well as she knew the alphabet. Nora had wept over the crème brûlée on the dessert menu, which had been their dessert, hers and James's. ("Who has a dessert?" Jenny said the next day. "A song, okay. A place. But a dessert? And the most boring dessert. Okay, maybe rice pudding is more boring, but, Jesus, Nor, at least cry for lava cake.") Of course the broker had never called her again.

Nora had lost track of all the ones who came after, and in retrospect she blamed herself. Her great love affair had ended under such an improbable cloud that she was suspicious of virtually every man she encountered. Every first date was second-guessing. There had been what seemed like a really nice lawyer, who brought a picnic to Central Park and took her to the Cloisters, and who for several weeks she thought might be in it for the long haul. Then he disappeared, and her friend Jean-Ann, also a lawyer, heard his name and mentioned that in her circle he was called The Phantom because he wowed every woman he wooed and then vanished without a trace. And Nora's distrust only deepened.

It was Jenny who had insisted she come to The Tattooed Lady. There was a TA at Columbia Jenny wanted Nora to meet, not, she assured her, for a real relationship, but for reliable sex. Jenny always liked to say that she didn't date, she slept with people, and once she had had a couple glasses of wine, *slept with* was not the term she used. Earlier that day she had helped Nora pick out her first leather jacket, and she made her wear it and wear her hair down, too. "What the hell with the ponytail, Nor," she'd said, pulling the elastic loose. "You'll be losing your hair by the time you're forty." Forty had sounded then like another country, like they would need passports and language lessons to live there.

The Columbia student was attractive in that peevish, elfin way that for some reason Jenny favored, and he wore ironic clothes, a vintage varsity jacket, brown-and-black saddle shoes. Charlie was his sort-of friend from Bowdoin, who, the Columbia student made clear in a series of asides, he had had to bring along after they'd run into each other unexpectedly. The TA chatted with Jenny while sizing up Nora sidelong, his index finger held in front of his lips in a way that looked disapproving. But Charlie bought Nora a drink and told her about a case he was working on pro bono, a school that was being dispossessed by the church in which it held classes. He'd just come from the office and he opened his briefcase to show her a drawing the first grade had made: THANK YOU MR. NOLLAND FOR HELPING OUR SHUL. "It's a Jewish school?" Nora said, but Charlie smoothed out the drawing with his hand and said, "No, they're kids—they can't spell. My name is Nolan, one *l*, no *d*." He had a Band-Aid on the bend of his arm, and when Nora asked about it he pulled it off and balled it up, said, "I forgot all about that. Company blood drive."

Charlie still gave blood once a year, maybe because Nora had said, a couple of months after that night, that the blood donation was one of the reasons she had given him her number. She couldn't tell him that, after all the bright young men who had talked about themselves manically as she nodded, the ones who were well and truly pissed that she wouldn't sleep with them in exchange for coq au vin and Cabernet, the ones with whom she had slept, including the guy who had given her an STD she now had to mention on almost every damn medical form even all these years later—after them all, Charlie one-*l* no-*d* Nolan, literal, guileless, all the things that would eventually make her sometimes want to scream, on that night, in this city, made her feel like that moment when you walk out of the waves, teeth chattering, gooseflesh from shoulder to ankle, and someone wraps you in a towel. That towel is just a towel, ordinary, humdrum, but at that one moment it feels like fur, better than fur, like safety, care, the right thing. Walking her back to the minute first-floor apartment into which she'd just moved, in a deeply unfashionable but not horribly dangerous neighborhood, Charlie had stopped at her corner and said, "You are great." When Rachel had rolled her eyes at the story, Charlie said it had never happened, but it had.

You. Are. Great.

Of course it now seemed forever ago. What had happened to all of them after they left behind those shabby little apartments, with the DMZ of boric acid showing white at the borders of cabinets and closets to ward off the roaches? When Nora had first met him at that bar Charlie had planned to practice environmental law, had instead been seconded to a junior partner in the corporate area, had traded in a job representing finance types for becoming one himself. Nora had meandered her way to something that might be called the top, she supposed, with her job at the museum.

The identities of everyone they knew were illusory: they considered themselves New Yorkers but all of them were from someplace else. And many of them had become people who loved to hate the city where they lived. But Nora had never stopped loving it. She still liked the sound of someone ranting on the street, someone screaming at a person who hadn't picked up after a dog, someone fighting over a parking space that two cars thought they had claimed with their blinkers, or someone simply spouting random crazy talk, although now, with cell-phones, it was sometimes hard to tell. In the old days a person speaking on the street was either a delusionary or an actor re-hearsing for an audition; now it could be someone taking a meeting through an earpiece. Nora still found it all oddly soothing, the idea that she was safe and warm and drinking a cup of tea and reading *The New Yorker* and outside some woman was screaming at her boyfriend that he never, *never,* paid atten-tion to what she was telling him (which had made Nora want to throw open the window and yell, "Duh!" into the raw and rainy night). She liked that she could hear the woman and the woman could see the light in her window and yet they were separate, unacquainted.

But even loving New York as she did, Nora sometimes felt it was like loving an old friend, someone who had over the years become different from her former self. Of course, Nora and Charlie had become different, too. It was as though, as the city had prospered and become less dirty, less funky, less hard and harsh, the Nolans and their friends had followed suit, all their rough edges and quirks sanded down into some New York standard of accomplishment. The price they had paid for prosperity was amnesia. They'd forgotten who they once had been.

Nora sometimes thought that if, through some magic of the space-time continuum, which she didn't understand but had heard Oliver and his geeky friends discuss through an entire year of high school, she might run into her younger self on her walk some morning, the two of them would scarcely recognize each other. The old Nora would have contempt for the new. The former Nora would be buying a hot dog with the works at the hot dog place on the corner of Broadway near their house, an outpost of sanity in a five-dollar-latte world, and the now-Nora would trudge by after picking up a salad, thinking of nitrates and acid reflux.

"The best hangover cure on earth is one of those dogs with cooked onions," Oliver had said his senior year in high school.

"Excuse me?" Nora said.

"Wake up and smell the mustard, Mommy," Rachel had said. Every time Nora walked past the hot dog place she remembered that, exorcising the nitrates. Wake up and smell the mustard. Or the pickles outside the last old deli on the Lower East Side, an area that had improbably become cool, as had the deli. Or the gyros that marked the moment when she turned onto the block where the museum hunched over the narrow street. The gyros were sold from a truck that played tinny Greek music starting at ten in the morning. Nora nodded at the guy at the truck window as she went by.

"Here she comes," called Phil, sitting cross-legged on the sidewalk. His sleeping bag was a dirty brown, his T-shirt gray,

his sign, black marker on tan cardboard: VETERAN NEED SOME-
THING TO EAT GOD BLESS YOU. The sky was as gray as his blanket.

"They're predicting rain this afternoon," Nora said.

"The driver for the big boss told me," he said. Bebe was the
big boss. Nora was merely the boss.

Nora couldn't complain to Charlie about the poop bags on the stoop because she knew he would once again talk about leaving the city, which had become his answer to everything from the clogged drain in the parking lot to the rise in real estate taxes to, she suspected, her meeting with Bob Harris. "When you start your new job," he would say sourly sometimes, no matter how often she said she had no intention of leaving the one she had. Charlie clutched his grievances close. He remembered every co-op building at which the real estate person had been high-handed, every restaurant at which they'd sat at the bar for too long while others were led to a table.

So Nora mentioned the poop bags only at her women's lunch. She should have known the others would be somewhat unsympathetic. All of them lived in apartment buildings, with doormen who would make short work of anyone trying to leave a tissue on the sidewalk in front, much less a bag of dog leavings. "Not while we're eating, for Christ's sake," Elena said when Nora was talking, waving her hand in the air.

"Do you know an architect named James Mortimer?" Suzanne asked Nora. "I'm decorating a house that he designed, and when I said one of my girlfriends had been at Williams he said that you two were friends in college."

"We were," Nora said.

"What kind of friends?" Suzanne said.

"What's the house?" Nora said, instead of answering.

"What can I say, a total nightmare. One of those hedge fund guys with a second wife bought two walk-up buildings downtown and had them razed to build something with eight bedrooms, a green roof, and a lap pool. Aluminum."

"Why would anyone want an aluminum lap pool?" Jenny said.

"Not the lap pool, the house. Very modern, angular, the kind of thing that will wind up in some magazine. The wife was an art history major and thinks she knows what she's doing. The only thing that's keeping her under control is that I think she's crushing on your friend James. I just hope she doesn't sleep with him and blow the whole deal up. It's a good job for me in a lot of ways. It will get a lot of attention, and they don't care what anything costs. And working with James—"

"I want a detailed explanation of how you're going to furnish this place," said Jenny, who had less interest in furniture than anyone Nora knew but wanted Suzanne to natter on about grass cloth and glass tile instead of James Mortimer, which was exactly what happened. As they walked out together, Jenny muttered, "Jesus, this city is like Mayberry. Everyone knows everyone else, especially the people you don't want them to know. Especially James goddamn Mortimer."

"It's fine, Jen," Nora said. "How's Jasper?"

"Good. He's auditing one of my classes."

"Really?"

"The one on fertility and pregnancy in various cultures. He

doesn't have time to come to class, but he does all the readings and he says he even wants to do the paper. Can you imagine a surer way to kill a relationship? 'Sorry, babe, but this is a B-minus at best.'"

"Are you actually in a relationship?"

"I think maybe I am. Isn't that weird? What about you? You seem a little fried."

"I'm fine. I just wish someone would stop leaving poop bags in front of my house."

"That's weird and creepy, and I say that as someone who has never even owned a dog. Is that the right term? Do we still own dogs, or is that, I don't know, speciesist? And if I can't say you own a dog anymore, does that mean we're all officially insane? We are, aren't we? Totally insane. I used to be a radical feminist, and the other day one of my students dismissed me as a straight establishment woman."

"Sometimes I think Homer owns us," Nora said. "I don't think we'd even live where we live if it wasn't for Homer."

It was true: in a way, Homer was responsible for their life on the block. His arrival had dovetailed with a period when Charlie had believed that he was on the verge of becoming (pick one, depending on degree of intoxication) a top gun, a macher, a rainmaker, a big swinging dick. They were living in a nice-enough three-bedroom apartment, and with a big bump in the real estate market their equity in their place had doubled. Add a boom-year bonus, and Charlie became obsessed with the idea that they should have a place more conducive to parties, dinners. He'd actually used the word *entertaining* two or three times.

But virtually all of the co-ops they looked at had a no-dog policy, and eventually their real estate agent had taken them to see the house. "No board approval, no financials," she said to

Charlie, as though they might be drug dealers, but the long vista of the second-floor double parlor answered Charlie's vision of successful cocktail parties. They had had a party the second year they'd lived there, and the wife of a partner at a law firm, with whom Charlie did a lot of business at the time, looked around with a glass of wine in her hand and said with a sigh, "I've always wanted to live in a house exactly like this." Charlie had expanded before Nora's eyes, as though the woman had attached a bicycle pump and, one, two, three, created a chestier, prouder, bigger man.

While Nora's ambition was a thing so ephemeral as to be nearly nonexistent, Charlie had had a strong sense of what he wanted, although Nora thought life would have been simpler if his goal had had a title: judge, senior partner. Instead Nora had realized early on that he simply wanted to be somebody. Charlie's father, an accountant who did the taxes of the locals in their smallish upstate town out of a basement home office with a separate side entrance, had an older brother who managed a steel processing plant, a towering figure among the Nolans, discussed as though he were a hair's breadth from great wealth and stature. Charlie had realized that Uncle Glenn's life, and not making an April 15 filing deadline for the principal of the high school and the chief of police, was what was desirable.

Nora had met Uncle Glenn exactly twice, once at her wedding, another time at a family reunion. It was considered a great coup that Glenn, who was so very busy, had managed to travel from Pittsburgh to Albany. After his third vodka gimlet, he had told Nora that he had always wanted to be a writer, but that, "events being what they were," he had been obliged to major in business in college. "And, well," he added with the Kabuki modesty that his extended family frequently lauded, "it all turned out for the best." Nora always suspected that his position was less than described, although enough for European vacations and a new Cadillac every three years, which at the time were definite markers of prosperity, along with a mink coat for the wife. But his legend was deep in her husband's DNA. Nora wondered if that was one of the things Charlie had come to like about the block: that on the block he was known, valued, somebody.

Nora had liked it there right from the beginning. Homer was young when they first moved in, and more tolerant of strangers, and, walking him, Nora met most of the neighbors. The Fisks had had the mastiff before the Rottweiler. The Fenstermachers had a standard poodle, a redhead called Elizabeth II, not after the queen, it emerged, but after Elizabeth I, who had herself been preceded by Charles. George had what he always described as a rescue pug, as though he were the champion of small, bug-eyed dogs everywhere. He often had two or three. They would dance around Homer on their pinpoint feet, wheezing and growling, while Homer looked out into the middle distance, his ice-blue eyes unfocused, as though thinking, "What are these things and why do they think I should acknowledge them?"

Homer was an Australian cattle dog, mottled and spade-faced, with a solid body and stance that telegraphed what he was, a working dog with no nonsense about him. Rachel had started to whine about a dog from first grade, when it seemed every playdate and duplex apartment came with a Labrador. "That's all we need," Charlie used to say, as though dog ownership were like a second mortgage, or bankruptcy. Then he'd blown it at a barbecue in Pound Ridge given by one of the senior partners. The man's wife bred dogs—"And looks every inch of it," said Nora in the car, although the woman had been perfectly nice in that bluff, collegial, WASP way—and Charlie had looked down at the cattle dog peering up into his face with an intelligent gaze, the dog seeing in Charlie's thick fingers an hors d'oeuvre possibly dropping, and said to his host, "Now, if we were talking about a dog like this, I would get a dog in a heartbeat."

Charlie had not noticed that Rachel was behind him, with the same glittery look in her eyes that Nora saw in people at the newsstand who were buying lottery tickets. That was how they came to arrive home from Westchester County six months later with a piglet of a puppy. Nora had been surprised at how attached she became to Homer, even when he needed to pee at the curb on a cold night, a little puddle that turned into yellow ice. Charity had been unpersuaded about Homer when he had first appeared, unpersuaded as well that Rachel and Oliver truly intended to take care of the dog in the way they both insisted they would. In this, of course, Charity was wise as she was in all else. "Lotta mess," she kept repeating as the puppy piddled on the parquet. "Whole lotta mess."

"You've been to Jamaica," Jenny said on one of their phone calls. "Dogs aren't pets there. They're feral animals who roam the streets."

So it had come as something of a surprise when Homer had become as singular and triumphant a figure in the Charity narrative as the twins had always been. Homer had found and killed a rat in the park. (Perhaps true, although Nora couldn't think of it without shuddering.) Homer had leapt into the air and snagged a pigeon. (Sounded apochrypal, was actually accurate, as Nora discovered when she picked up a poop full of feathers the next day.) Homer was an object of desire for a professional football player in one of the high-rises, who had offered thousands of dollars to buy him. (Almost certainly embellished, although there was a pro player living in one of the nearby buildings.)

"If she says that Homer dragged a couple of kids out of a burning building, are you going to keep agreeing with her?" Charlie asked one morning when Charity had insisted that it had not been Homer who had taken the block of Cheddar from the counter.

("Why does that man leave cheese out?" she asked Nora later, Charlie usually being referred to in the vaguest possible terms. When she had first interviewed Charity, Nora had asked if she was married. "Who wants that mess?" Charity had said with a snort.)

"If it makes Charity happy," she'd said.

Charity, too, remained insensible of the bags being left on their stoop. One morning at the corner Nora had confided in Linda Lessman. "That feels like such a hostile gesture," Linda said. "If someone was doing that to me I'd be tempted to let the court officers know."

"Thank you. That's just how I feel. It's not about litter. It's a message, right?" Nora looked at the aged panel van double-parked up the street. "I'm going to ask Ricky if he's seen anyone," she said.

That morning Nora had come out of the house and stepped right into an encounter between a traffic enforcement agent and one of Ricky's guys, whose English didn't extend to much beyond "Señora! No! Señora!"

"Don't Señora me," the agent, a broad-shouldered woman who was wielding a pen like a deadly weapon over a pad of tickets, replied.

Ricky came running down the block, waving his arms. "Oh, please, no," he cried, looking from the double-parked van to the agent, who had the look of concentration on her face you usually saw in teenagers working on an essay in AP English. It was well known throughout New York that once the tip of a traffic agent's pen had so much as touched the surface of the paper, there was no going back. Jack Fisk's favorite line was "I know the mayor." It never worked.

Ricky had always been one of those skinny, ropy guys who never gained a pound, but his pants hung loose now, and it looked as though he was losing weight. Nora was sad to see it because she had once seen a different Enrique Ramos, the one they didn't know on the block. She'd met him several months before, when it turned out the dishwasher wouldn't drain, no matter how much she bailed water, and she'd been reduced to using the apple corer to try to unplug the downspout. Twice she asked Charity to get Ricky, and finally Charity said, "No one sees that man this week. His little boy is terrible sick."

Nora dropped the corer into the murky gray soup at the bottom of the dishwasher. "How sick?"

"That thing, whatcha call it, Ollie had." And here Charity made a sound as though she were trying to eject her own lungs.

"Croup?" Nora said.

"That one," Charity said.

"Tell me when you see him and I'll give them my humidifier. That made a big difference. It's down in the basement, isn't it?"

"Upstairs. Rachel use it sometime to open her pores, that kind of nonsense."

But Ricky had not appeared, and Nora decided to take the humidifier to him. It was too unwieldy to take on the subway.

"The man can buy his own humidifier, the prices he charges," said Charlie on his way into the office on a Saturday morning, apparently because some deal was falling apart.

Nora still remembered that day as a disaster in every way possible. She had had a hard time getting the car out of the narrow opening to the lot, and had to be directed out by George, who was pleased as could be to have the opportunity to condescend. Then she had misread the signs, taken the George Washington Bridge into New Jersey, and found it hard to find a place to turn and head back in the right direction. Construction in the Bronx had closed the exit her directions had given her, and the Indian man she asked at the gas station kept nodding and smiling, repeating "Grand Concourse," until she realized she was actually on the road she had been trying desperately to find. She slid into a parking space in front of a bodega and locked the car while two teenagers with three inches of boxer shorts above the waistband of their jeans stared at the two feet between her car and the curb. She heard them laughing as she carried the humidifier in her arms. It was heavy.

In front of her a man strode down the street, greeting the old people who sat in the shafts cut into the front of the apartment buildings, getting as much light and air as there was to be found on a side street in the South Bronx. A kid leaned out a window and called something to the man, and he waved but walked on. He was wearing a leather jacket and snug jeans, and there was a swivel in his walk, like he was hearing music in his head the way Nora often did during her walk to work, although she was certain she had never moved quite like that. Four older men were playing dominoes around a card table on the sidewalk, hunched in coats that were too heavy for the weather. They raised leathery hands to the younger man as he walked by.

Nora said, "Twelve fourteen?" to a woman in a wheelchair with a New York Yankees blanket over her legs. The woman pointed at the man. "Follow him," she said. Nora passed a sign on the next building that said NO LOITERING. VIOLATORS WILL BE PROSECUTED. The man in front of her bent down to pick up an empty beer can from the sidewalk and flipped it into a trash can at the curb. It wasn't until she got to the steps of the last building on the block that he turned, and she realized it was Ricky—but a different Ricky, a Ricky at home, in his zone, not in uniform, not in character, or perhaps in his real character, a lighter, brighter cousin to the Ricky she knew, almost unrecognizable until he saw Nora Nolan standing behind him. The way his face changed made Nora sad, as though just by showing up she'd turned this buoyant character into the leaden facsimile he took downtown each day for work.

"Missus, what are you doing here?" he said, taking the box out of her arms.

"I'm sorry," Nora said, only in that moment realizing to her dismay that there were lines between people as clear as the median on Park Avenue or the narrower one she'd almost run over on the Grand Concourse, and that you were supposed to respect them.

"No, no," Ricky said. "No problem." But it was. It was a problem.

"I heard your boy had the croup. And Oliver had the croup when he was five—it was just awful, that sound of him coughing, I remember staying up all night with him in the bathroom, with the shower running for an hour so the steam would fill the room. It was the only thing that helped, and then the pediatrician said, Get a good humidifier, a good one, not one of those cheap ones from Duane Reade, and we set it up in the room and I'm pretty sure that's what got him over the hump, the steam all night long, so that all that stuff in his chest got loosened up—"

"Rico!" yelled a voice from above them. "What the hell?"

A woman was leaning out a window. Her arms were folded on the sill and she was hunched over them so that she had stupendous cleavage. Her mouth was as tight as her eyes were hot.

"This is Mrs. Nolan," Ricky said.

"Nora," Nora called, waving. "You must be Nita. I've heard so much about you." Charity had told her that Nita was a home health aide, moving from elderly person to elderly person in the Bronx as each one died. Looking up at her flamethrower of an expression, Nora wondered if she helped kill them.

"You're taking your sweet time," Nita said.

"I brought a humidifier," Nora said. "My son had the croup. It really helped."

"Thank you," Ricky said.

"You deaf, Rico?" Nita shouted.

"I have to go," said Nora.

"That humidifier really helped a lot," Ricky had said when he came to fix the dishwasher Monday morning, the handyman Ricky now, not the man who had strutted down the street in a leather jacket. Nora should have minded her business. On the way home she remembered a story Cathleen had told once during their lunch group, about running into one of her high school nuns at the beach wearing a black bathing suit. A one-piece with a skirt, but still. Both the nun and Cathleen had been so embarrassed they'd pretended when school resumed that it had never happened.

Nora had embarrassed that other Ricky, who was cool and loose, a swivel to his step, tight jeans and high-top sneakers.

Ricky on her block didn't dress that way, didn't walk that way, didn't even talk that way. He was all business, methodical and neat, or maybe that was just when he was on the job, the way his posture and clothes were different there. Nora remembered being at Charlie's firm's Christmas party and having one of the administrative assistants say that being married to Charlie must be a pleasure because he was so neat and organized. Nora had had to bite back a snort of incredulity. That Charlie apparently lived in the office with the big cherry desk, the matching credenza, the oatmeal-colored couch, the landscape on the wall. Perpetually messy Charlie lived in her house. Maybe it was the same with Ricky, no cap on the toothpaste, coffee cups with muddy dregs on the table, socks on the floor. Maybe that's the Ricky Nita knew, but the one who worked for Nora never left a tool out, always used a dustpan and brush when he was done with a repair, even though Charity always stood there frowning, waving the DustBuster and breathing hard.

Now Nora had to add Ricky to the list of things going awry on the block. The ocher shadows under his brown-black eyes were darker and deeper, and he had the kind of graven marionette lines that many of the women Nora knew had had plumped by a dermatologist. He still said, "Good morning, missus," whenever he saw her, but he'd lost his light. Usually when she gave him items the twins had outgrown, soccer shirts, picture books, passing them along for Ricky's own children, he turned them over in his scarred hands and smiled. Now, no. When she told Linda Lessman she had watched him being ticketed, Linda sighed. "Please don't ask me to fix the tickets," Linda said.

"Of course not. But the poor guy. He'll go out of business if this keeps up."

Nora stopped to talk to him while she was walking Homer and he was leaving the Rizzolis' later that evening. The Rizzoli oven had apparently gone kaput, but Ricky had cleaned out the automatic pilot, and heat had returned to the stove. Homer sniffed Ricky's pants leg. Nora jerked him back, and Homer turned slowly and looked at her with reproach. The idea that he would ever urinate on a human leg was insulting.

"No problem, missus," Ricky said, shifting his tool bag. "He just smells my dog. I got a pit bull mix, her name's Rosie."

"Rosie doesn't sound like a pit bull name," Nora said.

"Nah, she's real sweet. Pit bulls get a bad rep."

"His wife not doing so good," Charity said later, shaking her head, and when she saw the confusion on Nora's face, adding, "She got the cancer in the breast. They do—" Here she made a motion that Nora assumed was meant to mimic a scalpel.

Nora couldn't help but remember the size of the breasts on the windowsill the day she'd brought the humidifier to the Bronx, or the fit Nita had thrown from her perch above them. It seemed unlikely she'd be a compliant patient.

"Maybe I can help with a doctor," Nora said. "I know people on the board of the big cancer hospital."

Charity shook her head, then burst out, "Help get people off his back with the parking! Mr. Fisk yelling at him, that stupid man across the street"—even Charity was contemptuous of George—"Mr. Nolan, too. He work so hard for everybody, night, day, weekends. He missed church for Mr. Lessman!"

There had not been such an outburst from Charity since Rachel had been denied the part of Dorothy in the school production of *The Wizard of Oz.* "The good witch has a beautiful costume," Nora had said as her daughter sobbed into her side, and Charity had hollered, "Not the biggest part! Not what was for Judy Gartner when she was in the movie!"

Not for the first time, Nora wondered what would become of them if Charity were to quit. There were always rumors of poachers, newcomers to the high-rise buildings that had grown up around the block like a forbidding fence, women who trawled the parks and grocery stores for nannies and house-keepers who could be lured away with bigger salaries or lighter duties. Since part of Charity's routine when she'd first started to work for them was to believe that Oliver and Rachel were the most remarkable children to ever be born in a New York hos-pital, Nora had been confident for years that she would not leave. When she had first started to think about the twins leav-ing for college, she had found herself poised on a dark chasm of sadness and uncertainty, because she would miss them so terri-bly and because she was convinced Charity would quit.

"No way, Mom," Oliver said.

"Homer," Rachel added. "Charity will stay until Homer dies."

"Don't say that!" yelled Oliver.

"Then she'll come work for me," Rachel continued.

"Can you afford Charity?" Nora said.

"No, but you can," Rachel said with a smirk. "And maybe by that time I can afford her myself. Homer is going to live for a long, long time."

"And Charity will stay for us, anyhow," Oliver added while he was attacking a plate of jerk chicken. One of the reasons Charity loved cooking for the kids was that Oliver consumed vast quantities, often as though he were killing as well as eating his food. He had been a picky eater as a child, confining himself largely to rice, Cheerios, and bananas, and Charity took credit for the change. She insisted that both her sisters, whose names were of course Faith and Hope, said that she was the best cook of the three, which was a way to brag without seeming as though she were the one bragging. Vance apparently agreed. Vance was the only son, the golden child of the family, whose night-school college classes had culminated in a job juggling numbers in some city department. Vance's opinion on any topic, from Middle East policy to the care of hardwood floors, was invoked by Charity and considered the last, best word on the subject. There seemed to be some concern that Vance had not yet found himself a woman, but there was also agreement that no woman, even the estimable Mavis Robertson, who played the organ at church, was truly worthy of his notice. At church they apparently used Vance's full name, which was Perseverance, but Charity said he had thought that was too much to use at work.

"That poor bastard," Charlie had said after eavesdropping on that conversation.

"Can you please all back off of Ricky?" Nora said that night to Charlie, at the end of a mostly silent Thai takeout dinner, occasioned, she knew, by what she now thought of as The Bob Harris Situation.

Charlie picked up his plate. "Do they work for us, these people, or is it the other way around?" he said.

"These people?"

"You know what I mean. We're paying for the spaces in the lot, and Ricky isn't. If he doesn't like it, I bet there are lots of other guys in this city who'd like the work. George says there's a guy who works on Seventy-fourth Street who's cheaper and better."

"Oh, not again. The last cheaper and better was the tree trimmer who butchered all the trees."

"You just don't like George," Charlie said.

"I don't like George. I do like Ricky."

"This chicken satay isn't great," Charlie said, standing up to get another beer.

IMPORTANT REMINDER

Only paid occupants of the lot may have keys to the
padlock that holds the chain in place. NO DUPLICATES OF
THE KEY SHOULD BE MADE UNDER ANY CIRCUM-
STANCES. The chain must be in place at all times except
when moving a car in or out of the lot.

George

There are sounds that a person never forgets. Charlie Nolan said he would always remember the sound of the earth falling onto the lid of his father's coffin, although Nora had secretly found it a somewhat soothing sound, like very heavy rain on a very solid roof. Ollie could close his eyes and remember the explosive sound of the first home run he'd ever hit, in middle school, at the field at Randall's Island; Rachel the involuntary squeal that had come from her mouth when she'd opened a nondescript envelope and seen a check for five hundred dollars after she'd won an essay contest her junior year.

Nora would never forget the high, querulous complaint she'd heard in the delivery room from her children, first Oliver, then Rachel, although Rachel had long ago insisted that Nora admit the two had cried simultaneously, and Nora had complied, and Charlie now even believed this was true because he'd heard it so many times, even though he had been there and knew otherwise.

Afterward Nora realized that the sound she'd heard that morning in December would fall into the same category for the rest of her life: once heard, it could not be unheard. First there was a percussive noise that she thought was a jackhammer, and then something different, something that sounded like big bags of sand falling from the upper story of a building onto a wet pavement. It wasn't until she got closer and the screaming started, screaming that went on and on and on, so that, like a child, she wanted to put her palms over her ears, that she realized the last had been the sound of Jack Fisk hitting Ricky in the side of the leg with a golf club.

"Jesus Christ, Jack," Charlie yelled as Nora sprinted down the block toward the lot.

What exactly happened that day, chapter and verse, depended, of course, on who was telling the story. There were only three people who actually were there: Jack, Ricky, and Charlie. Naturally George told everyone, as he trolled the block all weekend long, that he had been standing right there, had seen it all with his own two eyes. He stuck to that until the police wanted an official statement and then it turned out he'd actually been taking the rescue pugs to the groomers to have their nails trimmed.

"Oh my God, oh my God, Charlie, do something," Nora yelled as she neared the entrance to the parking lot.

She had just finished doing her long run, her Saturday-morning-through-Central-Park-buy-an-everything-bagel-on-the-way-back run. Just under seven miles, just under ninety minutes. Nora liked that feeling about halfway through, when a trickle of sweat ran between her shoulder blades beneath her insulated shirt, at the same point when she had lost all feeling in her nose because it was thoroughly frozen. Then the shivers, coming out of the bagel shop, and the slow lope home. On a shorter run she had time to obsess, about what the twins would do after graduation, about whether they would move away or move back in, about whether Jenny had not called because she was irritated at Nora or away somewhere for work—it was always the latter—about where she and Charlie should go on vacation and whether she wanted to go on vacation with Charlie at all.

But for some reason the longer route eliminated obsession and pared her brain down to purely the motor part of the cortex. Sometimes she would get home and realize she could not remember a single part of the run, that she was like a self-driving car, following a prescribed route with no one behind the wheel. She had been in that sort of fugue state when the screaming started.

By the time she got to her husband, Ricky was lying next to his van, the leg of his khaki-green pants pitch-black with blood, the knee at a peculiar angle that made Nora afraid she was going to be sick when she looked, then looked away. His screams had turned ragged and breathless, his face a terrible putty color. The golf club was on the ground next to him. Nora knelt. She wanted to put a hand on Ricky's foot but she was afraid anything she did would make him jerk away and hurt himself still more, if that was even possible.

"I hear a siren," Charlie said.

"Did you call 911?" Nora said, looking over her shoulder. She saw Jack Fisk bent over the curb with his back to her, his hands on his knees. "Jack, did you call 911?"

Charlie shook his head.

"What did you do?" Nora screamed at Jack. "Are you insane? What did you do?" From behind Jack she saw Linda Lessman running out her front door and into the street, stopping at the curb opposite and looking up at the end of the block. Nora heard that terrible sound again in her head, the heavy thing hitting the softer thing, hard, and she turned back toward Ricky, who was sobbing, tears making tracks down either side of his face. "They're coming," she said. "They're coming." The sirens were louder.

"He gonna lose that leg," yelled one of the men looking down from an open window of the SRO. "It's all messed up, man. He gonna lose that leg, for sure."

"Get up, Bun," Charlie said, his voice shaking. He bent down to pull her to her feet and she saw the cherry lights strobing behind her from two patrol cars. Suddenly there were men in uniforms all around them. Nora stepped back next to Jack, who was arguing with two of the cops. "Calm down, sir," one of them said.

"Him!" yelled the man from the SRO, and when Nora looked up at the window she saw that at least five of the residents were standing, staring down. "Police! He's the one who hit him. He hit him real hard."

"Give me a minute to get you a goddamn business card," Jack was yelling at the cops. Charlie put a hand on Jack's upper arm, talking first to him and then to the two police officers standing in front of them, their eyes narrowed. Linda and Nora had stepped back and were standing shoulder to shoulder, as though they were holding each other up. "Jesus Mary and Joseph," Linda said, craning her neck to look toward Ricky. "Should I go get Sherry? Where is she? She should be here."

Between the wintry air and all of them breathing hard, even the cops, the area around them was as foggy white as the train station in an old movie. An ambulance pulled up and two EMTs ran to Ricky. The one man at the window of the SRO kept repeating, "He hit him! He hit him hard! Officer! Officer! It was assault with a deadly weapon."

"Shut up, you moron," Jack shouted back. "It was a goddamn golf club!" The two cops, nearly as young as Nora's own children, tried to speak, and one laid a hand on Jack's arm. Jack wheeled, looked as though he was going to hit the young cop. Another police car came down the block fast.

"They letting him go," the SRO guy yelled, leaning out so the others at their windows could hear him. "They letting him go because that guy that got hit, 'cause he's black, and the other guy, he's white. And rich."

"He's not black," one yelled back. "He's Puerto Rican."

"You don't know he's Puerto Rican. Why, 'cause he's brown? He could be a light black, like Lena Horne or what's-his-name, the ballplayer."

"He speaks Spanish, dude," said the other man, leaning so far out his window to eyeball the other, one floor up and two windows across, that Nora thought he might fall out.

"That don't make him Puerto Rican, man. He could be from Mexico, or maybe Panama, one of those other places."

"Officer!" yelled a third man. "Officer!"

"What?" the younger cop yelled back.

"I was at Attica in seventy-one."

"Ah, Jesus, Benny, not the Attica thing again," one of the other SRO guys said.

"Don't put your goddamn hands on me," Jack suddenly yelled, and the next thing Nora knew, he was up against the patrol car, face against the window, the officers holding him flat and snapping on handcuffs. Linda grabbed Nora's hand and whispered, "I'm going to get Sherry. Don't leave. Don't let Charlie get in the middle of this. Don't let him say anything to the police."

"They taking him now," said the SRO guy, talking to the

others. "White or no white, they taking him. He messed with the po-po."

"He'll get off, man, you know he will. These people, man, they pay the cops off, they get lawyers, they get out. The work-ingman, now, he goes to Rikers."

"I was at Attica in seventy-one."

"Shut up, Benny. You're too young for Attica. You're just a nut bar."

It was amazing how quickly it was all over. The ambulance backed down the street fast, an EMT visible through the lit window bending over a gurney, and the police cars followed, two with the backseat empty and one with Jack bent over in the back. Nora could tell he was yelling even though she couldn't hear him. The cords on his neck looked like trusses holding his head up. Linda ran back toward Nora. "There's no one answering the door at their house."

"I've got to go inside and sit down," Nora said. "You didn't see his leg. I feel nauseous."

"Did you see what happened?" Linda said. Nora shook her head. Charlie nodded. "I'll make some calls and then come over to your house," Linda said. Nora looked down at her left hand. She was still holding the bagel, wrapped in white paper, but she had crushed it flat and her hand was slick with melted butter.

Charlie's was the first version of the story Nora heard afterward, and then Jack's via Sherry, who had been away at a professional conference and had to get on a train in Boston fast. Both of them went like this:

Jack was scheduled to meet a client at his weekend house in Bedford. The client was important. Jack was running late. Ricky's van was parked in the entrance to the lot in its usual place, the one Ricky insisted put it far enough to one side so that anyone could get past it, the back half of the van just inside the lot line, the front half jutting onto the sidewalk.

Jack had tried to ease past. The top of his side-view mirror became entangled with the bottom of the one on Ricky's van at a moment when Jack was looking at his other side-view mirror and stepping on the gas.

(Nora could see it, could hear it, that horrible sharp sound of the mirror being torn off, the horrible sharp sound Jack would make deep in his corded throat as it happened.)

Jack kept going until his car was in the street, both his side-view mirror and the one on Ricky's van hanging from a tangle of colored wires. In a rage, he leapt out and opened the trunk of his car, where he kept his golf clubs, and took out his three iron. Apparently everyone agreed it was a three iron.

"I tried to grab his arm," Charlie said, which Nora knew was a foolhardy act when Jack Fisk was in a rage.

"Charlie's just lucky Jack didn't brain him," Sherry said afterward.

What had sounded to Nora like a jackhammer was the sound of Jack hitting the side of the panel van with his three iron. Charlie said that was when the men from the SRO came to their windows and started yelling. Between that and the sound of the golf club hitting the van, Charlie insisted that no one heard Ricky yelling, "Stop! Mr. Fisk, stop, please!" until Ricky was right behind him and had jumped at Jack to try to grab his arm. By then the side of the panel van, once convex, was concave.

Who knew what the truth was? Jack said Ricky ran right in front of him, that he hit him by accident when he meant only to hit the side of the van. Ricky told the police Jack wouldn't stop hitting him, which sounded not like an accident but like assault, which was what the cops charged Jack with when they took him downtown.

"Remember that time Jack told Ollie to be cooperative and polite if he was ever picked up by the cops?" Charlie said. "He should have followed his own advice."

Ricky's leg was fractured in two places, or three, or four, depending on who was telling the story. Jack had spent the night in a holding cell downtown, had been released immediately to one of his law firm colleagues, was at Rikers, was at home, depending on who was telling the story. Nora spent the day shaking on and off, hearing that sound again in her head, now that she knew what it was and what it had done. "It was an accident," said Charlie, on his second vodka, and Nora put up a hand and said, "Don't say that to me again. Don't."

"You are the only person who has been sensitive enough not to ask me a million questions," Sherry said when Nora saw her at the corner three days later. "You, and Alma. She sent over a pan of chicken tetrazzini, which was nice, although it did suggest that someone had died. Jack ate most of it. He hasn't left the house since it happened."

"He's taken off from work?"

"They've put him on some sort of leave until, in the managing partner's words, this is all sorted out. It's only the second time they've done something like that. The other time was a partner who was accused of beating his wife. He never came back."

Nora was at a loss. Finally she said, "Do you want to go get a pedicure?" It was all she could think of, what Rachel always said to her friends when they were feeling low. Nora felt foolish as soon as she'd said it.

Sherry smiled sadly. "I'll be all right. The good news is that there are enough Fisks in this city that it apparently hasn't occurred to any of my patients that I'm married to the assailant. At least no one has dropped me yet."

Right after the police had pulled away, Charlie had gotten into Jack's car and backed it into his assigned space in the lot. Nora noticed that he had no trouble getting past Ricky's van, although she wondered if that was because the van was narrower with the side bashed in and its side-view mirror hanging loose.

"Jesus Christ," Charlie had said, looking down at Jack's car keys and then putting them in his pocket. "Should I leave a note for Sherry that I've got these?"

"Don't forget we have your keys," Nora said to Sherry. "I can bring them over."

"I don't need them," she said. "I've got mine, and as far as I'm concerned the car can sit there and turn to rust. I hope I never see it again." Her voice shook slightly, and she compressed her lips "Have you seen the tabloids?" she said.

Nora had. So had everyone else. There were only so many dead-end blocks in Manhattan, and everyone they knew knew the one the Nolans lived on. Jenny had called her, every woman in the lunch group had called her, even Bebe had phoned from Florida. Nora had been short with all of them except for Jenny, who knew that Nora was what she called block-friendly with Sherry Fisk and had said, "I'm just calling to say that when you feel like talking about this I'm here, and if you never feel like talking about this, that's fine, too."

"And that's why you're the world's best best friend," said Nora, who didn't feel like talking about it.

She certainly didn't intend to discuss it with a reporter, although there had surely been attempts. Nora was walking Homer after work and a young man in a down jacket stooped to pet him. "Cool-looking dog," he said. "I've never seen one with eyes like that."

"He's an Australian cattle dog," Nora said.

"And you're Nora Nolan," he said. "From the jewelry museum."

"Do we know each other?"

"No, I just recognized you from pictures. Can I talk to you for a minute? I'm doing a story on the golf club assault and I understand you were there."

"And you seemed so nice," Nora said sadly, and she turned and took Homer back inside. Naturally, when she looked out the window fifteen minutes later, the reporter was talking to George.

"You are hateful," Nora said aloud.

Charlie and Nora had agreed not to tell the twins what had happened, which Nora realized indicated how naïve they could be. When her phone showed Rachel calling at 8 A.M., Nora snatched it up so quickly that it slipped from her hand and into Homer's water bowl. "No!" Nora shrieked, fishing it out, shaking it off. Incredibly it still worked, although by day's end it started to sputter and crackle like experimental music, and by the next morning died, despite an overnight in a bag of rice.

"I can't believe Mr. Fisk tried to kill Ricky!" Rachel screamed.

Both New York tabloids had featured the story prominently, and both sounded remarkably the same. Jack Fisk (whose real name apparently was Joshua—who knew?) was a wealthy partner in a white-shoe law firm. Ricky was a struggling neighborhood handyman who lived with his wife and two young sons in the Bronx. The assault took place on a dead-end block on the Upper West Side. Several years before, one of the tabloids had done a story on dead-end blocks, and had described theirs as so neighborly that on Halloween, candy was placed outside on the stoops for trick-or-treaters. Now neighborly had become isolated, insular, circling the wagons, which was reporter-speak for "residents who won't talk to us." Jack was wealthy; Ricky was from one of the city's poorer neighborhoods. Neither characterization, Nora was certain, was exactly accurate, but it made just the right kind of story that way. Ricky's leg had been "shattered" by Jack's golf club, both papers using the same verb. Ricky's wife, Nita, was at his bedside and said he couldn't talk because he was in too much pain, although the more florid of the papers said he was in agony. Jack's attorney, Marcus King, said, "When all the facts are known, my client will be cleared of all charges." Nita said, "Somebody has to pay for this."

"Your father was there. He says it was an accident," Nora said to Rachel.

"Mom, please. How do you accidentally break someone's leg with a golf club? This is all because of that stupid parking lot, isn't it? Have you gone to see Ricky? Is he going to be okay?"

Nora had asked Charity the same question. She had refused to answer directly.

"Faucet dripping in Rachel's bathroom," Charity said darkly.

"Dryer vent not working so good."

"Drain slow in back."

Charity had a marked tendency to be aphoristic—Charlie had once asked if they could buy her some verbs for Christmas—and when she returned to work Monday it had deepened noticeably. She made it sound as though all the things they would have called Ricky to fix over the course of six months had now happened at once, now that Ricky was gone, his men with him. Charity said that he was still in the hospital.

"Which one?" Nora asked.

"Big one," she said. "Uptown." Charity seemed to hold Nora at least partially responsible for Ricky's injury.

"Charity will be so upset," Nora told Rachel.

"She should be upset. Mr. Fisk is a scumbag. We used to pretend he wasn't, when all he was doing was screaming at Mrs. Fisk, but come on. He put Ricky in the hospital. And Dad is standing up for him? Um, excuse me, but if Dad had been blocking the entrance to the lot Mr. Fisk would have come over and discussed it with him. He wouldn't have beaten him with a golf club. And Charity won't quit because, duh, me and Ollie. But she should quit. This is all because Ricky is brown and poor."

Nora did not speak. She and Charlie had made a pact long ago that they would maintain a united front with the children no matter what. She had never been so tempted to throw the agreement aside, to say to Rachel, your father is wrong, Jack Fisk is a terrible person who did a terrible thing, I can barely stand to look at your father when he defends him.

"Mom?" said Rachel.

"I keep wondering how Ricky is feeling," Nora said.

"So go see him and find out. Tell him Ollie and I are worried about him. Tell him none of us believe this ridiculous accident story. I'm going."

An hour later it was Christine on the phone. "Have you seen the papers?" she said.

"Of course I've seen the papers. I'm beside myself. I'm exhausted by the papers."

"Exhausted? I'm excited. We're going to have people working double shifts to meet the demand."

"What are you talking about?" Nora said.

"The First Lady. You didn't see the First Lady? She led an exercise class wearing the *Candide* pants and top. We're going to be swamped."

Nora owned both. The pants said "The best of all possible worlds" in the waistband. The shirt said "Cultivate your garden." Nora sometimes wondered what Voltaire, resurrected, would think of all this, but the shirt was a slim cut with raglan sleeves and the pants had a good rise and laundered well, so she'd decided not to fret about dead French philosophers.

"What did you think I was talking about?" Christine said.

"The golf club attack."

"You lost me, Non." Nora was relieved. At least Jack, Ricky, and the block had not gone completely national. Nora narrated the story, and because it was Christine, she also told her she thought Jack's version was a self-serving lie and that it would serve him right to go to jail.

"Isn't Jack Fisk that really obnoxious man with the loud voice?" Christine said. "He was yelling at his wife because she was going to make them late for a restaurant reservation or something?"

"He's horrible," Nora said.

"Ya think?" Christine said.

"Mrs. Alma wants you to call her," Charity said.

"Mrs. Fenstermacher wants me to call?" Nora asked.

"What I said."

"Obviously I chose a bad weekend to visit the grandchildren," Alma Fenstermacher said, pouring tea. Nora should have known that when Alma invited you to tea, it wasn't boiling water and a bag in a mug. There were individual single strainers, tiny cucumber sandwiches, scones, and clotted cream. It reminded Nora of the tea she'd once had at a hotel in Oxford. "The Randolph," Alma said when Nora said it aloud. "The best afternoon tea in the British Isles. Sometimes we take the train from London just to walk around the colleges and have tea there."

Nora realized that what had happened on the block was monumental if the Fenstermachers wanted details. Alma never gossiped, never stood with her dog on the pavement and muttered, "Did you hear what those new people are doing to the backyard of Four forty-five?" Nora described what she'd seen, and Alma sighed and said, "I'm sorry it came to that. I hope Ricky's injury is not too terrible. We never used him much, but he seemed like a lovely man." Nora had noticed that the Fenstermachers rarely used Ricky, but she assumed that that was because nothing in their house ever broke.

She also assumed they never read the tabloids. The *Times, The Wall Street Journal*—neither had written about what had happened, but the tabloids had sunk their pointed teeth into it and wouldn't let go. Part of that was bad timing. Two weeks before, the police had stopped a man in upper Manhattan and shot him six times after, they said, he pulled a gun from his pocket. The gun turned out to be a cellphone; there had been a demonstration on 125th Street at which thousands of people had held their phones in the air. An accident at the George Washington Bridge, caused in part by the traffic occasioned by the demonstration, had resulted in the paralysis of a mother of three from Westchester County.

The Smoking Phone story, as the *Post* had termed it, had run out of steam several days before. Nature abhorred a vacuum, and so did the tabloids. Their block was such an easy and convenient target. Had none of them ever noticed that everyone who lived there, every single one, even the renters, was white, and that everyone who worked for them, every single one, was black or Latino? Nora remembered telling her sister that when she had advertised for a nanny, not a single applicant was white. "So, wait, you were worried when you hired Charity because you somehow thought it was racist to offer a black woman a good job?" Christine had said. "Does that make any sense? Especially if she wants the job?"

"All the nannies are black and all the children are white. Does that make any sense?"

"I guess kind of," Christine said. "Charity is an immigrant, right? Immigrants work hard for us to someday get to be us. Someday their children will be hiring nannies of their own. Besides, if these women need the work, who are you to second-guess them? That's racist for sure."

"So you have lots of people of color working for your company?"

There was a silence. "Well, it's a smallish business," Christine finally said.

"So that would be a no?"

"Are we counting Asians?"

"No," Nora said.

"Why are you suddenly worrying about this?" Christine asked. "This is like the time your lunch group had that big discussion about whether it was wrong to call Charity *your* housekeeper instead of *the* housekeeper."

("I don't understand why," Suzanne had said. "I call Hal Bancroft my lawyer and Dr. Cohen my gynecologist."

"My trainer," said Jean-Ann.

"My waxer," said Elena.

"Your waxer?" Jenny said.

"You blondes have no idea," Elena said.

"Honestly, Nora, I love you, but you're overthinking this," said Jean-Ann.)

"Or," Christine added, "that time you called Charity an African-American and she got huffy and said she wasn't African, she was Jamaican, and you raised her salary by fifty dollars a week because you felt guilty."

"I'm just trying to be a good person here!" Nora cried.

"First of all, you are a good person. And second of all, what does any of this have to do with being a good person? And third of all, I think you pay Charity more than most of our designers here make."

"The haves vs. the have-nots," the *Post* said. "The deadly dead end." Charity was annoyed at being described as a have-not. Charlie kept complaining that *deadly* suggested Ricky had been killed. He was also annoyed by the *Daily News,* which had come up with a picture of Jack at a golf course somewhere, with the headline WELCOME TO THE CLUB!

"That's not even the club he was carrying," Charlie said at breakfast, when he saw it.

"Charlie, do you think anyone cares whether he almost beat a man to death with a wood or an iron?" Nora said.

"He didn't beat him almost to death. He was hitting the side of the van. He hit Ricky when Ricky stepped in front of the door."

"That's his story and he's sticking to it," Nora said, throwing the paper down so that it landed half on Charlie's cereal bowl and spit milk onto his shirt.

"I was there, Nora. I saw it happen."

"And he'll have one of those sharpies from his firm represent him and he'll wind up getting off."

"If it was an accident he should get off."

"As long as we don't have to pretend we think that's what happened."

"It is what happened. I told the police that, and if I have to, I'll say it in court."

"Are you crazy? You know Jack Fisk. He's got a temper so bad that he flies into a rage if a cab doesn't see him at the corner. He was screaming about Ricky and his van for months before this ever happened. An accident? I took the party line on the phone with our daughter, and I was embarrassed afterward."

"I know what I saw, Nora," Charlie said, putting his suit jacket on. "Just because you have a different version doesn't mean you're right."

"It's not a different version," Nora said as the front door slammed. "It's the truth."

The Fenstermacher holiday party had for many years been a grand tradition on the block. It was always held on the second Saturday of January, and featured the sort of food everyone loved and no one served anymore: baked ham, biscuits, macaroni and cheese that tasted of cheese, not as though it had been leached of all flavor by the roving band of punitive nutritionists and gluten purists who had taken New York by storm. The guest list was confined almost entirely to the residents of the block: a judge, a shrink, some finance guys, some lawyers, two doctors, a freelance writer, a freelance graphic designer, a freelance artist, and the director of a museum. There were no public school teachers or police officers, for the obvious reason that by any sensible non-Manhattan standard, everyone in the room was what had once been called rich. They were rich, but they had no money; it was all in their houses.

At the door Harold Lessman said to Nora, "I'm told you, too, are going to work for the legendary Bob Harris."

"That's what everyone says," Charlie said.

"It's not true," said Nora, hoping the party hadn't just been ruined for them both as her husband went in search of eggnog.

She was frankly a bit surprised that Alma had not canceled the party. It was a month since what had now come to be referred to on the block, if it was referred to at all, as "the parking lot incident," and although the reporters had moved on, there was still an oddly uncomfortable feeling among them all, as though they were somehow complicit in what had happened. On the other hand, the cancellation of the Fenstermacher holiday party would have been an enormous concession, a dark turning point. Apparently the party had been going on for decades, long before the Nolans had moved onto the block. It was not exactly difficult to score an invitation, but the guest list was selective, composed of what Alma once called habitués. A renter would be hard-pressed to be included unless in residence for some time, usually with a family and a pleasant way of greeting people on the block, almost always with a dog. Even a new buyer of one of the brownstones might have to wait a year or two after taking title. Apparently there had been one couple who had lived on the block for five years and had never been invited because somehow Alma knew that the husband also owned a co-op on Riverside Drive in which his girlfriend and their young son lived, and she was not having any of that.

That first year the Nolans lived on the block, when she felt she was still auditioning to be a block habitué, Nora had asked Edward Fenstermacher if they had ever missed a year, but he said no, never; they had thought about canceling the party in 2002 but Alma had concluded that after the destruction of the World Trade Center and the pall it had cast over the city and its people, the party was needed more than ever. That year they had invited all the firefighters from the nearby firehouse, which had lost seven men when the Twin Towers collapsed, and nearly all of them had come. "I'll be the first to admit it—I wept when

I saw them," Linda Lessman had said. Five years ago there had been a blizzard the night before, snow wafting down like enormous feathers for hours until the cars were nothing more than soft, curved contours up and down the block. The caterers canceled, but Ricky and two of his men showed up to clear the sidewalks, and Edward Fenstermacher sent them out for pizzas, and with all of the cookies and candy Alma had made for the holidays arrayed on the table amid the poinsettias, it had actually been very jolly. When Nora and Charlie had left that party the block was still impassable, quiet and lovely as a church, the tunnel of street trees leaning conspiratorially toward one another with their burden of snow, the plows a distant buzz on the busier thoroughfares, Oliver and Rachel and some of the other kids pulling one another down the center of the street on sleds, and they had all agreed that it was a special occasion, the perfect end to the season.

The Christmas holidays were, like so much else in the city, both wonderful and weird. Most New Yorkers complained incessantly about the traffic and the crowds that clogged Fifth Avenue looking at the holiday windows, and yet almost without knowing it, a Christmas spirit crept into their activities, tree-trimming parties, garlands and wreaths at the doors. The city exerted its customary fiscal hold on its residents and turned Christmas into a bonus round, with envelopes for the postman, the super, the housekeeper, the doorman. Every year Nora gave Ricky a fat envelope with instructions to dispense as he saw fit to his various men. "You're naïve," Jack Fisk had said. "He'll just keep it all himself." Charity, who was given two extra weeks' salary every year and her family sent a fruit basket—the closest Nora had ever come to visiting Charity at home was typing her address into the order form—snorted at Jack's remark. "That man don't know Ricky," she had said.

One day Nora stopped in front of Phil, the faux-homeless man, who had a new sign: NO ROOM AT THE INN. MERRY XMAS.

"You are completely shameless," she said, and he grinned.

"Come on—I'm creative, admit it," he said.

"Does it help?"

"Hard to tell," he said, blowing his nose. "Everybody says you take in more between Thanksgiving and Christmas."

"The holiday spirit," Nora said.

"Guilt," Phil said.

"You know there's a man at the other end of the block now?" Nora said.

"Yeah, I know. It's fine."

"Is he a real homeless person?"

"If you mean does he live in a shelter, then, yeah. If you mean does he spend all the money he makes on booze, that, too. If you mean that you would prefer that I be that kind of guy, I'll pass. You have to ask yourself why you care about that so much."

"Authenticity?" Nora said.

Phil snorted. "We're in New York," he said. "You want authenticity, move to Des Moines."

"You think people are more authentic in Iowa?"

"Nah, not really. That's just one of the things we tell ourselves, right?"

Nora looked up the block. The man at the far corner looked like a pile of old clothes someone had put out for the trash. You could scarcely tell that there was a person inside the heap of sweatpants, flannel shirts, jackets, and hats. "He's going to freeze to death," she said. Nora looked up at the sky, which was the color of an old T-shirt, the kind Charity turned into a cloth to oil the furniture. Looking up at the sky was an effort. You had to search for an opening—cranes, water towers, high-rises, cornices . . . ah, there it was.

"It's not really that cold yet," Phil said, "and he's got a good down jacket. It has a little rip in it but he put some duct tape over it. You people throw out a lot of good stuff."

"You people?"

"Yep."

Charity thought the same. Twice a year she muttered about how crowded the basement was getting, barely room for a person to move, hard to iron things right. This was Nora's cue to stack up clothes that were no longer needed, usually hers, usually because they had been a mistake in the first place. She often wound up wondering why she ever thought she would wear something pink, or pale blue. It was as though, from time to time, she imagined herself a completely different person, not who she really was, in her black and occasional gray. Even her dog was black and gray, with the dolor relieved by the odd patch of white. She had always been the same weight, a little slender, a little hippy, so that her blouses were a size smaller than her pants, and she had worn her hair the same way for three decades, shoulder-length, cut blunt, ponytail or bun. Once, years ago, she had gotten a shorter, layered cut, and when she went to pick Rachel up at school Rachel had burst into tears. She never made that mistake again but she somehow continued to buy clothing from time to time that would have been perfect for someone else living somewhere else, somewhere where people wore pastels.

Charity took these misguided purchases to her church, which apparently was unusually active during Christmas week, and where apparently everyone loved a lively yellow or a horizontal stripe. Charity was agnostic about most holidays, even Thanksgiving, but she always took off the last two weeks of December. Before she left she would bring them two of her traditional fruitcakes, which had been percolating in a closet somewhere in her apartment for the entire year, the process of making them beginning as soon as the preceding Christmas celebration was done. Once a month, a jigger of rum was poured atop and then the cake put back into hibernation, and while Charity insisted that the alcohol "got gone fast," as she liked to put it, the aroma of the cakes was so strong that once they arrived, the kitchen smelled like a tiki bar for a week. The great Christmas lecture the Nolans had had to give their children, along with the warning that if they revealed to their younger cousins there was no Santa there would be terrible consequences, was that they had to tell Charity how good the fruitcake was, although after the first year, when Charlie and Nora had tasted it and spit it back onto their plates, it had gone directly into the garbage disposal. Not the garbage, since Nora invested Charity with magical powers and believed she would be bound to find the garbage bag with the cake inside.

"What if we brought the fruitcake to the Fenstermachers'?" Charlie had said the first time they were invited to the holiday party across the street, and Nora had said, "Are you insane?" Now every year he said it as a joke.

"And so another year has come and gone," Alma said, standing at the foot of the mahogany banister in a green velvet dress with a bejeweled holly brooch on one shoulder, opening her arms. Her hair was always freshly done in a style that hadn't been popular for thirty years and yet looked fine on Alma. Nora's mother had had an expression: "She looks like she just stepped out of a bandbox." Nora did not know then and had never learned since what a bandbox was, but she was certain Alma looked like she'd just stepped out of one.

It was funny, how different it was seeing people you saw every day on the sidewalk at a party instead. There were air kisses, some one cheek, some two. People who had grown up in Kansas City greeted one another in New York as though they were Parisian. There was even a man in Charlie's firm who kissed three times: cheek, other cheek, original cheek. You never knew what you were going to get.

There were big vases full of pine boughs, and garlands on the landing and mantels. The Fenstermachers had a tree in their front window that charmed from the street, its constellation of white star lights glimpsed through the glass, and a phalanx of poinsettias down the center of their very long dining room table.

"We should have a holiday party," Charlie said every year, and Nora just ignored him. That royal we always meant, I like the idea, which meant, You should take care of it. We should get a new sofa. We should replace the garbage cans. Besides, anyone on the block who attended the Fenstermacher party knew that to hazard their own was an exercise in hubris.

Nora always enjoyed the party, and she thought it was telling that the twins complained now that their school schedules meant they could not attend. Even when they were in high school and sometimes acted as though they would prefer to eat ground glass rather than go anywhere with their parents, they always stopped in at the Fenstermacher holiday party, although they arrived and left on their own.

"You should get her mac-and-cheese recipe, Mom," Ollie had said once.

"Oh, my goodness, honey, that whole party is catered."

"Really?" Rachel said. "It doesn't feel like it is." Which was perhaps the nicest thing a born-and-raised Manhattan child could say about a meal.

"Ms. Marathon," said George, sidling up to Nora at the drinks table, which unfortunately was in a corner, which meant Nora was trapped. Forced proximity to George was the only downside to the holiday party.

"Is Betsy here?" Nora asked.

George's wife, Betsy, was an almost mythic figure on the block. She was a thoracic surgeon, apparently involved in lung transplants for children with cystic fibrosis, the kind of job that made Nora feel thoroughly ashamed of what she herself did for a living. Occasionally when Nora was running very early because of a breakfast meeting, or coming home very late because of an event, she would see Betsy across the street and wave. Seeing her always made Nora wonder three things:

- How hard was it to find a pair of lungs to transplant into a small child?
- Did transplanted lungs grow along with the child, or did you need to someday replace them with a larger, adult-size pair?
- Why would anyone who was a thoracic surgeon be married to someone as annoying and apparently aimless as George?

"Unfortunately, no," said George, as he always did. "She had a patient who spiked a fever. In her line of work, that can be a life-and-death issue."

No one was sure what George's line of work was. Like most people in New York whose profession was murky, he described himself as a consultant. But no one had ever seen him in a suit and tie, and the only thing he seemed to consult about was the business of the block.

In the interest of a uniform appearance, it has been suggested—by whom no one had any idea—*that the tree surrounds on the block be provided with the same plantings throughout. A garden wholesaler in Westchester County*—probably some friend of George, to the extent that George had actual friends—*has agreed to provide flats of impatiens and wax begonias at wholesale prices, which would be picked up by Ricky and installed by him at a reasonable cost.*

Nora would never forget that one. She had gone out the same day, bought masses of pink geraniums and planted them thick around the tree just outside their front door.

"Someone didn't get the memo," George said the next morning, and instead of feigning ignorance, Nora said curtly, "I hate wax begonias."

The holiday party was one of the only places Nora could not avoid George. She started to move away, eggnog in hand, trying to ignore the mustache of cinnamon and nutmeg on George's upper lip, but George body-blocked her. "Did you get a chance to say hello to Jonathan?" he said. "Jonathan," he called across the Fenstermacher dining room. "Jon! Mrs. Nolan! Come say hello."

"He hasn't been home in a while, has he?"

"Busy living the dream," George said as Jonathan threaded his way toward them, holding a clutch of carrot sticks and celery in his hand.

"I wish Ollie and Rachel were here," Nora said to him. "They love this party. Ollie swears by the mac and cheese."

"Animal fat and carbs," Jonathan muttered. "Fat and carbs."

"I suppose," Nora said. "But worth it."

"No, man," Jonathan said. He was wearing a T-shirt for a

band called Municipal Waste, and flip-flops. His ensemble was disconcerting, not so much, Nora thought, because it was just above freezing and threatening snow, but because Jonathan lived in a place where she assumed it was always freezing and threatening snow at this time of year.

"How's Colorado?" she asked, to be sure he hadn't moved someplace tropical.

"He's living the dream," George said. "He's into wellness and physical fitness. Clean eating. Clean living."

"Eat plants," Jonathan said. Nora was pretty sure that the twins were right, and that Jonathan spent as much time smoking plants as eating them.

"He was up all night talking to his mother, weren't you, Mr. Mountains? Yakking it up with your mom."

"Whatever," said Jonathan, shuffling toward the buffet table, perhaps to pass judgment on the ham and biscuits, animal fat and carbs. Nora could only imagine what he would think of the chocolate-and-butterscotch Yule log cake. She had taken a picture of it and sent it to the twins. *Mommy stop* Rachel had texted back.

"He seems good," Nora said, because even in George's case the travails of parenthood forced her into kindness.

"Betsy got him back here. He's always too busy to visit, and he isn't really a city boy. Mountain man, you know? Hiking, skiing, rappelling, the whole ten yards." Nora looked at Jonathan, who was scrutinizing a cherry tomato as though it were a crystal ball. Somehow she doubted it.

"I wanted to ask you a question," George said. "Exactly how much were you paying Ricky?"

"You mean how much am I paying Ricky?" Nora said. "How much will I be paying Ricky when he comes back to work?"

"Whatever you say," George said. "I get it. I hear you. Your better half told me you were Team Ricky."

"I'm Team Don't-Bash-People-with-Golf-Clubs," Nora retorted, then looked around the room.

"They're not here," said George. "Don't worry."

"I'm not worried," Nora said, although she was—about upsetting Sherry, who, she figured, already had enough to put up with.

"You're avoiding the question," George said.

"Don't we all pay Ricky the same?" Nora said. Actually, she knew that this was not exactly the case. Some people on the block, the Nolans included, paid Ricky in cash because that was what he preferred and there was no downside for them. Charlie said that even if he was asked to serve as deputy mayor for finance—"Really?" Nora had said once when they were bickering over expenses, but backed off when she saw the look on his face—he could say that Nora had handled paying Ricky and that he had assumed it was being done properly. Nora had asked Bebe about whether she needed to start paying Ricky on the books because of the job at the museum. "Are you going to be running for office anytime soon?" Bebe had said, one eyebrow arching above the rim of her bright-red reading glasses like an exotic punctuation mark.

But the Lessmans paid Ricky by check because Linda was a judge, and so did the Fenstermachers, when they used him, because their household expenses were paid out of some odd little family corporation. For those who insisted on what Charity called "that government nonsense," Ricky levied a small surcharge.

"I think he's been jacking some of you up," George continued, shaking his head. "I'm trying to get a sense from everyone on the block of what they're paying him so I can make sure we really want to take him back and that he hasn't been abusing his position here."

"What position? The man does chores for all of us for what seems like a fair wage. It's not like we're doing him a favor. Especially under the circumstances."

George ignored her. "Now, I know what your housekeeper is making—"

"What?" said Nora, and apparently hearing this as a question and not an exclamation, George came out with a figure far in excess of what they paid Charity, leading Nora to think that Charity either was paid far below market rates or was ginning up her salary for public consumption to inflate her standing on the block.

Alma Fenstermacher, flawless as always, appeared at Nora's elbow and led her away. "Thank you," Nora breathed. "What a nice person you are, to tolerate him every year."

Alma smiled. "Oh, I believe every party needs one crashing boor," she said. "And Betsy is lovely."

"She has a patient emergency."

"She always has a patient emergency. I don't believe I've actually spoken to her for almost two years. There was a period there during which I suspected he had killed her and buried her under the back patio."

"Do they have a patio?" Nora said. George lived on the opposite side of the street from the Nolans, one house removed from the Fenstermachers.

"Some awful artificial flagstone. Unfortunately, I can see the yard from our bedroom." No one had ever actually been inside George's house, but it was widely understood to be a complete mess. George would hire contractors and then wind up trying to finish the job himself, badly. It was commonplace for New Yorkers to stiff the people who worked for them, but most of them were canny enough to wait until the job was completed and then offer fifty cents on the dollar. George was apparently dumb enough to argue with workmen before the job was completed, when they could see the stiffing coming. His house was half stripped to its original stone, half still covered in a layer of liverish red paint, because he'd so harangued the refinishers that the boss had just told them to pack up their scaffolding and leave. Jack Fisk had once said George's name was on more legal papers than the U.S. Attorney's.

The Fenstermachers' house, on the other hand, was, predictably, lovely. All the original detail had been restored to quiet glory, and the decor was vaguely Victorian without being slavishly so. New Yorkers who owned old houses tended to go in one of two directions, museum or tabula rasa, in both cases perhaps intimidated by the weight of history. Nora remembered when the insurance adjustor had come to assess the replacement value of the Nolans' new house soon after they'd closed on it. "You know that's a joke, right?" he'd said, frowning down at his clipboard. Nora knew. You couldn't replace this sort of house. People tried: old brick from a magical place somewhere in central Pennsylvania, oak flooring salvaged by the Amish, new cornices designed to look like old, mantels taken from other houses. Somehow you could always tell.

With a house as old as theirs in a city as fluid as New York, the idea that it belonged to you was relative. Maybe that was why some people ripped everything out: smooth, clean walls, steel banisters with bluestone treads, undeniably theirs in a way nicked wainscoting turned from butterscotch to caramel with age never could be. A curator who was an expert in city history had told Nora at a book party that while the house where the Lessmans lived was once a brothel and the Dicksons' a small-time hat factory, the Nolans' house had been owned for almost ninety years by a single family. The Taylor house, he called it, as though to emphasize the Nolans' transience. The Taylors: a father, a mother, the mother's mother, three daughters, a son. Apparently, you could find them memorialized in copperplate in some great leatherbound census book. The three daughters married and moved to what was then the country, now the suburbs. The parents died. The son stayed, single, and made his surroundings smaller and smaller, until finally he was living in what was now Oliver's bedroom. He had had a hotplate, a cat, and six locks on the door. Only after they closed did Nora find out that he'd died there, information she had kept to herself and would never reveal to a living soul.

"With houses this old, every single one has had someone die in it," Alma Fenstermacher said when Nora first met her, unsolicited, as though to take the curse off, and Nora wondered whether Alma had actually known the last of the Taylors.

Elizabeth II, the poodle, nuzzled Nora's hand, in which she clutched a cocktail napkin spotted with a bit of mustard. "No," said Alma, and Elizabeth backed off and sat down.

"One more thing," George said, coming up behind Nora and Alma, but Alma said, "Oh, George, I think Edward had something he wanted to ask you," and she and Nora circled around to the dessert table.

"Did you ever consider canceling?" Nora asked, choosing a cookie.

"Edward and I discussed it," Alma said. "I think we would

have done so if it had been closer to the actual event. There's been such an atmosphere, hasn't there? But I thought canceling would make the atmosphere worse somehow."

"That's what I thought, too," Nora said.

"I'm glad you agree. I think Linda was a bit disapproving, but then she's so judgmental. Which, from a professional point of view, makes perfect sense for a judge. She and her husband are here somewhere."

"And the Fisks?"

Alma sighed, her brooch rising and falling and catching the light from chandelier and candle. "I think I put a foot wrong there. I called Sherry to urge her to come. She looks so beaten down, poor thing. I said, Sherry, please, we want you there. She said, 'What about Jack?' And I paused."

"She can't really have wanted to bring Jack here."

"I don't think so—I think it was a kind of litmus test. I suppose I failed. In any event, they're not here. Someone told me they've moved to their weekend place in Bedford for a while, or maybe he has and she goes out there from time to time." Alma sighed again. "I hate it when things are unsettled on the block," she said. "Let's retire the subject. I've got some food in the freezer for your children. They've always been so appreciative of the party, and I know they'll be home again before long."

"They've always loved this party," Nora said, and she was not merely exhibiting Manhattan party politeness. She was still convinced that Rachel had dropped the determination to celebrate both Hanukkah and Christmas after just one year because of the centrifugal force of the Fenstermacher party. Christmas was an oddly a-religious holiday in most of the city, although when she walked Homer on the evening of the twenty-fourth Nora was always faintly surprised and, if she was being honest, buoyed by the number of people she saw entering the Catholic church on the next block. The Fenstermachers actually had a crèche, but they kept it upstairs in the den, so few guests ever saw it. Her own children had played with it one year as though it were some sort of fancy toy village, and Alma, coming upon them, had insisted that they continue.

"I always wondered what you did with all the leftovers," Nora said.

"Most of them go to the SRO. They have a party the day after this party. The decor is not the same, sadly, but they seem to enjoy the food."

"You're too good to be true," Nora said.

"Well, we all have to do something," Alma said, picking up a petit four. "I hope Sherry will be back next year. But not her husband. I draw the line there."

"I hate February," Nora said to Charlie at breakfast.

"There are places where we could live that are warm even in February," Charlie said. Nora wouldn't make that mistake again.

"I hate February," Nora said to her lunch group, and Elena rolled her eyes. "Everyone hates February," she said, snapping a breadstick. "Have you ever heard anyone say they loved February? If you did, would you ever have anything to do with them again?"

"God, you're in a great mood," Suzanne said.

"I hate February," Elena said, and winked at Nora.

"The good news is that whoever was putting dog poop on my stoop has stopped," Nora said.

"Again with this?" Elena said. "How many times do I have to say, Not at lunch, babe. Not. At. Lunch."

"You sound like Charlie," Nora said.

"That's just mean," Elena said, and they all laughed.

"The really good news," Nora said, "is that my assistant quit."

"That's the good news?" Jenny asked.

"Oh, I hear you," said Elena, who ran a PR firm. "I had one

kid, when he aced his LSATs and decided to go to law school, I was happier than his parents. I was so glad to see the back of him."

Jean-Ann said, "One of my partners, I swear it's his favorite part of the job, calling some young associate in, saying, 'You may want to consider employment elsewhere.' I've just never developed the knack. I'm always so relieved when they decide to quit and I don't have to fire them. You're so lucky, Nora."

"This is a depressing conversation," Jenny said.

Nora's assistant now was a temp named Richard. He was so thin that his clothes all looked as though they were still on hangers. When she had gotten in that morning, picking up the folder for a meeting with a vodka company that wanted to sponsor an exhibit of the Danish crown jewels, he held up a hand. "Your daughter is on the phone. She says it's urgent," he said, and then, seeing the look on Nora's face, added, "in a girl way."

"Do you have a sister?" Nora asked him as she went into her own office.

"I have six sisters," Richard said.

It seemed to Nora that it was always when she was late for a meeting that the phone rang and Rachel was on the other end with a crisis at once so profound and yet so fleeting that if Nora ignored it it would be added to the grievance bank, and if she took it seriously Rachel would say when she brought it up again that her mother exaggerated everything. "In a girl way," she thought to herself. Richard had been working for her for only three weeks and she already liked him infinitely more than she ever had Madison.

"I'm in so much pain," Rachel wailed, as though Nora could

do something about it, with Rachel four hours away in Williamstown.

"Oh, buggy-boo," Nora said, a relatively safe reply.

"I was in this rugby scrimmage yesterday—"

"A rugby scrimmage? Why were you in a rugby scrimmage? Aside from everything else, it's not even rugby season." Not a safe reply.

"Mom, why do you always ask questions instead of just listening to me? I want you to listen to what I'm saying and instead you just grill me, like I'm a criminal or something. I don't know why I bothered to call."

Nora was not sure, either. She supposed she should be glad that Rachel still called her when she was overwrought, when she got a B on a paper in her major, when she and the current boyfriend had quarreled, when she'd strained something—it sounded like a hamstring, although Rachel was bound to think it was a compound fracture—in a rugby game. Sometimes Rachel called Christine about these things, which hurt Nora's feelings, although she would never say this to either one. Oliver seldom called, and only with emergencies that he refused to characterize as emergencies. In a boy way, Nora supposed. "Mom, do you know where my passport is?" he'd asked the week before he was due to go to Oslo for a semester abroad. Luckily Nora was well acquainted with a place that could, for a price, provide a new passport in forty-eight hours, having used it twice before for Oliver, once for Rachel, and even once for Charlie, when he had to fly to Tokyo on an emergent business matter and discovered that he had somehow let his passport expire. In New York City you could find anything. There were women who would pick nits from a child's hair if there was an outbreak of lice at school, as there so often was. Christine had thought she was kidding when she first told her. Nitpickers. Now they had them in Seattle, too.

The last time Rachel had called Nora at work, Bebe had stood in the doorway of her office tapping a foot in a black slingback stiletto. There were people who were careful not to let judgment register on their faces, particularly where mother-hood was concerned; Bebe was not one of them. Her whole body was a semaphore: get off the phone this is ridiculous what am I paying you for.

"Kids," Nora said, putting down the receiver and shrugging.

"There were so many reasons I never had them," Bebe said. "Or had any interest in doing so. Husbands don't really care for them."

"And yet so many of them become fathers," Nora said coldly.

Bebe waved a hand. She was wearing a square-cut emerald so big no one would bother to steal it because it shouted "fake!" It had once belonged to some Indian royalty and had been Bebe's engagement ring, and so "for sentimental reasons"— "the woman is as sentimental as a crocodile," Nora had told her sister—she had decided not to give it to the museum. "Until I'm dead," she'd added, unsentimentally.

"They become fathers because their wives insist on becom-ing mothers. Although most of the ones I know had only one, just so they could say they had, you know: little Lindsay has changed my life, blah blah blah, night nurse, nanny."

Thank God Bebe was away now and couldn't hear Nora talking to Rachel nor see Phil sitting in a spot cleared by their facilities guy with the snowblower. The last time Bebe had no-ticed him was just before the holidays, as she stopped in to the museum before she flew south.

"Go away!" she'd yelled.

"Good morning, Mrs. Pearl," he said. "Nice morning."

"It's fucking freezing," Bebe said, pulling her mink coat tighter around her midsection.

"Don't you ever take a snow day?" Nora had said to Phil when she got to the office.

"I've got all-wheel drive," he said.

"How did you wind up doing this in the first place?"

"Ah, you know—like most things, it was a confluence of events," he said.

"A confluence of events?"

"What, because you're homeless you have to be stupid?"

"But you're not homeless. You have a home."

"Maybe I have a home because I do this." He grinned. "You gotta love a country where there are rules for being poor, and rich people make them."

"I'm not a rich person," Nora said.

"I'm inclined to take your word for that," he said. "You're one of the only regulars who makes eye contact. Even a lot of the people who give me money won't make eye contact."

"So what was the confluence?"

"A divorce, the economic downturn. Some medical issues. A problem with alcohol. I got it together, but it took a couple of years. When I first started, I was more, you know . . . like you think I ought to be."

"That makes me sound terrible."

"Nah, you're okay. Like I said, eye contact. Plus, like, right now, you're having normal conversation."

"Don't you ever consider . . ."

"What? I sit on the sidewalk with a sign. Maybe you think it's humiliating, but it's only humiliating if I feel humiliated, and I don't. What did Eleanor Roosevelt say? 'No one can make you feel inferior without your consent.' And, by the way, everything on the sign is true."

" 'Need something to eat?'"

"Hey, everybody needs something to eat. What about you? Don't you need something to eat? You walk all the way downtown in this cold?"

Nora had. The garbage in the gutters was frozen into agonized attitudes as though the Cheez-It bags and drinking straws had died of hypothermia. Even George's pugs stayed indoors in this weather, allowed to relieve themselves in the backyard because George insisted that they suffered terribly from the road salt that got into the tender creases of their paws. But still Nora walked, waiting for the cold to weaken and wane. When the weather warmed she would resent the bicyclists who suddenly reappeared, the runners who had been inside on treadmills while her earlobes were anesthetized by cold. But she always noticed that when the temperature warmed, she lived in the world more surely, looking at the buildings and the people around her. As soon as the winter wind began to blow up the Hudson corridor, her head went down and her shoulders up. It was not something she noticed, really, until she felt her body unclench sometime in March, although, this being New York City, people had even begun to pathologize the phenomenon. "He suffers from terrible seasonal affective disorder," a woman had said about her husband, who was a poet and thus assumed to have enhanced sensitivities. ("He's a pain in the ass even in June," said Jenny when Nora mentioned the exchange.)

In the meantime she bought one pair of gloves after another, slapping her hands together as she came down the block to restore feelings to her fingers, seeing Linda at the corner in a gray coat waiting for a cab, wondering where Sherry was and whether she was away or simply avoiding the rest of them. There was an odd disconnect between their professional selves, in dress shoes and tailored jackets, and their everyday selves on the block. Those selves were the great equalizers, just men and women in sweatshirts wondering why the recycling guys always spilled half the plastics on the street, who it was who persistently refused to properly bag their garbage. (George had once said he would mount a spy camera, but either he hadn't done it, it hadn't worked, or he hadn't caught the culprit.) They could have been anything: German professors, nephrologists, sculptors. Nora had discovered that Linda was a judge not during conversation at the holiday party or on the street while walking their dogs, but by reading a story about a sentencing in one of the tabloids. She was certain she had once had a conversation with Linda about getting out of jury duty, but Linda had in no way suggested at the time that there was anything wrong with that. It was as though each of them was two people, at a minimum. Once Nora had hypothesized jokingly that Alma Fenstermacher was a CIA operative. "If so, it's the best cover I've seen yet," said Sherry Fisk.

"Yet?" Nora had yelped.

All that was quite different from her own parents, who each was only ever a single person, as far as she could tell. Her mother was always a Connecticut housewife, partial to bridge parties and celery with cream cheese filling to serve at them, and her father, when at home, was not a different man from his work self but simply waiting to be that self again, like a windup doll whose key had been removed from its back. When his appendix had burst, he was confined to his bedroom for a week after he left the hospital, and Nora and Christine hurried by the half-closed door as though, if they raised their heads, they would see something shameful: Douglas Benson in pajamas on a Tuesday afternoon.

Their mother had always seemed to think of being a mother as a kind of pastime, like bridge or tennis. Most nights at dinner she asked them to describe the best thing about their day, and most mornings at breakfast she paged through their copybooks, although it was not clear what she was looking for except for conspicuous misspellings, which had to be erased and corrected on the spot. But sometimes when she was reading a magazine in the living room in the afternoon and they appeared, she would look up with a faintly puzzled expression on her face, as though they were neighbors she'd invited for coffee and then forgotten about.

Nora had felt sometimes that she should be grateful for her mother's vague and cordial disengagement. Jenny had shocked her by offhandedly telling stories of how her mother was always slapping her face, putting her on punishing diets, flirting with her boyfriends, how she had looked at one college rejection letter and said, "I never understood why you thought you'd get in there in the first place." Nora had come around to thinking that it was better to bear no marks at all than claw marks. The most resonant memory she had, for some strange reason, was of her mother leaning toward the bathroom mirror, patting her face lightly with a pink chamois powder puff over and over again as though she were somehow comforting herself.

While many of her friends had agonized about hiring help for their children, nailing themselves to the cross of motherhood and learning to resent their kids in the bargain, Nora had not thought twice about engaging a nanny—because of her own childhood, and Mary. For cookies after school there was Mary, and for help with sharpening pencils, and for soup on winter vacation days and ice pops on summer ones. Mary made cinnamon toast when they were sick, sewed the badges onto their Girl Scout sashes, and stacked the cotton underpants in their top drawers. For cuddling under the covers and talking about this and that, the two sisters had each other. "You don't know how lucky you are," Nora had said one evening to Rachel, when they were huddled under the lavender duvet talking about how mean the new girl in the fourth grade was. "I don't think my mother ever got into bed with me or my sister."

"I wish I had a sister," sighed Rachel, who hated being told how lucky she was. "I love Aunt Christine."

Nora believed that her sister was a better mother than she was, or at least a more natural one, and she knew why this was so. When Nora was ten but her sister only six, their mother had died. She had done that in the same halfhearted way that she had been a mother, fading out over the space of a few winter months, propped in bed in a lilac-colored housecoat surrounded by magazines. "She should be in the hospital," Mary said, and for the final weeks she was, so that she disappeared from both their lives overnight, and then, after Mary had cleaned out her closets, almost completely. There remained the hand-tinted wedding portrait hanging at the end of the upstairs hall, in which both of their parents looked stiff, a little uncomfortable, almost as though they had not yet been introduced.

Nora always thought that her story was the opposite of every other dead-mother story she'd heard since. A year later their father had gone to Christine's parent-teacher conference; six months later, when school was out for summer, he had married the second grade teacher. Of course everyone talked about how, in what seemed like an instant, the universally liked Miss

Patton had become the second Mrs. Benson. When Nora and her friends would go into the game room at the tennis club for sodas it would sometimes fall silent, like a thud, and she would know that's what people had been discussing at the card tables. And naturally, since she was eleven, the beginning of a time when, Nora now knew from experience, girls are as mean as sleet and should be cryogenically frozen and then reconstituted later, Nora had done her best to torture her stepmother: to begin with, she insisted for months on calling her Miss Patton.

She had refused to let herself be persuaded of the reality until one day when she had come home late from field hockey practice. The house had a rich brown smell that turned out to be pot roast, and in the den her sister and her sister's former teacher were sitting close together on the leather chesterfield, reading *Anne of Green Gables*. On the coffee table was a plate of brownie crumbs and two mugs that had held cocoa. Cocoa with marshmallows— not the big ones that made an unwieldy lump in the cup, but the tiny ones that melted into soft, little, elevated puffs of sugar. Mary worked only part-time now, so the pot roast, the brownies, and the cocoa had all been produced by Miss Patton, whose name was Carol. "You can call me Carol," she had said when her father had suggested "Mother." But Christine already called her Mommy. Carol was more of a mother than their own mother had ever been. When Nora was in high school she had heard Carol and her father talking in the living room one night when she came downstairs to get herself a banana from the bowl of fruit that always stood now on the kitchen counter. "Did that honestly never occur to you?" Nora heard Carol say, and her father said, "I think it's a coincidence. Stella wasn't literary enough for something like that." The sentence hadn't meant anything to her until college, when one of Nora's suite-mates, a drama major, had said to her, "How weird—you and your sister have the same names as the two main characters in *A Doll's House.*"

"Do you think it's possible that our mother named us after characters in an Ibsen play?" she'd asked her sister during semester break.

"You knew her a lot better than I did," Christine said apologetically. She always said that. Christine worried that Nora resented her closeness to Carol, the notion that, in a way, they had had different mothers.

"I don't think that's true," Nora said.

She supposed it had shaped her view of marriage as well as motherhood. In the way that children always did unless there was screaming and hitting involved, she had thought her parents were perfectly happy, watching her father drape a mink stole over her mother's narrow shoulders, seeing her mother tap her father on the arm when she thought he was going on too long about work. But then her father had married Carol, and she had seen what happiness really was. When she was a little girl Nora had gotten a party favor that was a tiny, undifferentiated nugget of sponge. The instructions said to put it in a bottle and add water, and sure enough, it grew, swelled, became identifiably a bear. That was what had happened to her father. Carol was the water. At their twenty-fifth-anniversary party, when Nora's father had stood to give a toast, his daughters had seen him cry for the very first time.

Now, while her friends discussed nursing homes and dementia, Nora kept quiet. No one wanted to hear that her father and his wife, just turned seventy-five, almost sixty-five, were on a river cruise up the Danube, sending texts to Rachel and Oliver: *Vienna is amazing!* and *Love from Budapest!* Twice a year they spent a long weekend in the city, always staying at a hotel but taking Charlie and Nora and, if available, the twins out to dinner and brunch. Nora remembered walking through Central Park with them after sundaes at Serendipity when the twins were small and still easily co-opted by hot fudge and free balloons, watching as Carol slipped her hand into her husband's and swung it slightly. Nora had felt such a spasm of envy that it almost made her faint.

It was one of the only marriages she'd ever encountered that wasn't a mystery to her. Even her own. When people divorced, she was often surprised, and when they stayed together, sometimes more so. She thought that people sought marriage because it meant they could put aside the mascara, the bravado, the good clothes, the company manners, and be themselves, whatever that was, not try so hard. But what that seemed to mean was that they didn't try at all. In the beginning they all spent so much time trying to know the other person, asking questions, telling stories, wanting to burrow beneath the skin. But then you married and naturally were supposed to know one another down to the ground, and so stopped asking, answering, listening. It seemed foolish, fifteen years in, to lean across the breakfast table and say, By the way, are you happy? Do you like this life? Familiarity bred contempt, she'd read somewhere, or at least inattention, but sometimes it seemed more like a truce without a war first: these are the terms of engagement, this is what is, let's not dwell on what's not. "Want what you have," it said inside the waistband of one of Christine's bestsellers, some patterned capri pants, and it sounded so life-affirming until you really thought about it, and then it just sounded like capitulation.

Sometimes Nora would look across the room at Charlie and

feel the same way she did when she looked at her old oak roll-top desk and remembered how thrilling it had been to spot it across a dusty plain at an antiques show, even though nowadays she mainly cursed its sticky drawers and splintery edges. That was how most people stayed married, she suspected, nine parts inertia and one part those moments when she spotted her husband sitting across a long table illuminated by a votive candle, bending his head to listen to the blond pianist next to him, bending as though he were deeply interested in her remarks about how terribly Juilliard had changed and how vitamins were really unnecessary if only you ate by the 1/2/3 method. Bending his fair head, as he once had at a table in Montreal, when they were seated side by side and he said, "Don't ever change a thing, Bunny mine. Not. One. Thing." Bending it now because he was beginning to lose his hearing a bit. All the men seemed more attentive at dinner parties these days because they needed hearing aids and refused to get them. You could tell them you'd won the Nobel, her friends said, and they wouldn't react because they hadn't truly heard.

"Although how any woman stays married after she wins the Nobel is beyond me," said Cathleen from her lunch group.

Charlie was still angry because Bob Harris had discussed a job with his wife, much less a Nobel Prize. Lord knows what he would do if he knew that Bob Harris had called Nora just the other day, left a long message, this time on their home phone: "I've been meeting with a mess of lawyers, all trying to hike up their billable hours, about this foundation thing. I think it would be good for us to talk again real soon so we can nail down your terms and title. Come on now—let's get this party started."

An eerie pewter light fought its way past the sheers into the bedroom, and when Nora went to the bathroom she could see the snow mounded on the pediment of the house next door, a perfect parabola. Downstairs Charlie had not started the coffee. Instead he stood, dripping, in the center of the kitchen, his down jacket on the floor, a pair of old ski pants unsnapped and unzipped at the waist. Nora wondered if this was because he had loosened them or because he hadn't been able to close them at all. He always gained weight over the holidays, and when he was unhappy.

"No smart-ass comments, all right?" he said, his cheeks red.

"About what?" said Nora, sliding past him and flinching as a slick of cold water was passed from the waistband of Charlie's pants to the back of her nightgown.

It always took her a few beats in the morning to remember what day it was, to make sense of the headlines in the paper. It had been a nightmare when the twins were small and the hour before they left for school had been full of things that needed attention: permission slips, misplaced homework, snacks that had been promised for a field trip, although not by her. As the coffeemaker began to hiss, Nora realized that Charlie had been digging the car out. The parking lot was still closed, the chain across the entrance secured with a new padlock, but George insisted it would reopen any day, and in the meantime he had persuaded Charlie to join him in parking on the street, as though it would be a defeat to begin to use the enclosed garage again. Charlie was chugging another glass of water as though he'd been running a marathon. "You do understand that you are shoveling snow at seven in the morning because of George?" Nora said.

"I'm well aware of your opinion," Charlie said, wiping his face with a dish towel. "Meanwhile, I've got to get to an off-site in New Jersey."

"Seriously? An off-site?" One of the things Nora loved about running her own operation was that she never had to authorize a retreat, a team-building day, or an off-site. At her last job there had been two off-sites a year, at which they had heard endless speeches from management gurus, done stress reduction exercises, and attended breakout sessions that consisted of writing your greatest fears on index cards and listening to them being read aloud in an NPR announcer voice by the facilitator: disappointing others (obviously a woman), not being promoted (obviously a man), death (everyone looked around the circle).

"Not ours. The old man thinks they're a waste of time. It's an invitation from—" Here Charlie mentioned the name of what was obviously a client with whom she was obviously supposed to be familiar, so Nora nodded and began to make oatmeal. Nodding was good. It was attentive, collegial. Charlie dropped client names as though they were celebrities—although he was unfamiliar with most celebrities, so she supposed it all evened out.

The twins had just returned to college after a Presidents' Day break. "I want more time off," Rachel had moaned the day they were due to go back to school, standing in the kitchen eating ice cream from the container.

"Me, too," said Oliver, who was dressed almost exactly like his twin sister, something that Nora had vowed, while staring at the sonogram, that she would never do to them herself.

"Me, three," Charlie said.

There had been a long silence. Nora knew that normally Rachel would have responded with a wisecrack, but she had been noticeably cold to her father since the Ricky incident. "If I run into Mr. Fisk, I can't be held responsible for what I might do," Rachel had said at dinner.

"I hope you've learned to always be civil to adults," her father said sternly.

"Not to adults who attack innocent people," Rachel replied.

Charlie blamed Nora for this, too.

So it was Oliver who finally said, "Dad humor. Lame."

Rachel continued to ignore her father and handed her brother the ice cream and the spoon.

"There's, like, two spoonfuls left," Ollie said.

"And I saved them for you, bro. Because I love you."

"None for me?" Charlie said, because he could not leave well enough alone, but Rachel just went upstairs.

"Women," Ollie said, ever the peacemaker.

The house was now still with that terrible stillness that came after raucous habitation. Nora could only imagine what Rachel's bedroom looked like. There appeared to be a dearth of food in the kitchen, and the cupboards looked as though they had been ransacked. She was sure there had been bags of granola that had found their way into someone's duffel bag. She wondered if there were still raisins. There were still raisins. God bless Charity.

"So I will probably be late," said Charlie, and Nora nodded again. Peanut butter and jelly for dinner, her guilty pleasure. She could scarcely wait.

She put on her waterproof boots and tucked her indoor shoes into her tote. In an act of insurrection Nora might wear the boots all day, although she knew Bebe hated them. Bebe never needed to wear boots herself since her relationship to the sidewalk consisted of the cleared walkway to the door of the museum, the cleared walkway to the door of her apartment building, and the cleared walkway to the revolving door at Bergdorf's. Nora would wear her boots because Bebe was in Palm Beach until Easter. "I hear it's snowing there!" Bebe would bellow jubilantly when she called in later in the day, in that way Florida people always did, as though temperate weather alone were equivalent to Lincoln Center, Broadway theater, endless museums, excellent restaurants, Saks. Although Bebe liked to say that the Saks in Palm Beach was very well curated, which Nora assumed meant it stocked only the really, really pricey things.

Nora knew that in a matter of hours she would be sick of the snow, sick of wading through enormous gray puddles of slush at the corners, of tracking the grit the plows laid down into the foyer as Charity rolled her eyes and got out the bucket. But when she first left the house with Homer she was struck by how beautiful the block looked, the scrawny street trees filled out by their white furry coats. The block was always near the bottom of the street-cleaning list, which made perfect sense since it was a dead end, although George vowed every winter to address the issue with their council member, and Jack Fisk insisted he could call a deputy mayor who would move them up the list like that: finger snap. Nora assumed that Jack's finger-snapping days were now over, his phone calls unreturned. Jack Fisk? Barely knew him.

"Isn't it lovely?" Alma called from across the street as the Fenstermacher poodle, wearing a tartan coat, sniffed at the curb. It occurred often to Nora that they all tended to be much more solicitous of their dogs than of their spouses, and she was not sure whether that was because their dogs loved them unconditionally, did not engage them in conversation, or simply didn't live as long. Sherry Fisk always said monogamy had worked better when people didn't live past fifty. It was a huge event on the block when one of the dogs had to be put down. They would always tell one another, as successive animals approached twelve or fifteen or, in the case of George's loathsome little yappers, eighteen, because the worst dogs lived longest, that they hoped the dogs would die in their sleep. But that never happened, and after that last trip to the vet there was always a moment on the block when a neighbor arrived home dogless. Hugs, murmured condolences. At their age, a parent could die with less ceremony.

It was while pausing to let their dogs sniff each other that Linda had asked Nora about Charlie's meeting with a real estate agent. Linda had heard from her husband, Harold, who had heard from George. (Who else?) Nora had not heard about it at all until then. "I just wanted to get a sense of the market," Charlie said, a bit abashed, but not very. "New York is a young person's city now."

"We're almost the youngest people on this block," Nora said.

"You know what I mean. All the reasons to live here—they don't make sense for us. How many times have we gone to the theater in the last year? Or a museum?"

"I run a museum."

"I mean a real museum," Charlie said. "No, no, you know—one of the major museums. No, you know what I mean—a big museum."

"You should stop talking," Nora said. It was as though he had seen her weakness and decided to poke her with a sharp stick, and it made her want to poke him back, to tell him she was ready to get Bob's party started. Now she would never mention what had happened earlier that day, after she had taken the stairs from her office to the third floor, where there was a new exhibit, *Turquoise of the Southwest*. It wasn't particularly popular, but that wasn't the point; it was one of their habitual attempts to seem serious. Nora had started an education program for children, with a demonstration from their gemologist and a disquisition about gems as an element of geology. She'd instituted a book club with so many women now enrolled that they had had to field three sections; they read a nonfiction account of the Duchess of Windsor's collection, a novel about a diamond cutter in Amsterdam, that kind of thing. "The Seven Sisters crowd," Bebe had said dismissively.

The turquoise exhibit was designed for the curators from other museums, the major museums, the big museums, many of whom had open contempt for the Museum of Jewelry, a contempt that had only grown with the Museum of Jewelry's attendance figures, which had surpassed the American Folk Art Museum and were now closing in on the Frick. Bebe was obsessed with outdoing the Frick, in a way that suggested she might have wanted to join the board there and had been rebuffed. Sometimes on weekends she would have her driver cruise by what she liked to call her museum on her way to somewhere else, a restaurant downtown, the private airport in

New Jersey, and if there was a line of people waiting to get in, she was in a good mood all week long.

An exhibit on the silverwork of the Navajos might impress, or at least mollify, the curators at the more established museums. It was actually a beautiful exhibit—the Museum of the American Indian had loaned them some clay pottery and a few ceremonial robes and headdresses, and the turquoise and silver glowed against a black fabric with a thick nap. But when Nora had gotten up there that afternoon it was empty except for an old woman with a walker, her long black coat almost dragging on the floor because her curved back and forward lurch had made her inches shorter than she once was. A younger woman in stretch pants holding a down jacket was pressed up against an exhibit case across the room. Old woman and paid minder: like twins, they, too, were everywhere in New York City. Every time Nora saw a pair together, indivisible, like skis and poles or salt and pepper shakers, a small voice in her head said, Not me. Behind that was another voice that said, I bet that's what they once thought, too.

Bang! Bang! Bang! The old woman was hitting the base of the display case with the walker with a strength belied by her stringy, spotted hands. Each time she did, the guard yelled, "Ma'am!" and the aide's shoulders jumped. Nora could imagine the aide going home every night, slipping her black lace-up shoes past her bunions, sighing, and saying to her husband, or her sister, or her kids, "That lady is a handful and a half." Nora wondered if even Ricky's wife, Nita, could have kept her under control. She couldn't blame the guard for doing nothing.

When Nora moved to the older woman's side, she swiveled with the walker in her hand and Nora stepped back a bit. "Can I help you?" Nora said quietly.

"That's mine!" the woman shouted, pointing to the large squash-blossom necklace that was the centerpiece of the exhibit. It was not particularly valuable, especially compared to most of what they had, but the center turquoise was very fine and the etchings intricate.

"And that," said the woman, gesturing with the walker as the guard moved forward behind her. "That, too." A bracelet. Another bracelet. Another necklace. They were all from Bebe's personal collection, although Nora had never been able to imagine her wearing them. "I can't abide silver," Bebe had told her once. "It's so ordinary. Forks and spoons, okay. Jewelry? Forget it."

"They're beautiful pieces," Nora said.

"Oh, good Lord above," said the aide behind her.

"They were purchased in Santa Fe," the woman said. "There's a lot of cheap copies for sale out there. These are the real thing." Her voice sounded like a door that needed its hinges oiled.

"Why don't we go to my office? You can tell me more."

For the first time the woman looked up at Nora. The whites of her eyes were a faded yellow, the irises a milky brown, as though if she lived long enough, the colors would meet in the middle. The look in her eyes was knowing, almost predatory, and her first thought, that the woman was senile and confusing jewelry she'd once owned with what they had on exhibit, evaporated.

"You run this place?" the woman said.

"Yes," said Nora, smiling.

"Shame on you," the woman said, and she tightened her hands on the bar of the walker, like the little claws of a parakeet on a perch, and clumped out of the exhibition hall, her coat sweeping the floor. "Thank the Lord," the aide said as they left.

Later, as Nora went over their coming events—a class on gem assessment for men buying an engagement ring, a lecture by a historian on Marie Antoinette's jewels—Richard buzzed her. "There's a woman here who is asking for a minute or two of your time," he said. "Her name is Deborah Messer. She says her mother was here earlier." Nora looked down at her computer screen. Richard had texted: *Mother disruptive in southwest exhibit.*

Deborah Messer turned out to be a handsome woman perhaps ten years older than Nora. Like her mother, she was a type, albeit a different type, well dressed, in beautifully tailored clothes that might have been in her closet for decades or be brand new, so classic as to be completely unmemorable and acceptable.

"My mother was here today," she said. "I understand she caused quite a kerfuffle."

"There's a word you don't hear very often," Nora said, but the woman didn't smile.

"I also understand she may have caused some damage, and I wanted to take care of that."

"There was no damage," Nora said. "She was just confused. She seemed to think that some of the pieces in an exhibit of Navajo silver jewelry were hers."

"They are."

"Excuse me?"

"I suppose it's more accurate to say that they were. My mother was Norman Pearl's first wife. I'm his daughter."

If Nora had not spent so many years being politic with older donors and museum trustees, she would have said what she was thinking: Holy shit. Bebe had once told her that most men truly wanted to have three different kinds of wives during their lifetimes: the first one, who was to make a home and a family; the dishy trophy wife, who could be enjoyed and then dispensed with when lust paled and died; and the third wife, who would be devoted but still interesting, admiring but not slavish. The point was that Bebe was that third wife. Nora didn't know if there had been a second, but it had certainly not occurred to her that Norman Pearl's first wife was even still living.

"I toured the museum soon after it opened," the woman added. "As far as I could tell, none of the things on display belonged to anyone but my father's last wife." Nora could tell by the way she said this that that was what she always called Bebe: my father's last wife. No "Bebe dear" from this woman, for sure and certain. "My father didn't acquire a taste for buying jewelry until after he and my mother divorced. She kept her engagement ring, of course, and a few other things, but there were some items at the weekend house that she'd either forgotten or was forbidden to fetch, depending on whom you believe." Deborah Messer sighed heavily, as though she was exhaling the poison of years and years.

"I don't know what to say," Nora said. She was painfully aware of the Andy Warhol four-panel portrait above the office sofa, the portrait that Bebe had had hung recently to, in her words, "dress up the place." The father's last wife, times four, in neon colors.

"There's no need to say anything," Deborah Messer said, standing with her camel-hair coat over one arm. "I didn't intend to make you feel bad. I was just concerned about damages. I'm relieved to know that there weren't any."

"Please tell your mother that I'm sorry."

"For what? She was the first wife of a rich man who got much richer after the divorce. It's not an unusual story. She has everything she needs. I don't know how she found out about these things, but I imagine they were just symbolic." She chuckled mirthlessly. "This whole place is symbolic, isn't it?" she said, and for a moment the mask fell. It happened so seldom in Nora's world that it was even more shocking than what had gone before. In an instant the placid water of good manners closed over the fury and erased it as though it had never been, but the mother's words had seemed reflected in the daughter's face: Shame on you.

A real museum, Charlie said to her that night. There couldn't have been a worse night for him to say that. There hadn't been a time when Nora had felt so uncertain of what she was doing. *Shame on you,* she heard over and over again, *shame on you.* And she knew if she told Bebe, the big boss, what had happened, she would say contemptuously, Oh, them. Those two. The detritus of the past, with their silver jewelry and wool coats.

"All those emeralds getting you down?" Phil had said when she passed him at the end of the day, and when she went on without a look or greeting, she heard him say quietly to himself, "One of those days."

But she shared none of that with her husband. There had been times when she and Charlie had aired their uncertainties with each other, but not this time. Instead she narrowed her eyes and said, "Let me give you the bottom line, Charlie: I am staying in my little job in my little museum living in my little house. I am not selling it. And since my name is on the deed, you can't sell, either. It's as simple as that. End of discussion."

"Bun," Charlie began, but Nora interrupted.

"I've had a really long day. I'm going to bed."

The lot is closed to all parking until further notice. Fees will be reimbursed at the end of the month on a pro rata basis. Any car found in the lot will be towed.

Sidney Stoller

New York hospitals were like telephone companies: they had started out smallish and local, and then merged and merged and merged so that they became behemoths. The greatest behemoth of all was the hospital in which Nora had given birth to the twins. From the bridge it looked like a small city, and inside it felt like one. Charlie had gotten lost in its hallways when Nora was recovering from her C-section and had somehow found himself entering neuro-oncology, which he'd only realized after he passed two rooms in which the occupants had shaved heads with railroad tracks of staples across them. It had taken directions from two nurses and an orderly to get him back to maternity.

It also turned out to be the hospital where Ricky was recovering from yet another surgery, which Nora had learned through various disapproving miming gestures from Charity. Nora was ashamed that she hadn't visited sooner. She stood paralyzed in the gift shop: Flowers? Balloons? A teddy bear whose shirt said HOPE YOU'RE BEAR-ING UP? She settled on a large box of chocolates. She figured that even if Ricky didn't have a sweet tooth, his children must.

"Eight-oh-two-B?" she said in one of the endless hallways, and someone hurrying in the other direction pointed.

It was a double room, but one bed was obviously unoccupied. Ricky was in the other, his leg encased in a cast to the hip, immobilized by equipment that looked not unlike one of the trusses on the bridge seen from the window of the hospital room. In the buzzing fluorescence of the terrible overhead lighting he looked waxy and slightly gray. She remembered that the doctors had wanted to keep Rachel for a few additional days after Nora had given birth because they said the baby had jaundice. "In this light, how can you tell?" Nora said to the doctors. "Everybody looks jaundiced. You look jaundiced." They said it was clear in the blood tests, but she'd taken Rachel home anyhow, even though she had looked a little yellower than Oliver.

Ricky's breathing was shallow, but he seemed to be sleeping soundly. A breakfast tray still held a plastic cup of that kind of orange juice that separated into watery top and bright, unappetizing bottom. "Like sunset in a toxic nuclear sky," Ollie had said once when he was holding a glass of the stuff in a dining hall during a college visit. "That's a little dramatic," Nora had said, but she'd never forgotten the turn of phrase.

Nora remembered that when Charlie had gotten lost in the hospital she was furious because she was so hungry and he had promised her a pastrami sandwich and chocolate pudding. When he finally arrived at her room, where a lactation consultant had just tried to explain how to breastfeed twins—in succession, which had almost killed her over the months that she'd done it—Nora was in a fine postpartum rage state until Charlie opened a greasy white paper bag and took out a glazed doughnut. It was one of those just-made doughnuts that tasted like a cloud composed of sugar and fat. Nora had bitten into it and started to cry. "I can't believe you brought me this," she said around an enormous mouthful.

"I got the sandwich and the pudding, too," Charlie said.

"No, no, this is perfect. It's so good. It might be the single best thing I've ever eaten in my entire life."

"Your hormones are out of control," Charlie said, unwrapping the sandwich on her tray table.

"I love you," Nora mumbled, stuffing the rest of the doughnut in her mouth.

"I love you, too."

Looking at Ricky's breakfast tray, she could almost taste that doughnut. Someone had told her that elsewhere in the hospital there were rooms with toile drapes, nice art, a menu from which you could choose your dinner. But she was quite sure Ricky's insurance wouldn't cover that. She had once thought hospitals were the great equalizers, but in New York even they could be stratified so that people with money seemed to be in a completely different place from people with none, or even people with less. She had once complained about how long it had taken in the ER when Ollie had cut the underside of his chin open on the edge of the tub. Another mother at school had said, "You took him to the ER? My pediatrician says to dose them with codeine and wait until morning to take them to a good plastic surgeon." Now that Oliver was a head taller than she was, Nora sometimes saw the small pink line where he'd gotten five stitches and wondered if she should have waited until morning and taken him to a good plastic surgeon. In Manhattan, finding one must be like finding a good latte. Just walk down the street with your wallet out.

She put the box of chocolates next to the breakfast tray and stood silently, looking at Ricky's face. He had a couple days' growth of beard, the way male models and movie actors did nowadays. She supposed shaving was beside the point. On one arm he had an IV line attached to one of those little boxes that she knew, from visiting Jean-Ann after she had had her mastectomy, allowed you to dose yourself with morphine. She was just starting to wonder whether she should leave, when Ricky opened his eyes. It seemed to take him a minute to focus them.

"I didn't mean to wake you," Nora whispered.

"No, no, that's okay. Sit down. It's nice that you came. Charity said you might come by."

Nora pulled up a chair. "Are you in a lot of pain?" she said.

"It's not so bad now. In the beginning—" Ricky grimaced.

"I'm so sorry, Enrique."

"Nothing to do with you, Mrs. Nolan," he said. "How's Mr. Nolan?" Nora wondered if Ricky knew that Charlie was parroting the Jack line to the authorities. Nora had shifted to saying, "Talk to your father," when the twins asked about it.

"Good. He was asking about you. He wanted you to know he's sorry, too." Not true, but suitable. "Everyone on the block really misses you." Absolutely true. The forecast was for a freak ice storm later in the week, and Nora knew that everyone was wondering who would salt the sidewalks, as though salting the sidewalks were a complex ritual that none of them could manage themselves since it involved a bag of salt and the ability to drop it in handfuls.

"How's the dryer vent?"

"The dryer vent?"

"Charity, she's not getting the clothes dry the way she's used to. The last time that happened, I cleaned out the vent with a Shop-Vac. Lotta people think, you take care of the lint filter, you got it covered, but a lot of lint winds up in that dryer vent, and then it doesn't dry so well." Ricky smiled, his eyelids at half-mast. Nora wondered whether he was high from the medication, and also whether when they'd lived in the apartment they'd gotten rid of a perfectly fine dryer that seemed as though it didn't work anymore purely because they hadn't used a Shop-Vac on the vent.

"She hasn't said anything to me. Maybe it's better. Or maybe she's just waiting for you to come back and fix it for her. You know the way Charity is. She doesn't like change much."

"Maybe I can get one of the other guys to go down. I gotta see how they feel about that, you know. Plus how they could get down there. You know, there are a lot of issues." Ricky looked away, grimaced again.

"Oh, I almost forgot," Nora said, reaching into her purse and pulling out an envelope. "Your Christmas bonus. I never got to give it to you." She laid the envelope on the tray table next to the chocolates. "I didn't want to wait until you were back to work."

"Ah, you didn't have to do that. But I appreciate it. It's tough, you know. I miss the job. Charity comes by, she tells me about something like the dryer vent, I feel bad. She's got to have a dryer that works, Charity. You don't want her to have problems with that machine."

"What the hell?" said a loud voice from the doorway. A small, round woman in acid-washed jeans and a T-shirt stood there, and Nora realized that until now she'd seen Ricky's wife only from the chest up and at a distance.

"Hi, Nita," Nora said. "I just wanted to see how your husband was doing. I brought some chocolates."

"What the hell—you're talking to him about fixing your

damn dryer, the shape he's in? Look at him. The man might never walk again, and all you care about is your damn dryer?"

"Babe, it's Mrs. Nolan. She's the one who brought the humidifier up that time. She sent the boys all that stuff, the soccer goal, the checker game. She's got Charity works for her, they got a problem—"

"They got zero problems, Rico. You're the one with the problems, your leg all busted up like that. You brought chocolates? You bring his van back fixed up? You bring the money he'd be making if he wasn't lying here in a hospital bed? You bring my rent money?"

A nurse stuck her head in. "You're disturbing the other patients again, Mrs. Ramos," she said.

"I should leave," Nora said. "I should let you rest, Enrique." Nita stood in her way, with her arms across her chest. Her cleavage was still gargantuan. Nora noticed that she had a deep, ropy scar along one cheek, as though someone who hadn't really learned how to suture skin had practiced on her a long time ago. She was wearing a gold cross, a Saint Christopher medal, and a nameplate necklace that said JUANITA. She followed Nora out into the hallway, which was bright, with even less flattering fluorescent lights and pale-green paint. All hospital corridors could double as operating theaters in a pinch.

"I just wanted to see how he was doing," Nora said.

"Maybe take it back into the room?" the nurse at the nurse's station said.

Nita ignored the nurse, who looked nervous. "You people," Nita said. "You make me laugh. How's he doing? His leg bone is broken in two places. He's got pins in it. Twenty stitches in his leg, and that's before they cut him open for the pins. A couple of torn ligaments that the doctors say might really be a problem in the future. In the future, they say, he could have some problems bending the knee. It's gonna be hard for him to fix your dryer then, huh?" She'd started out in almost a normal tone of voice, but now she was yelling. The nurse stood up. Obviously the staff was familiar with Nita.

"I'm so sorry about what happened."

"Yeah, you're all so sorry. What about that son of a bitch who did this? He sorry? He gonna pay? Rehab, lost wages, pain and suffering? Compensation?" She sounded like the personal-injury lawyers who advertised on TV. Nora wondered if she'd already hired one.

"I hope your boys are okay," she said.

"How you think they are? You want to explain to them why some crazy person beat their father up so bad he put him in the hospital?"

Put that way, it sounded as though Nora had wound up on the wrong side of some battle line. She said, "All of us on the block like Enrique and miss him."

Nita pushed past her, and though the hallway was wide, she came much too close, elbowing Nora aside. Nora felt stupid for coming in the first place. "How many more worthless assholes from where you live coming here to pretend they care whether he lives or dies?" Nita said over her shoulder.

"He seems like a nice man," said the nurse behind Nora at the nurse's station in a low voice. "She's a piece of work, though."

Nora took the subway back downtown afterward. She remembered taking it up there when she was pregnant, to visit her doctor, to tour the hospital. It had been terrifying. It wasn't just that she was so big that she felt she might pitch forward off of the platform, onto the tracks. The subway was scarier then.

The twins and their friends rode it now at all hours. "Every once in a while you get a weenie wagger, but if you pull out your phone to take a picture, they usually stop," one of Rachel's friends had said.

The train was the great equalizer now, not the hospitals, not the neighborhoods, the way they'd been when she first came to the city. The Upper West Side had had students and old people, Puerto Ricans and Orthodox Jews, strollers and shopping carts filled with the ersatz acquisitions of people who lived on the streets. Now it had black cars waiting for corporate pickups at the curbs, and expensive mountain bikes in the park. No one tried to steal car radios nowadays, and no one feared having the bikes stolen. Nora supposed this was an improvement. She was packed tightly into a subway car with medical students still wearing their scrubs, hipsters in short, tight pants, a few of what looked like Columbia professors carrying leather book bags, brown girls, black guys, a man who said he was collecting for the homeless and looked homeless himself and played a harmonica. It was like a casting director had said to herself, Something for everyone. Like a diorama of New York City life. A teenage girl with cornrows and a City College sweatshirt offered Nora a seat, and she shook her head, and felt old because of the gesture, and stupid for going to the hospital in the first place.

As she came down her block, she saw a young man pick up a black trash bag from in front of the Fisks' house and hoist it over his shoulder. "Reporters go through people's trash now?" she said, enraged, while the man blinked behind his glasses. "Is that what journalism has come to? Do you people have no shame?"

"This is my laundry," he said quietly.

"What?"

"My laundry. I'm taking my clothes to the Laundromat."
That's what the renters did. Laundry in trash bags, boxes of
empties after parties.

"Whatever," Nora said as he looked at her quizzically. It was
the rudest she could remember being in years. Nita had undone
her. How pleased she would be to know that.

"Are you nuts?" said Charlie that night when she told him
about the hospital visit. "Those people are going to sue the
Fisks, and you went up there to see how they're doing?" While
Charlie's face was normally ruddy, it had turned practically
purple.

"He's a person who worked in our home," Nora said. "He's
a good person and I like him. Jack is a bad person and I don't
like him. So, yes, I went up there to see how he's doing. And,
by the way, he's not doing very well. That leg is a mess, which
is what I suppose happens to your leg when someone keeps hitting it with a golf club."

"Nora, Ricky is a person who did odd jobs for us. He's not
our friend, he's the neighborhood handyman. Jack is our
friend."

"Jack's not my friend. I think he's a terrible person and he
deserves whatever he gets."

"What are you thinking? Are you trying to take sides against
our neighbors?"

"Aren't you interested in doing the right thing, Charlie? You
talk all the time about Jack's version of events. Aren't you interested in the truth? What about the truth?"

"Oh, Jesus, Nora, you're on such a high horse with this I
don't know how you'll ever get off. Just don't drag me into
whatever crazy liberal guilt thing you've got going on."

"I don't have a crazy liberal guilt thing going on," Nora said. "I have a human thing going on."

Sherry Fisk was annoyed, too. Nora felt sorrier about Sherry's reaction than Charlie's, but not sorry enough to regret what she'd done. "I just wish you'd mentioned it to us, Nora," Sherry said when she ran into her on the block. "Apparently Ricky's wife told their attorney that you said Jack was to blame for what happened."

"I absolutely did not say that, or anything like that."

"She says you told her you were sorry for what Jack did."

"I said I was sorry. I never mentioned Jack's name or the particulars of what happened."

"She also said you gave them money."

"I gave him a Christmas card with his Christmas bonus in it, Sherry. That's all. He shouldn't have to lose his Christmas bonus."

"Well," Sherry said, sighing, "it's just unfortunate. We're in the middle of trying to work something out with them so that this whole thing can be nipped in the bud. The timing of your visit wasn't great in terms of those negotiations."

"I'm sorry if I upset you," Nora said. "His wife talked as though I wasn't the only one who had visited."

"Yes," Sherry Fisk said. "George went up there and apparently told Ricky that if he didn't say the whole thing was an accident he would never work on the block again. That wasn't helpful, either."

Nora felt her face grow hot. Being lumped in with George was a terrible feeling. "Apparently Ricky's wife came in and hit George with a crutch. It's the only good thing to come out of this whole sorry situation." Sherry started to laugh a little tentatively, as though she hadn't laughed in a while and was trying to get the laugh motor running again. "I have to admit, the idea of someone hitting George with a crutch made my day. She didn't hit you, did she?"

Nora shook her head, although she suspected Nita had wanted to. As Nora was going toward the double doors that led to the elevators, walking fast, although what she really wanted to do was sprint, she had heard footfalls behind her.

"Hey!" Nita called, and Nora turned to see her with the candy box in her hand. "You leave these?"

"The food is pretty terrible here, right?"

"Not bad enough to eat these," she said, shoving the box hard into Nora's chest. "And all that stuff you give Rico for the kids? He sells it all on eBay. Ice skates? Who you kidding, lady? Ice skates?"

Nora and Charlie were a little surprised to find themselves going to a dinner party, but it saved them eating alone together, which had become difficult since they were barely speaking, and it was an invitation that could not be denied. Charlie still had hopes of another rung on the ladder at Parsons Ridge, and the dinner was being given by one of the so-called rainmakers, Jim DeGeneris. There had almost been a snafu; Charlie had looked at the date and time, but not the address, and until the afternoon of the dinner had planned to meet Nora at the DeGeneris apartment, a rather bare but enormous place with elaborate moldings and fireplaces off Fifth. But his assistant had reminded him that Jim and his wife were now separated and that Jim had moved to a loft in Tribeca, neither of which Charlie had known, making it even more important that they attend the dinner party. "A Tribeca loft," said Nora. "Where rich guys go when they ditch the first wife. When he remarries someone younger he'll move to Madison Park."

"Maybe table the cynicism for tonight," Charlie said on the phone. "This could be important for me." Nora had lost count of how many times her husband had said this. They each found the other's work inconsequential, for very different reasons. But hers was shinier in public. Charlie was interested in what she did when he could proffer it for possible professional gain, or at least reflected stature. He needed the card to play. He was afraid that he was never going to be one of the big men, the ones whose names popped up in *Forbes* or the *Journal*. He was usually the third guy to be introduced to the major client in the conference room.

"Is Jim cooking?" Nora asked.

"I have no idea," Charlie said. Charlie had never cooked a thing in his life. When she left him something to reheat, on those evenings she was out with a prospect or a friend, he would always text: *What temp how long?* Several years before, she had written on the chalkboard in the kitchen *350/30 minutes.* It was still there. She'd once seen a quote on someone's inspiration board—"Kill me if I ever have an inspiration board," she'd said to her sister, who'd responded with a silence so weighty that Nora instantly concluded that Christine had one—that said "Insanity is doing the same thing over and over again and expecting a different result." She actually sometimes thought that was the definition of marriage.

"Everyone attibutes that quote to Einstein," said Jenny, standing in the wreckage of what had been her old kitchen and would become her new one. "It's not Einstein. Maybe it was Einstein's wife."

"Was Einstein married?"

Jenny had nodded. "Can you imagine? You're not married to a man who thinks he's Einstein, you're married to a man who *is* Einstein."

"God, this looks great," Nora said when Jenny showed her the cabinet door samples. "This finish is beautiful. Jasper really knows what he's doing, although I assume you get special treatment."

"That's what happens when you're fellating the craftsman," Jenny said.

"Oh, my God, Jen," Nora said.

"I love that you're still shockable. Seriously, he's really talented. And I don't just mean in the obvious way. He reads all the time. He cooks, too."

"Oh, please, save me from the man who allegedly cooks."

"This is completely different, Nor. He's not a guy who talks about cooking, or buys a ten-thousand-dollar stove and then tells you you can't make osso bucco properly on anything else. He's a guy who goes through the cupboards, stops at the butcher, and makes real food that tastes good without making a big deal about it or expecting you to act like he cured cancer."

Jim DeGeneres was the other guy, the guy who acted as though making a meal were akin to nuclear fission, who produced food that tasted of nothing, or too much of something you couldn't identify and didn't particularly like. Nora knew this new place would have a monumental kitchen, and it did. The Tribeca loft was cavernous and modern but, oddly, done in Swedish antiques, all white and blue. It was the kind of downtown place that, for a few years after September 11, would have gone begging. Everyone who lived below Canal Street had been traumatized; everyone who had considered buying or renting there had gone elsewhere. But though everyone was fond of saying that New York, and New Yorkers, had been changed forever by the terrorist attacks, forever in terms of real estate lasted about thirty months. A shiny new tower stood where the Twin Towers had crumpled to the earth, and the downtown real estate market had bounced back. At some point Nora expected Jim to say, "I don't want to tell you what I paid for this place," and then proceed to do just that.

"Nora!" Jim said. "You cut your hair!" Not a good beginning; over the years Nora had learned that when a man said you'd cut your hair, it was less an observation than an indictment. She decided to parry with a generalization, since she had in fact been wearing her hair the same way for a decade: "It's been too long, Jim. I hope you're cooking."

"Of course," he said. (Thank God for big lunches.) "You haven't changed a bit."

Why did they all say that to each other? There was the fact that it was so patently untrue; Nora had looked at herself in the bathroom mirror as she was applying mascara and realized that her skin had begun to look like silk after you washed it, still serviceable but without its sheen. She had never been vain and had never felt she had reason to be: strangers were always asking her whether they knew her from high school or the ad agency or this or that suburb because she looked like a generic woman of a certain age. Even the people she knew who had taken pre-emptive action to maintain their looks had changed more than a bit. And that was only the exterior. "I used to really like him, but Jim's a different guy now," Charlie had said on their way downtown. As was Charlie, of course. And Nora as well.

"How's the jewelry business?" Jim said.

"You're in the jewelry business?" said a thin blonde behind him.

"Not really," said Nora.

"I want to hear all about what happened on that block of yours," Jim said. "What a story! Everyone's been talking about it." And Nora suddenly realized exactly why they had been invited. Luckily Charlie was placing a drink order with the cater waiter and hadn't heard.

"Charlie, come sous-chef," Jim cried. Charlie shucked his jacket, took off his tie, and rolled up his sleeves so that he was dressed like Jim. Nora was dressed in her dinner party uniform: black dress, statement necklace. "Are those real?" said the blonde, peering at the stones.

"If they were I'd need an armed guard," Nora said, but the blonde continued to peer and didn't crack a smile.

There were two other men there, one above Charlie in the pecking order, another young but, from the sound of him, promising, with the kind of party patter that was smooth and memorable, a few witticisms, a recommendation for a *New Yorker* article, the kind of bright young man her husband would have once befriended and now hated and feared. His wife was a lawyer—"semiretired"—who had just had her second child and wanted to talk only about private-school admissions. Nora was tolerant. She had passed through a phase in which she did the same, until the twins had been accepted to a school that had been founded just after the American Revolution and that, most important, ran from kindergarten to the end of high school. The semiretired lawyer's eyes lit up when Nora mentioned it. Jennifer? Jessica? The husband's name was Jason, she was certain of that. It was so hard to remember. Nora's assistants had always been told to give her flash cards to tuck beneath the napkin in her lap when she was hosting a donor lunch so that she could keep the names straight.

"Charlie, when's the last time you diced an onion?" she heard Jim say in that kidding way that had an edge of exasperation. Mumble, mumble: Charlie was probably saying he didn't cook as much as he used to. Nora glided away from the kitchen, an open-plan stainless-steel number that looked as though it had been lifted right from one of those restaurants whose layout demanded you admire the chef's technique.

Since Nora had first moved to New York, dinner parties had mainly evaporated. In the beginning there had been one a week, exercises in competitive cooking. "Whose is this?" they would ask one another, the way they now asked it about a particularly sharp coat or pair of boots. Marcella. Julia. Cookbook intimacy that passed for friendship. At the end of every evening they were wrecked by the need for perfection and the assumption of judgment.

Then they'd made some money and graduated to virtual cooking. Nora discovered that, like manicures and pedicures, cooking was something she could do herself but preferred to have someone else do for her. She was one of the first to discover HomeMade, a company that delivered meals with little cards that described how to prepare them. Like dress designers supplying gowns for a big gala, the women who ran the company kept a computerized accounting of who'd ordered what to avoid unfortunate duplications. When Nora sent along a list of guests, one of them might say, If you're having the Roysters don't get the Chicken Marengo; they served it themselves last week. It all seemed like cheating, but Nora prided herself on the fact that at least she didn't lie and pretend the HomeMade dinners were homemade. In the beginning, lots of other women did, but after a while it became impossible, the roster was so well known, although Sherry Fisk's sister-in-law swore her Apple Brown Betty was her grandmother's recipe when it was exactly the same dessert, in the same ramekins, that they'd all had elsewhere.

"She claims her nose is original, too," Sherry had once said.

Eventually they had all started meeting at restaurants, so that no one had to hide the pill vials in the medicine cabinets from nosy guests. It seemed the only time they went to dinner parties now was when the men had taken up cooking. Everyone acted as though that were akin to Christ turning water into wine at Cana.

"Risotto!" the women exclaimed joyfully when Jim brought it to the table in an enormous shallow serving bowl, which Nora knew meant by the time it got to her it would be luke-warm. Which was fine. It was crunchy, too, which meant she wouldn't eat much.

"You need to work on your husband's knife skills," Jim said, pointing his fork at her. Knife skills: this was a new badge of honor, a status symbol for guys who had finally—finally!—become tired of talking about wine. The slightly aberrational spouse was a status symbol, too. The husband who cooked. The wife who played golf. The husband who took his children to school. The wife who ran her own business. Of course, it was chancier with the women than with the men. You couldn't push it too far. The marathoner wife who made partner—perhaps. The wife who could bench-press her own weight and made the cover of *Fortune*—too emasculating. The men, on the other hand, got unlimited mileage out of performing so-called women's tasks as long as they also had substantial disposable income and significant business cards. Occasionally a woman would say of her husband, "He's a stay-at-home dad," and everyone would smile and think, He doesn't have a job.

Jim's wife had been a significant woman, a doctor who treated people with addiction issues, which probably explained why he was a wine aficionado. Nora could hear Polly now, saying to her husband, "Nora might have better things to do than work on her husband's knife skills." Charlie and Nora had been close friends with Jim and Polly, once upon a time. They had lived in similar three-bedroom apartments, not far from each other, and had children around the same age. There had been a couple of years there, when, one Sunday a month, they had had takeout dinners in each other's places, the children throwing Lego blocks around in the next room while the grown-ups ate Peking duck or sashimi. Jim and Polly had nothing that Charlie and Nora wanted except for a wood-burning fireplace, which Polly said was more trouble than it was worth. "We have to start a fire hours before anyone arrives because the room fills with smoke," she said. "Can't you smell it?"

By the look on Jim's face when she said this Nora could tell it was one of those low-level arguments that married couples had frequently. "What good is a wood-burning fireplace if you don't have a fire?" Jim said.

Nora had enjoyed those evenings. The men would talk across the table to each other about work, and the women about their children. Then someone had canceled, and someone else had canceled, and Jim had become a bigger deal than Charlie, which Nora only figured out at the cocktail party Jim and Polly had had as a housewarming for their new place, which no amount of partying could warm, with its marble entrance foyer and elaborate window treatments. She and Polly agreed, when the Nolans were leaving the party, Charlie impatiently holding the elevator, that they would schedule lunch, they would, and then they never did. And now Nora never could. Having lunch with the estranged wife of a man your husband wanted to think well of him was a no-go.

Charlie had never liked Polly. He had always said he thought she was difficult. Also not sexy. He was seated now with the thin blonde on one side. Alison? Alyssa? The conversation was a hubbub, like modern music, discordant, with odd bleats and no melody. People in New York never really listened to anyone else; they just waited for a break in the action so they could start to speak, push off with their own boat into the slipstream of talk.

"Your wife is in the jewelry business?" Nora heard the blonde ask Charlie.

"How large is your endowment?" said young Jason, who obviously knew precisely what Nora did, the kind of man who researched his fellow guests before a dinner party.

"Substantial for the size of the museum," she said. "Plus we own the building free and clear, which is certainly an advantage."

"And your annual budget?"

Nora tapped the table with her dessert fork and laughed. "Are you really interested?"

"I'm interested in board service. I'm trying to decide where."

"That's interesting. People are usually much cagier about that than you are."

"Should I be cagier?"

She laughed again and saw Charlie narrow his eyes across the table. She realized she had to hit some sweet spot between being nice to Jason and appearing to be too cozy with him.

"I'll be candid with you," she said. "Our board is largely decorative. The founder of the museum picks its members for optimal society traction. She makes all the decisions herself."

"I'll be candid right back," Jason said. "I'd be interested in being involved with Bob Harris's foundation."

"I don't know anything about that," Nora said.

"Really? Because he talks as though he's certain you'll be running it."

"Running what?" Charlie said from across the table. Luckily dessert was served, lemon tart and raspberries, and Jim tapped her arm, so she turned from Jason. "I want to hear all about this crazy thing on your block," he said. "I don't know Jack Fisk, but I know lots of people who do, and they say he must have lost his mind. I told them, Well, I know someone who will be able to give me all the details."

Later, as she pulled her nightgown over her head, Nora said to Charlie, "Did Jim ask you about Jack Fisk?"

"It's all he wanted to talk about," Charlie said sourly. "It's the same deal in the office. Someone comes in and I think they want me for a meeting or on a call, and instead it's all, What the hell happened there? Plus they all think it was a tire iron. Why the hell would Jack swing a tire iron?"

"A golf club makes more sense?"

"And what about you and Jason?" her husband said as though she hadn't spoken. "There's a guy who's an operator. His middle initial is *H*. I think it stands for Howard, but we all say it really stands for Hungry. He's one of those guys you're afraid to turn your back on. He's sort of Jim's boy, which is why he was there. I guess he knows something I don't about you and Harris."

"Oh, for God's sake, Charlie, he's just ambitious, like everyone else in town. He doesn't know anything. And Jim needs to learn how to make risotto. It was like chewing gravel. And how he could trade Polly in for whoever she was . . ."

"He didn't," Charlie said in the darkness as she got under the covers. "One of the other guys in the office told me this morning. Polly left him. She was apparently having an affair with some other doctor for years, and once their youngest kid was out of the house she figured, What's the point. I hear he's really a mess."

"He didn't act like he was a mess."

"Yeah, like he's going to fall apart with the people at that table? He got wasted at some cigar bar last week and told one of the guys that he has sex with that girl all the time because when they're not having sex she talks to him, and he can't stand to listen to her."

"He'll find somebody," Nora said. "He's rich, he's nice-looking. Maybe he'll even learn to cook."

"What do you want to bet Jason knows how to cook," said Charlie. "He probably studied at the Cordon Bleu after his Rhodes scholarship."

A petition is being prepared to request that the lot be reopened at the same rate as previously. Please let George know if you are willing to sign.

The lot is closed to all activity until further notice.
Any cars in the lot will be towed at owner's expense.

Sidney Stoller

The empty lot was a constant reminder. That, and the fact that nothing worked in any of their houses. A dripping tap in the Nolan kitchen kept on dripping. Harold Lessman tripped over a flagstone in the patio that had heaved up during the winter freezes and spring thaws and sprained his ankle. The Fisks were mainly at their house in the country, but their housekeeper, Grace, told Charity that there was a leak in the skylight and she had to put a bucket in the hall. Ricky had made himself essential. They had all made themselves helpless.

"I hear you know the golf club guy," Phil said, sitting outside the museum with a new sign that said STILL CRAZY AFTER ALL THESE YEARS.

"Don't you think that one will put people off?" Nora said, pointing at the cardboard placard.

"You know, people our age love this one. I'm thinking of using nothing but song titles from now on. Maybe 'Born in the U.S.A.' When does the big boss come back from Florida?"

"You really keep up on things," Nora said.

"I'm a student of my surroundings," he said. "Who's your new guy? The skinny one?"

"He's a temp," Nora said. "My assistant quit."

"The snooty tall one? I can't believe you put up with her for a minute. She never said hello to me, not once. This new guy is a good guy. Smart, too. You think you'll keep him?"

"I'm thinking about it," Nora said. Richard was still technically working for the temp agency, but Nora had made it a point to sit down and talk to him after he had rearranged her computer files so that finding anything made infinitely more sense.

"My parents came here from the Philippines," he had said. "Seven kids, and here's all they want: a college degree, and then a job where you don't get your hands dirty. All they know is that right now I work in a museum. No dirt, right?"

"A museum, but not jewelry?" Nora asked.

"I'm not sure they'd get it," Richard said. "I'm not sure I get it, to be honest. But I like working for you. Where did your last assistant go, if you don't mind my asking?"

The Met, of course. The pinnacle of New York museums. Madison had sent Nora a note on stationery engraved with her initials. "I learned so much from you," she wrote, a student of the no-bridges-burned playbook. Apparently she had told Bebe's assistant that she didn't think there was sufficient room for growth for her, that the museum was a one-woman show. The woman she meant was not Nora.

"There's a man on the phone for you," Richard said as Nora took off her coat. "He won't give his name, but he said to tell you"—he looked down at his notepad—"fasten your seatbelts, it's going to be a bumpy ride."

"A bumpy *night*," Nora said. "It's going to be a bumpy *night*. It's a line from a movie. *All About Eve.* Everyone gets it wrong."

"I thought he said 'ride.'"

No, he didn't.

"James?" she said into the phone in her office.

"Moneypenny," he replied.

That's what he'd always called her, James Mortimer, ever since they'd ripped through three James Bond movies the month they first met. She was Moneypenny and he was James. Never Jimmy or Jim or, God forbid, as he had once said early on, at a crowded party full of lacrosse players, Jimbo. "You're blessed," he said then. "No one can turn Nora into anything else."

"My sister calls me Nonnie," she said.

"That's different," he said. "My sister calls me Manchild. Mannie for short."

His sister lived in London, his parents in the suburbs of Philadelphia, or that's what he called them, which sounded fine until he and Nora had started up the long driveway on a snaky street where none of the houses were visible from the sidewalk. Nora was too young to know then what she knew now, that on the outskirts of every American city there were areas in which the houses were invisible from the road, and that that was where the richest people lived. Grosse Pointe, Bel Air, Buckhead: during her years raising money for museums and schools she'd been to almost all of them. The Mortimers lived in Gladwyne. They were stereotypical bad parents, almost stock characters from a film, which might have been one reason their only son so loved old movies. She drank, he screwed around. She shopped, he managed their investments. At dinner in the morning room, which had wallpaper that looked like a trellis and a table that sat only six, as opposed to the dining room, which could hold twenty in a pinch, they had both been pleasant enough, although when Nora had mentioned that she and James had met in an art history class Mr. Mortimer rolled his eyes. He said that the town where Nora had grown up had a decent golf course, and Nora agreed that it did, and Mrs. Mortimer asked if her parents lived on the water, and she said unfortunately not. The food all tasted somehow like canned vegetable soup, even the salad. It was awful, and there wasn't enough of it.

Nora had been given a guest room with yellow walls and white furniture, but it was right next to James's room, which still had a pennant from his boys' school above the twin bed, and she'd barely gotten under the covers before he slipped in next to her. The guest room had twin beds, too, but they were used to it from the dorms. Nora could remember it all so well, better than she remembered what she'd done yesterday, how smooth and warm his skin had felt against hers. She'd realized that that was how life was, that certain small moments were like billboards forever alongside the highway of your memory. There was a strip of moonlight through the curtains that moved across James's back—waist, shoulder blades, waist, shoulder blades—as he moved. And then suddenly she heard a thud, thought for a moment that they'd knocked the bed frame loose, and he stopped, and she heard shouts and doors and other sounds that couldn't be identified but that sounded like pitched battles from one of those old movies he had taught her to like, *My Man Godfrey* or *The Philadelphia Story,* which James said was about a family who had lived not far away from his parents' house. It went on for a long time, and after that James didn't finish, went back to his own room.

"Now you know why I'll never get married," he'd said after an hour-long silence in the car. Nora stared out the passenger side window and let the tears fall onto her barn jacket, but deep inside she was thinking, I'll change his mind.

Almost two years together, three more disastrous visits to his parents, one visit at school with his sister, who had said, "You took her to the house?" as though her brother had exposed Nora to a communicable disease. Dinners with Nora's father and Carol and Christine, who all loved him. "No wonder you are the way you are," James said after the first such dinner. "Which is what?" Nora said, hoping for "wonderful" or "irresistible." "Uncomplicated," James said, and somehow it seemed like an insult. It still felt that way, the few times Nora remembered it. No one in New York ever said about anyone interesting, Oh, yes, that So-and-so, she's uncomplicated.

"What a dick thing to say," Jenny had said one night when Nora had gotten drunk and told her about it, and about James, and everything that followed, while Jenny held the tissue box.

The truth was, she had been uncomplicated, and naïve. Would she know even today, nearly thirty years out, that a good-looking young man who at twenty swore by French cuffs, who spoke much of the time in the language of old movies, and could sing all the lyrics to "I'll Be Seeing You" might not be suited to be her boyfriend, or that of any woman? She imagined Rachel describing him, bringing him home, and alarms ringing between her ears as though the house were on fire. But perhaps that was just retrospective. Or stereotypical.

He had already graduated, moved to New York, put off her two scheduled visits to him there over the summer. She remembered the day in early August when he drove up in his VW convertible and took her to a nondescript local place for lunch, not the inn where they'd had dinner on Valentine's Day, and she wanted to say, No, no, the choice of restaurant a door slamming in her face. James was incandescent. When he finally spoke, it was not only as though he'd rehearsed his words, but as though he was jubilant at being able to deliver them.

"I love you, Moneypenny," he said. "I'll always love you." Even in everyday life James had a tendency to talk like a movie, perhaps one with Ray Milland or Dana Andrews. They'd watched *Laura* at least half a dozen times.

Then he added, "And I like sleeping with you. But I really want to sleep with men."

"How do you know if you've never done it?" she sobbed.

There was a long silence, and it contained so many things that she didn't want to know that it took years for her to color in all those lines, one terrible realization at a time, one suspicion, one acquaintance, one prep-school friend, one swim-team member. Finally James said, "I just know."

Of course she had moved to New York, too, and from time to time she would see him, or hear of him. What were the chances that she would be at a party with a friend of a friend at an artist's loft three years after graduation and see his black-and-white photograph on the bedroom wall, shirtless, laughing, beautiful? It turned out things like that happened in New York all the time. Things like what happened to the artist happened all the time when they were young, a big success, then no new paintings, then the obituary, age forty-one, dead of AIDS. Nora couldn't help it; when she had seen it in the *Times,* part of her had been oddly, shamefully glad: her replacement was gone. Then she'd gotten tested, been negative, which managed to convince her that James had not been sleeping with the artist and her at the same time. She and Jenny had the kind of friendship in which they told each other everything, and yet it had taken her nearly two bottles of Chardonnay atop two margaritas to tell Jenny that. "Oh, honey," Jenny had said, stroking Nora's forearm. "Here's the thing: he didn't really break up with you. He broke up with the lie that was his life."

"I had no idea. What sort of woman am I, that I had no idea?"

"Lots of the women I know slept with gay men in college, before they knew they were gay. Or before they admitted they were gay. One of my colleagues said it was the best sex she ever had."

"Oh, thanks a lot, Jen. That bodes well for the future," said Nora, who was already with Charlie by then.

In retrospect it seemed that American colleges were the opposite of English boarding schools, where boys who would wind up married to women and surrounded by children were said to try it on for a time with other boys. All of her female friends now talked about the men they knew at Williams or Columbia or Oberlin who had had college girlfriends before they realized, or acknowledged, that they were not really interested in women in that way at all. Nora sometimes thought that if only she and James had been young fifty years earlier, they would have married and had children and been as happy as most people and she would only wonder sometimes why he had run out of steam in the sex department and took so many business trips (which was no different from being married to a straight man, if it came to that). Instead they had had the good fortune—or the bad, from her perspective—of meeting at the dawning of the age of enlightenment. But when she'd said that to Jenny that drunken night, her friend had looked at her sternly and said, "You need to check yourself, Nor. That's just crazy. There's a reason those kinds of arrangements went out of style."

"Flexual," Rachel had told her some of her friends at school called themselves, which she supposed meant whatever. James wasn't whatever. After the artist there had apparently been a fellow architect, and then an actor. From what she had heard from their mutual friends, each relationship lasted less than the length of time theirs had. She wondered if any of them had gone home with him to Gladwyne, and suspected not. If his father had been contemptuous of art history, the likelihood was small that he'd welcome a young man starring off-Broadway in a play that required him to have his hair dyed blond.

Nora had run into James several times over the years, when she was pregnant with the twins at the screening of a documentary, at a restaurant in midtown, she arriving for lunch, he leaving. "How is your sister?" Nora asked. "You have a sister?" said the man who was with him. Nora couldn't help but notice that James was aging oh so gracefully, but as he got older, the guys stayed the same age, just slightly older than the age he'd been when he'd broken up with Nora. What had been a charmingly unstudied urbanity when he was in college had hardened into something approaching a performance. Nora hadn't needed Jenny to tell her that one of the things that had drawn her to Charlie was that he was the un-James. When Nora met Charlie he had never even seen *Casablanca*.

It infuriated Nora that the sound of James Mortimer on the phone, just a single word, still gave her that telltale and shame-making frisson. Nora had married Charlie on the rebound from something else, something impossible and profound that probably would have become just as everyday as everything else. She knew, had always known, had always told herself, that she had made the right decision. Even today Charlie would say or do something, usually with the kids, that would remind her of why she'd chosen him. He had always been a good father, not one of those who handed off a baby when the odor of full diaper shattered the potpourri air of the living room. He genuinely liked amusement-park rides and Saturday-morning cartoons and tossing that Frisbee around. He was happy to play in the father-son game, which had been changed to the father-son-daughter game, then to the parent-child game because not everyone has a father. Some of the upper-school girls had later decided that the word *child* was demeaning but by upper school their kids didn't want to have anything to do with sports events that included their parents. It was bad enough having them stand on the sidelines. "Mom, I can hear you!" Rachel had said after one basketball game at which Nora had thought she'd been relatively contained.

She could almost see James in front of her as she sat with the phone in her hand, although she suspected that he might be a bit more weathered since she'd seen him last in person. "This is a surprise," she said, and even she thought she sounded a bit harsh.

"Now, now," he said. "How would that nice husband of yours feel if I was calling you all the time?"

"Don't be facetious," she said. Charlie was exactly the sort of guy James had disdained in college, the sort Nora should have been dating in the first place.

One night after a long week at work, Charlie had come home drunk, and she could never remember how they got there, maybe because someone at school had come out at an assembly, but he'd muttered to the twins, who were teenagers by that time, "Hey, you never know. Your mother's college boyfriend was a gay blade." After he'd turned off the light and before he'd begun to snore what she thought of as the drunk snore, Nora had said, "If you ever say anything like that again,

I swear to God I will walk out of this house and never come back." Perhaps having seen the look on their mother's face, the twins never asked about it, either, even Rachel.

"The reason I'm calling," James said, "is that I have this friend who's a journalist. He's working on a magazine cover story about that block you live on, and I told him I would ask you to talk to him."

"Oh, my God, it's been months now. The story is so over, which is nothing but a good thing as far as I'm concerned. Even the tabloids haven't touched us for ages."

"I understand, but I think he's envisioning something more expansive, more global. The incident as the peg for a real New York fin-de-siècle narrative. White-collar. Blue-collar. The golf club. You have to wonder whether it would have gotten as much attention without the golf club."

"I try not to think of the golf club. And I haven't talked to any of the reporters."

"I understand, but this writer is quite talented, and I think what he has in mind is something bigger and broader than the newspaper reports. Somewhat literary, I suppose."

"He's a friend? What kind of friend?" Nora said.

"Don't be facetious," James said. "It's an interesting idea, isn't it? Culture clash. How the other half lives. He says your block has this strange Brigadoon feeling. Hermetically sealed. The land that time forgot."

"If you were supposed to sell me on this idea, you're failing miserably," Nora said. "I like where I live, and I like the people who live there. Why would I want to sell them out for a magazine piece?"

"I told him you might feel that way, but that I would ask." Nora wondered how James had described her. A college classmate? An old friend? Nora wrote the writer's name on her desk pad, and below it she wrote "James Mortimer" and underlined it twice.

"How's the aluminum house?" she said.

"Ah, so your friend Suzanne mentioned the millstone around both our necks. It's fine. It in no way relates to anything around it, the contractor complains constantly about how difficult the job has been for his men, maintaining it in the future will be an extraordinary chore, and the client is difficult. But it will get a lot of attention."

"And that's all that matters."

James sighed. "Moneypenny, has anyone ever mentioned that you telegraph judgment effortlessly with your tone of voice?"

"My daughter."

"How is she?" James said.

"Rachel is graduating from Williams soon," she said.

"My Lord," James said. "Did it ever occur to you, all those years ago, that someday you would have a daughter there?"

The silence was her, coming up with a reply. But all the possible responses were so unspeakable, or lame, or humiliating, that instead she said, "I have to go. Tell your 'friend'"—even she could hear the quotation marks she put around the word—"that if he doesn't get a return call I've decided not to cooperate."

She pushed down the button on the phone, then impulsively hit one of the speed-dial buttons.

"What?" said her daughter.

"Just checking in, honey. How is everything?"

The silence was Rachel, taking her temperature. "Mommy, are you okay?" she said. Her daughter could be combative, egocentric, impossible. But she could read Nora's voice as no one else could, even Charlie. Especially Charlie.

"I'm fine," she said.

"So am I, actually. Actually, I'm really good. You know that paper I told you about, about the British suffragettes, the one I was worried about because the instructor is so harsh? I got an A, and she wrote 'excellent work' at the bottom."

"You smartie."

"Right? I was pretty excited. So I'm more or less all done for the year. One open-book test in poli sci, one paper but not that big a one, and that's kind of it. I think I might have an A-minus average this time, and graduate with honors. I won't know for a couple of weeks, but it looks good."

"You smartie. I'm so proud of you."

"Plus Oliver is here and we're making a big dinner for my friends tonight. Bolognese and a salad and Ollie says he's making some kind of brownies, but I'm a little worried because he's never made them before. And before you ask, not pot brownies."

"The thought had not occurred to me," Nora lied. "That's so nice that he came to see you, that he misses his sister."

"Yeah, right. He misses Lizzie. You know, the one with the curly hair who stayed with us over break? The one whose mom you met once because she was friends with that friend of yours?"

The remarkable thing was that Nora knew exactly who Rachel meant, a small girl with enormous gray-green eyes and a laugh that sounded like it belonged to a much larger, perhaps male person. *Heh heh heh heh* from the den as they all watched television.

"I didn't know that he and Lizzie were actually seeing each other," Nora said.

"Oh, my God, Mommy, seeing each other, really—what is that, even? So in the beginning it was kind of a random hookup, but then they both decided to just hook up but have it be exclusive, and now I guess they're kind of a couple or something."

"Wow. I guess I'm happy?"

"Definitely. Nice, smart, not clingy, not crazy."

Nora laughed. "I guess that covers everything."

"She has that really annoying laugh. But, yeah, she's cool."

"Oliver and Lizzie," Nora said wistfully.

"You sure you're okay? You don't sound okay."

"I am," Nora said. "Don't worry about me, Bug. Still crazy after all these years."

"What?"

"Never mind," Nora said. "Love you."

Please contact me about the block BBQ.

George

"I thought you had the barbecue this year," Nora said when she saw Linda Lessman that evening walking her cocker spaniel.

"We do. Or we did. I talked to Sherry about it, and we both think we should either put it off, maybe until right before Labor Day, or cancel it entirely."

"Oh, wow," said Nora. "That's kind of a big deal. I mean, we were going to miss it anyhow because it's at the same time as some commencement things. But even then the twins wondered if we could somehow make it back for the last hour or so."

"I know, but what can we do? Can you imagine the newspaper coverage? Sherry says their lawyer told them Ricky is back in the hospital for another surgery. I just pictured a photo of his wife at his bedside juxtaposed with all of us with hamburgers in our hands, standing and smiling at the spot where it happened."

It was the clearest indication yet that the block itself had been wounded by what Jack Fisk had done. Along with the Fenstermacher holiday party, the barbecue had been a major communal event for them all. The first year the Nolans had lived on the block, they had gone to visit Charlie's family, always a teeth-gritting affair. That Monday Nora had run into Sherry Fisk with their then-dog, Nero. "You all missed the barbecue!" she said.

"What barbecue?" Nora asked.

That was how it had always been on the block, a sense that by osmosis a person would know to apply for a spot in the lot, decorate the front door at Christmas (or "the holidays," as they all called them, in deference to the Jewish residents), and set aside the last Saturday in May for the barbecue, rain date Sunday. As Sherry Fisk spoke, Nora had realized that the night before, lying in bed as someone on the street sang "America the Beautiful" without really knowing the words, she had noticed a faint tang in the air that she now knew was the scent of residual charcoal. Apparently, five big grills were set up at the end of the block: hot dogs, burgers, chicken, kebobs, and whatever veggie stuff passed for barbecue food. The neighborhood children jumped around in one of those bouncy tents that someone had rented, and the adults sat on the nearest stoops, eating and chatting as though they didn't see one another every day. The Nolans had never missed the barbecue again.

Responsibility for the barbecue moved annually from family to family, which really only meant responsibility for calling the people hired to make it happen. Even George had not been able to kill the block barbecue, but he had come close, officiously putting up sawhorses at the head of the block to close it off and drawing the attention of the police, who asked to see his permits. Since almost no one drove down the block anyway, they decided after that to leave it open for the barbecue, and someone was always willing to guide a driver who drove in by mistake and needed help backing out. The twins had loved going to the firehouse to tell the firefighters that if they got a call about smoke on their block, it was just from the line of grills.

Even the renters were invited, and most of them came, to eat a hot dog or two. But they tended to be younger than the permanent residents, and they treated the barbecue a bit like a street fair.

One year a group of Swedish kids staying at a hostel a few blocks away swarmed the street and ate as though they hadn't eaten since they arrived at Kennedy, and they were so good-humored, grateful, and, honestly, good-looking that no one had had the heart to tell them it was a private party. But afterward George had sent out one of his notices:

Only homeowners are permitted to attend the barbecue.

Nora had felt at the time too new to the block to respond, but both Sherry and Linda had given George hell about the mean-spiritedness of this, and the next day another notice had followed:

Please disregard previous notice.

The barbecue was how Nora had become block friends with Linda Lessman instead of just dog-walking acquaintances. Several years after the Nolans had moved in, the city passed a law that, while couched in the kind of legalese that made so many rules and regulations impenetrable, came down to this: large-scale outdoor barbecueing was now forbidden except by restaurants and licensed caterers. A small deputation complained to the two police officers who ate lunch in their patrol car at the end of the block most days, and a community service officer invited them to the precinct. "I wish I could let you go ahead with it—I know you do it right, clean up, keep the noise down," the officer said, leaning across his desk. "It's not for you people, it's for the people who take advantage—you know what I mean? You should see what they do under the highway at A Hundred and Fifty-fifth Street. The music, the cars, old beaters with a keg in the trunk, blankets all over the grass, baby strollers all over the place."

"Hot dogs everywhere," Linda said drily.

"You have to see it to believe it, Judge." Oh, Nora thought to herself, that's why we got asked in. Linda's shoulders stiffened, and Nora realized she didn't like someone using her title in this setting, particularly a police officer.

"I hear they will actually sometimes roast an entire pig," Linda said.

"You hear right," said the officer, who clearly didn't recognize sarcasm when he heard it. But Nora did. She'd initially found Linda a bit cold and she'd never known what to talk to her about because she seemed so serious. But suddenly she liked her, admired her, even. On the other side of Linda, Nora saw Sherry Fisk holding her hand in front of her face to hide her smile. The three of them had walked back to the block from the precinct. "It's not for us," Linda said from between clenched teeth. "It's for those people."

"We could hire a caterer," said Sherry. "Caterers can get a permit." For a year they had held out, hoping the law would be repealed, writing letters, organizing petitions. But one year without the barbecue was plenty, and Sherry hired a catering company called Charcoal Briquettes, which basically did nothing but barbecues, although in the winter they turned into Church Supper and did crockpot food for people who had grown up on it but hadn't actually had it in years. They all had to admit that the catered barbecue was not as laborious and that the food was better, although it felt somewhat less like the block barbecue than it had before.

"So if there's no barbecue, why did we get a note from George about contacting him?" Nora asked as Homer marked the spot where Lady had just peed.

"Oh, he's so irritating," Linda said. "I swear, I know Betsy is supposed to be saving lives, but if I were married to him I'd arrange to be away from home all the time, too. When I told him we were putting the barbecue on ice, he insisted that we had to send out some letter to everyone, and when I didn't jump to it, he came to me with this horrible thing he'd written that talked about the accident, and the events, and the recent unpleasantness, just the sort of thing the papers would have loved to get their hands on and probably print in its entirety if the case ever went to trial. I went slightly ballistic. I mean, this is so not a good time to pretend that it's business as usual around here."

It was not. Jack was rarely seen on the block, particularly after the day he had been out getting coffee and had run into Nora and Linda. It was the first time Nora had seen him since he'd been put in the back of the police car, and she was uncertain how to respond. Linda was not at all uncertain. "Good morning, Jack," she said with the frostiest voice imaginable, without any indication that she would stop and chat even when Jack had squared up in front of her on the sidewalk. Either he was growing a beard or he had forgotten how to shave.

"Judge, you of all people should know there are two sides to every story," he said loudly.

"I certainly do, Jack," Linda said. "But I've learned over the years that the two sides are often not of equal weight."

Nora did not speak until they were half a block away. "I feel so sorry for Sherry," she said. "I think she's still angry at me for going to see Ricky in the hospital."

"She shouldn't care," Linda said. "Nobody knows better than her what he's like. Did you ever hear the story of when they first got Brutus? Jack didn't want to neuter him. That says it all. One day Sherry looked up and Brutus had his leg lifted and was marking all down the hallway on this wallpaper that it had taken her months to find. She took the dog to the vet that afternoon, and Jack went crazy. I think that was one of the times she left him. The mystery is why she came back. Although I suppose it's not really a mystery. Two children and all that."

The Lessmans had no children. "It's a big house for just two people," someone had said years ago at the Christmas party, the constant refrain of those whose children were grown and gone, and Linda looked at Harold and he looked back at her and they both smiled and said, "It certainly is." Charlie liked to posit that the Lessmans were one of those couples of restrained dress and manner who had a dungeon in their basement. Maybe he was right. Or maybe they were just what they seemed to be.

"You don't think he hit her?" Nora asked Linda.

"Amazingly, no. His abuse was always verbal until the encounter with Ricky. He's the kind who abuses down the social ladder. Cabdrivers, waiters. He's relatively civil to surgeons, senior partners, and CEOs. Have you ever gone to dinner with them? It's a nightmare. One substandard piece of fish and it's

World War Three. I've put up with it for years, but not any-more. This was it for me. I told Harold, I'm done. Sherry, yes. Jack, never again."

"You are tough," Nora said.

"What? Oh, it's mainly professional posturing. Not for this, though. I mean it. Really, it's unforgivable, what he did."

Nora had to agree. So did all the people who worked on the block. Grace, the Fisks' housekeeper, had quit. She had told Sherry that it was because she was used to being able to work alone in the house, both Sherry and Jack at work, and that hav-ing Mr. Fisk around all day when he wasn't at the country house, criticizing the way she cleaned the steam shower and telling her Mop & Glo was dulling the floors, was making her crazy. And Brutus had growled at her twice. George had told Charlie that Brutus had been placed on medication to combat his anxiety about the atmosphere at home.

"You think they'll be able to find another housekeeper?" Nora had asked Charity.

"For sure and certain," Charity said. "People always needing jobs."

Grace had begun to get angry months ago, when Sherry asked her not to take a get-well card from house to house for the other housekeepers to sign for Ricky. "We got free speech like everybody," Grace told Charity.

"Please don't talk to reporters," Nora had said at the time, and Charity made her explosive dismissive sound, although Nora was not sure whether it was aimed at reporters or her request. They had had a terrible time when the Rizzoli grand-children had been interviewed on their way down the block from the school bus. Their sitter had stopped to talk to Grace, and so the magazine writer James had mentioned to Nora had had a few minutes to pretend to be merely a friendly passerby with a cellphone set to record in his hand.

"When I had strep throat, Ricky gave me honey candies and they made my throat feel better," the little girl apparently said.

"My mom says Mr. Fisk needs to learn to get his temper under control," said the boy. "She says let this be a lesson to me to use my words and not my hands."

So Sherry had also stopped speaking to the Rizzolis. She had suggested to the wife that her children were inadequately supervised, and the Rizzoli wife had said that it was clear the person in need of supervision was Jack Fisk. And so on and so forth. It was the first time anyone could remember the block erupting in this kind of discord. It had always protected its own, the facing houses seeming to agree, cornice to cornice, window to window, that intimacy and privacy could exist together. For years, the elder Mrs. Rizzoli had attended both the Fenstermacher holiday party and the barbecue as drunk as a woman could be and still remain upright, and no one had said a word. Nor had they taken notice, except covertly, when she disappeared for several months and came back for a year of sparkling water with lime, followed by the addition of the occasional glass of wine, followed by the holiday party, at which she'd fallen into the tree, and then another stint away. Because of her senior status on the bench, Linda was able to take off the entire month of August and move to their beach house, Harold driving out late on Thursdays, and no one mentioned that Harold spent many weekday nights away from their house on the block, which could be because he had a sofa bed in his office (unlikely) or stayed with his sister at her townhouse in the Village (perhaps). Or it could be that while August was a time for

Linda to play tennis with her friends and have her nieces come and stay, it was a time for Harold to spend the night with his girlfriend, who, in the way of girlfriends everywhere, would hope that August would turn into December, girlfriend into second wife.

Or maybe it wasn't girlfriends at all. Maybe it was boyfriends. All of it was none of their business. Nora thought that her friends who lived elsewhere felt free to gossip about their neighbors because they didn't know them, and about their friends because they knew them too well. But the people who lived on the block existed in some weird nether region between the two, and that made all of them protective of one another. They had been able to turn aside from one another's secrets and setbacks until Jack Fisk had taken that three iron from his car trunk.

"I hate to say this," Linda Lessman had told her, "but I think we need to hire somebody else to do things around the house."

James's friend the magazine writer had written a loathsome piece about the block, suggesting that it was a bastion of white privilege served by people who were frequently mistreated by those for whom they worked. He had asked Charity if the Nolans paid her on the books. "Go away, fool," Charity said, snapping a finger in his face, "or I'm gonna hit you." He had seemed to take special pleasure in comparing the holdings of the Museum of Jewelry with Charity's public-television tote bag and imitation leather jacket. Nora took pleasure in the way Charity had schooled him, and in the fact that what was supposed to be a cover story had merely been two pages near the back of the issue.

"Boy, this guy was really out to get you," Charlie said, looking up from the magazine.

"I'm sorry, Moneypenny," James said when the story appeared. "I should have known he was a class-A little pissant."

"He's turned into a little pissant already? What was it, a couple of months? Am I the longest romantic relationship you've ever had?"

There was silence, and then James said sadly, "I suppose that's true, but it's not a fair point. In the beginning they all died."

"And now?"

"They're all so young," he said.

"You could fix that."

"I suppose that's true, too."

When she first woke Nora had one of those moments in which she wasn't sure where she was. A sharp sliver of silver daylight had broken through closed drapes and maneuvered itself across her face, or maybe she'd maneuvered her face out of the shadows and into the glare as she slept. She rolled over and heard Charlie singing in the bathroom. He was giving it his all. Then she realized she was in a hotel room, and hoped that the walls were solidly built, not just because Charlie was singing so loudly but because they'd had sex the night before, and her headache and the soreness in her thighs made her suspect that both of them had been loud then, too.

Charlie had always had a thing about hotels, maybe because he'd lost his virginity in a Holiday Inn on prom night his junior year. Nora remembered taking the twins to college that first time and a hotel room in Boston, where she and Charlie had had frantic sex while both of them wept drunkenly. They'd even broken a lamp. She looked at the bedside tables. Both lamps were intact. That she would have remembered, although she was powerfully hungover. Nora had a thing about hotels, too, but it was entirely different from her husband's. Sometimes she had a momentary fantasy of never checking out, of living forever in a state of constant impermanence, no address, no lightbulbs or shampoo to buy, no shopping, chopping, or cooking for breakfast. French-press coffee and a vegetable omelet on a tray with butter in little curls. Then she packed up and went home.

Asheville, North Carolina, was famous for a large resort built around what had at one time been the largest private house in America, before everybody and his brother was trying to build the largest private house in America. When they first arrived, Charlie went out onto the terrace and spread his arms wide. "God's. Own. Country," he said, inhaling audibly. "For what it is, it's nice," Bebe had said dismissively when Nora said she was spending a weekend there. It *was* nice, with a view of the mountains and an enormous bed with high-thread-count linens. The fact that she could tell this about the sheets made Nora feel ridiculous.

"Good last night, right?" said Charlie, coming out of the bathroom in a towel, and Nora was not sure if he meant the food, the wine, or the sex. Probably all three. The minibar had Advil, thank God.

The day before, after Charlie had left to play golf with the president of a local bank who had been a fraternity brother, she did a long trail run, had a massage and a facial, and sat out on that terrace, drinking an eleven-dollar smoothie and reading a fashion magazine full of clothes no one she knew would ever wear. She called Jenny to tell her that her newest book, *Witches and Wise Women,* was mentioned in one of the fashion magazines.

"Why are you reading that?" Jenny said, and Nora explained where they were.

"I'm exhausted by Charlie's midlife crisis," she said, sipping her smoothie, but Jenny was oddly unsympathetic.

"I'd like to see the midlife crisis get more respect," she said. "Everyone talks reverentially about terminal illness or bipolar syndrome. Why do we all blow off the midlife crisis as nothing but red convertibles and hair plugs? It's a perfectly reasonable response to increased life expectancy and the demands of modern life."

"Is this your next book?" Nora said. "Because you sound like it's your next book. It would just work better for me if it wasn't a bad mood twenty-four/seven and the determination that I should trade New York for a picture window on a golf course."

"Well, that's not going to happen," Jenny said. The two of them had decided years ago that even a move to Brooklyn on one of their parts would be a geographic betrayal. At one point Emory University had tried to lure Jenny to Atlanta with more money and a teaching schedule that basically consisted of not teaching at all. The provost had taken Jenny to what she said was a wonderful restaurant, but when she was invited back for a tour of the campus and another dinner, this time with the president, Jenny decided it would be dishonest to go any further.

"You're not even considering it?" Nora had said.

"You're stuck with me, babe," Jenny replied.

After Nora hung up the phone, a woman in a white uniform came to the door of the hotel room with a wheeled cart of supplies and gave Nora a pedicure on the terrace while she started in on a mystery novel. She felt totally content, although she would not tell Charlie that, since he would think it was yet another sign that they should move here, or someplace like it. After her pedicure she sat there alone. When she had first met

Charlie, part of the appeal had been that she found New York such a hard place to be by herself. In the ensuing years Nora had discovered that by herself was a condition she really liked.

In the afternoon they went out to lunch at the kind of first-rate pretentious little bistro that garnished the food with flowers. "What are these again?" Charlie asked.

"Nasturtiums," Nora said. "I'm so glad they stopped doing this in New York."

"You're from New York?" the massage therapist at the spa had asked. "I love New York."

"Are you from Asheville originally?" Nora asked.

"Buffalo," the woman said, shivering slightly. "I don't miss the snow."

"But now you get it here, too, don't you?"

"It's true. This winter we had two inches one day, and they had no clue how to handle it. But the same day my mother said they had a foot in Buffalo. So, no contest, right?"

They had dinner in the main dining room, and Charlie ordered a bottle of wine so good that Nora knew the dinner bill would be larger than the bill for the room. They chatted determinedly, but they avoided the obvious oil slicks: Bob Harris, Jack Fisk, the estimated value of their house, the lack of parking on the block, the persistent drip of their kitchen sink. Nora knew that they were there that weekend to convince her that a life elsewhere would be wonderful, but Charlie didn't even mention how pleasant the weather had been that day. She told him about Oliver and Lizzie. He told her about the fraternity brother and his wife. When they were first married they had vowed they would never be one of those married couples who sat silently at dinner because they'd run out of things to say.

They were determined that they would never run out of things to say. So they repeated themselves a lot.

A hotel car drove them a half hour outside town for a house tour. Several of the houses on the tour appeared to have been designed to give the resort a run for its money in the square-footage sweepstakes. One kitchen had three sinks, two refrigerators, a cooktop in the center island, an eight-burner stove, a wall oven, and two microwaves. "The caterers must love this place," Nora said.

"Don't be cynical," Charlie said.

"I'm a New Yorker," said Nora. "Cynicism is my religion."

"I just love New York," said the tour guide, who had an accent so thick the consonants appeared to be chewy nuggets in the butterscotch pudding of her voice. "Is that where you all are from?"

"Nobody's really from there . . . Carolyn," Charlie said. Charlie always tried to personalize things, with the rental-car clerk, the bagger at the grocery story. If a person wore a name tag, Charlie would use the first name, although it had become less offhanded and neighborly now that his vision was shot and he had to take that telltale minute to narrow his eyes and parse the letters. "Everybody in New York is really from somewhere else." And there was the problem in a nutshell. Nora had been a New Yorker from the very first usurious security/first-month/last-month check on that ratty apartment. When she thought of the gifts she had given her children, one of them was that for the rest of their lives, when a form said "Place of birth," they could write "New York City."

There were three types of people in New York: people like Nora, who had found their home there; people who talked about how much they hated it and would always live and eventually die there; and people who always had one foot over the border, to Scarsdale or Roslyn or Boca Raton. Once upon a time those last had been driven out by muggings and cockroaches. Now they left because of five-figure monthly rents, three-figure restaurant lunches, and the covert realization that if you weren't a big winner, you were a loser. Nora suspected her husband had unconsciously consigned himself to the last camp.

All the qualities that made people love Charlie—"Charlie Nolan, the best," so many of them said—were the same ones that would ensure that he was never a major player. So he blamed the block, the firm, the city. If only they were somewhere else, he would be someone else.

And he was right. It was hard to be important in New York. Sometimes Nora felt guilty because she knew he would have been aces elsewhere, the president of a small bank in a city in North Carolina chairing the United Way campaign, the mayor of a town of fifty thousand people who would always respond to citizen calls. Once she'd suggested that he might want to try something else, perhaps become a teacher or a coach. "Yeah, that'll pay the maintenance on this place," he said, but Nora had been able to tell that he was insulted. You could argue they'd lost their way, in their choices, their work, their marriage. But the truth was, there wasn't any way. There was just day after day, small stuff, idle conversation, scheduling. And then after a couple of decades it somehow added up to something, for good or for ill or for both.

On the plane Charlie put his hand over Nora's and said, "Come on, Bun. They have art galleries and chamber music and a marathon you could run. I could golf year-round. Aren't you tired of all the craziness?"

"All what craziness?" Nora said. "The only craziness is restaurant reservations."

"Things on the block are crazy. You can cut the atmosphere with a knife some mornings." Nora had to admit that this was true. People who had once easily met and chatted on the street now passed with stiff, perfunctory greetings, or even crossed to the other side.

"There's a financial outfit in Charlotte that has an office there," Charlie added. "They'd hire me in a minute."

Nora settled back in her seat and closed her eyes.

"Just think about it," Charlie said as the plane lifted off, and then again as they came down the escalator to where the scrum of limo drivers gathered, like undertakers in their black suits. NOLLAND, said one sign in capital letters.

"They can't even spell, these people," Charlie muttered.

"No whining on the yacht." That's what Christine always said when Nora complained about lousy food in first class, or a manicurist who had nicked her cuticle, or a luxury hotel. "Spotty wireless and a wait for room service? Poor baby," Christine would say. Success had not spoiled her.

Both of them leaned back against the headrests in the SUV. "Do you have a preferred route, sir?" said the driver.

"Take the tunnel," Charlie said, as Nora said, "Take the bridge."

Nora laughed. Charlie didn't. "It'll be a nightmare either way," he said.

Homer didn't greet them as they wheeled their suitcases into the foyer. He emerged slowly, almost painfully, from his kennel, blinking in the light. "How would you like to have a big yard?" Charlie said, scratching behind his ear. "How would you like to spend the rest of your life off the leash?"

"Oh, come on," Nora said. "Really? Using the dog?"

"Fine," Charlie said, trudging up the stairs. "You take him for a walk."

She supposed if she wanted to move to a gated community with a tennis club and a pool in the backyard this was one of the cards Nora would have played, too. The last dog walk of the night was always more or less unpleasant, trying to pick up after Homer wearing gloves in winter, watching him sniff at and then try to snag some piece of garbage when the weather warmed. He was almost thirteen now and had slowed down so much, especially at the end of the day, that a walk to the corner and back took even longer than it had when he was a puppy and she had felt foolish telling him what a good good good dog he was, making pee-pee off the curb, pooping outside instead of in the house.

"You *are* a good dog," she said aloud, remembering those days, but Homer didn't turn his head, although his pointed ears swiveled back slightly. Just before the Lessman house, he pulled suddenly forward, hard, and Nora yanked him back. "What are you doing?" Nora asked, and then watched as a large rat trundled from curb to sidewalk and into the shadowed steps down to the well of the Lessman basement. Homer finally turned then because Nora had shrieked without meaning to, a kind of adrenaline charge through her whole body and out her mouth. She had unconsciously put her hand on her heart.

"Oh, my dear God," she said out loud, and a man at the end of the block turned to look at her.

Back at their house she peered into the stairwell toward their basement door, wondering if the door's join at the sill was tight enough. She thought of the dryer vent to the backyard with horror. Hadn't Ricky put chicken wire over it so that nothing could get in? What if he hadn't? Who would do it now? In the foyer she wondered whether to tell Linda Lessman what she had seen, or Charity.

"I will never go into the basement again," she said to Homer, who trudged back into his kennel and fell onto his pad with a heavy sigh.

Several buildings have been cited for vermin infestation. These citations are being challenged before the Department of Health. It is imperative that all garbage containers have tight-fitting lids. Only if all buildings conform to these specifications will the citations be quashed. An inspector will be on the block Tuesday morning at 9 A.M. to advise all interested homeowners about how to mitigate the situation.

The health inspector was a man named Dino Forletti. He wore a windbreaker with DEPARTMENT OF HEALTH stenciled on the back, steel-toed boots, and a Mets cap, and carried a laser pointer. Their customary little knot of concerned homeowners had broken down into a string of beads around him. George stood apart from the others with an elderly pug under one arm, perhaps because he thought he was somehow in charge, and Sherry arrived only at the last minute and didn't join Nora and Linda, who had one of the Rizzoli sons and his wife with them. Nora had been afraid Jack Fisk would show up just to show he could, but he was nowhere in sight. One of the landlords was there, too, and he'd tried to get friendly but no one would bite. It was generally agreed that it was the rental buildings with several tenants and not enough trash cans that were causing the problem.

The inspector made a humming sound in the back of his throat; the group trailed him down the block as if they were fourth graders on a field trip and he their teacher. He said nothing, but sometimes the humming got a little louder or faster and Nora looked around to see if there was a reason for that. She hadn't wanted to do this in the beginning because she was afraid that somehow the inspector would pull a rat from a hole the way a magician pulled a rabbit from a hat, but Charlie insisted he was too busy at work and he didn't see the point, that that's why there were exterminators, and if you lived in New York what could you expect.

The inspector didn't speak until he had entered the parking lot and walked from the front to the back, stopping to stoop down here and there. They waited for him at the entrance. Nora couldn't help it; in her mind's eye, just for a moment, she saw Ricky broken on the ground, clear as anything.

"People park their cars here?" the inspector said, and there was a collective sigh.

"Not anymore," said Linda Lessman.

"It will be open for parking again soon," said George. "Very soon."

"Yeah, they like to go under parked cars," the inspector said. "You've probably seen them come out from under one at the curb at night."

Nora wasn't sure she was going to make it through the session. Her stomach was somewhere between morning sickness and roller coaster at the very idea.

"Anyhow, I've seen worse," Dino Forletti said. He turned on the laser pointer and indicated the back of the SRO, with the pints of milk and bags of bananas perched on the windowsills. One of the residents was peering down at them. "The food storage situation there is obviously an issue, especially since it looks as though some things fall into this area."

"I knew it," said George. "That building is an eyesore."

"But it's not the biggest issue," the inspector continued. "The building they're doing the gut renovation on at the end of the facing block is a big part of the uptick. Once they start digging up underground waste lines, excavating the foundation—" He shrugged. "The rodents get displaced." The laser pointer traced a thin red line along the perimeter of the parking lot to the dull brick of the building on the far side. It ran along what Nora had always thought was a line of dirt. "You got trails here," said Dino Forletti. "They like to rub along the sides of the walls. I saw one of those light-colored limestone buildings on the East Side once, it was like someone had used a piece of charcoal to draw a stripe."

"On the East Side?" said the Rizzoli daughter-in-law.

"They are no respecters of class, believe me," the inspector said solemnly. "I remember we got a call from the mayor's office because one got into a lobby on—"

Involuntarily Nora made a little flapping motion with her hands, and shivered all up and down her body. "Are you all right?" whispered Linda.

"Aw, you got a thing," the inspector said to Nora. "It's okay—lots of people have a thing. My girlfriend has a thing. She tells everybody I'm a homicide detective because she thinks it's easier for people to deal with. I always tell her, If you got to understand them a little better, they're actually really interesting, they've got a family structure, social habits, they're really not—" Nora flapped again, her eyes wide. It was an automatic reaction, like a sneeze or hiccups, even though Nora was not a particularly squeamish or timid person. She and Charlie had spent a week at a vineyard in Tuscany for their twentieth anniversary, and Nora had gone running through the forest and encountered a wild boar. She had no idea what you were supposed to do when faced with a wild boar: Keep running? Stand still? Climb a tree? Yell loudly? For an instant she thought she remembered she should rap it on the nose if it came close, then realized that that was what she had always heard you should do if a shark approached, which was absurd. Who would have the wherewithal to hit a shark? Or a boar, for that matter.

The boar made a noise like an old man clearing his throat and then disappeared into the undergrowth with a tremendous amount of thrashing that made her realize, a bit late, how large it really was. The people who owned the vineyard were horrified, although they had been serving boar in various guises at nearly every dinner. Pappardelle with cinghiale. Cinghiale ragù. They wanted Nora to stop running every morning. "Good luck with that," Charlie had said to one of the owners.

"As long as it's not rats," Nora said.

"Rats?" said one of the owners with an accent that turned the word into something else, not as recognizable or somehow as terrible.

"Or snakes," Charlie said.

She shivered again, standing at the entrance to the parking lot, although the sun was warm on her shoulders. Dino Forletti shook his head.

"I've done a lot of research," George said. "One for every person living in New York City, correct?"

"She's got a thing," Dino repeated, putting a dot on Nora's chest when he turned the laser pointer toward her. "Maybe not the best conversation for a person with a thing. Besides, no one's done a census—you know what I mean? We're just making assumptions."

He put the pointer in his back pocket. "The bottom line is, there's a lot you can do here. I'll make sure we keep the bait boxes current. All of you be vigilant about the garbage cans. Bags, lids. Don't offer them access to food, you know? Get whoever works on your house to go into the basement and make sure there's no way to get in. I'm a big fan of the feral cat, but you can't convince New Yorkers on that. Next thing you know, someone's rounding them all up, taking them to the shelter, spaying, finding homes. I say let feral cats be feral. They'd take down all except the biggest ones."

"What about dogs?" George asked.

"Oh, they won't mess with a dog."

"No, I mean what if a dog goes after them? Should we let them?"

Dino Forletti looked at the pug. "I wouldn't," he said. He'd turned back to Nora. "I'm sorry, I didn't know anyone had a thing," he added.

It had gotten to the point that Nora could scarcely bear to walk Homer at night, although she couldn't say anything to Charlie because she didn't want to add to his big-house-in-the-warm-south arguments. Even after Dino Forletti had had a pair of his men bait all the backyards, speak to the contractors on the building under construction about not leaving trash around and being sure to cap waste pipes, cite the landlords with too few or flimsy trash cans, she still responded to every stray ad flyer blowing along the curb, every shadowy break in the pavement, as though it were a bullet of a body, a thread of a tail. When she was running in Riverside Park one Saturday and saw an enormous hawk overhead, dappled and proud, one of the men picking up trash in the playground had ruined the sight by saying with a grin, "That guy eats his weight in rats every damn day."

"It's become like the plagues of Egypt," Nora said on the phone to her sister, forgetting that Charity was in the kitchen wiping down the cabinets. "The dog-poop bags are back on the stoop, there are rats running rampant on the sidewalks, and two of the men in the SRO died in the last month. Not to mention what happened with Jack Fisk and Ricky."

"New York is like the plagues, Nonnie, which is why lots of us won't live there. But it's your place. It's always been your place."

"There are times when I can't imagine why," Nora said. "My husband certainly can't imagine why. His attempts to make me leave have reached critical mass."

"Even if he wanted to move to Seattle I'd have to veto it. You belong there. It's like chemistry. You either have it or you don't. There's no explanation."

"Rachel asked me about that last year. 'Mommy, can you develop chemistry with a guy if it's not there in the beginning?'"

Christine laughed. "Oh, that. The really nice guy who is like kissing the inside of your own arm. I hope you told her no, absolutely not, if it's not there, it's not there."

"What else could I say?"

"So, okay, on this other thing. The guys in the SRO are old and are bound to die sometime, and the bags on the steps are just a nuisance even though you're making them sound so sinister."

"They feel sinister. They feel hostile, as though someone is out to get me."

"Okay, whatever. But the other thing—"

"Which one?"

"I won't even say it or you'll freak," said Christine. "I mean, it's not like I don't get this. We had a huge spider in one corner of the garage last summer, and I didn't put the car inside for two months. The boys acted like I was a monster because I wanted them to go in there with a broom and knock its web down. 'Maybe it had babies,' Jake said. Reading *Charlotte's Web* has been terrible."

"Did you kill it?"

"I ran in there one day really fast and emptied an entire can of Raid onto it. They're still mad at me. I thought I could get away with it but, boy, the smell of that stuff really lingers."

"Plagues of Egypt numbered ten," said Charity dismissively once Nora was off the phone, passing through on her way to the basement. "From God. Rats we take care of with poison. God takes care of Mr. Fisk."

"So now we're on top of the situation," George said triumphantly the morning after the Health Department visit, when he ran into Nora. He seemed to be baiting her, trying to tell her how many litters a year, how many babies in the litter. She was accustomed to George's nonsense, but she had found Dino Forletti disconcerting. He seemed more agnostic about rats than Nora would have expected, or appreciated. She couldn't imagine anyone talking about how termites built their homes, or what stamina cockroaches had. "Live and let live" had been his valedictory words.

When Nora got to her office, she went down to the basement, the bowels of the building, to the windowless office where Declan, the facilities manager, sat in front of a wall of grainy security monitors. Declan was a small, very precise ginger-haired man with leprechaun tendencies so obvious that Bebe had signed off on his hiring with the words "I hope the road-show production of *Finian's Rainbow* where you found him won't want him back."

"Declan, do we have rats?" Nora asked. Even the word made her shiver.

"To my knowledge we have never seen a rat inside this building," Declan said, his brogue making the horrid word sound like a small throat clearing.

"Thank God," Nora said, turning to go.

"Is this about the charge for the exterminator in my monthly budget?"

"What? No."

"Because he does come on a regular basis. This is New York City. We are near the river. I have to be prepared for every contingency. It would be a disaster if one of those ladies saw a wee beastie."

"Stop," Nora said.

Nora had been delighted to discover that Richard, too, had a rat thing. "Mrs. Nolan, no offense, but can we not talk about this?" he'd said. "Absolutely," Nora said. Charity did not want to discuss it, either, except to say that on her island there were no rats or snakes because the mongoose killed them all, and that there would be no rats on the block if only Mr. Fisk had not attempted to, in Charity's words, "bash Ricky's whole head in."

"I just had a drink with Jack," Charlie said one night. "He says Charity hates him. He says Charity is why Grace quit."

"You went over to see Jack?" Nora said. "Did he tell you that he refused to write Grace a recommendation after twenty-one years?" Which had been immaterial, because Sherry had written a fulsome recommendation, according to Charity, and Grace was already working for a couple who lived on Central Park South and, according to Charity, were paying her more for less work.

"Don't start with me about Jack. And tell Charity to leave the Fisks alone." Nora would do no such thing, although she felt a slight spasm of sympathy for Sherry. Having Charity angry at you was like being caught in a thunderstorm.

Charlie didn't know about the men in the SRO or the dog leavings, which had stopped all winter long and now had appeared again. But George had told him all about the rats, and Nora suspected that Charlie was glad of the news. He was certain there were no rats in gated communities in North Carolina. "I bet there are lots of snakes," Nora had muttered to herself.

"You're not really moving, are you?" Rachel, home for a few days, had said that morning.

"What do you think?" Nora said as she packed up her tote bag and waited for Rachel to find her jacket, which was somehow under the coffee table in the den, and was somehow actually Nora's jacket.

"I think Daddy is a little crazy for some reason. I think pretending he believed Mr. Fisk's ridiculous story made him crazy. I also think if you move to the places he's talking about moving you'll scarcely ever see me because why would I go there?"

"I hope you told him that," Nora said as they left the house.

"Are we getting a cab?" Rachel said.

"I always walk," Nora said.

"Okay," Rachel said.

"It's a long walk," Nora said, and Rachel just shrugged, which was how Nora knew that something was up. Even if Rachel was amenable to a walk, tradition would dictate that she should argue about it: a cab was more comfortable, what about the subway, no one else walked to work, whatever.

"Doesn't she know that she's only feeding rats?" Rachel said when they came upon the woman with the baguettes, surrounded by a gaggle of geese and a cloud of rapacious gulls.

Nora shivered. She could still see the rat in the Lessmans' stairwell, the shadow of its long, hairless tail. Rachel was almost as crazed about rats as her mother. "I don't get you guys," Oliver had once said; he had spent a good deal of time with lab rats. "I bet if you got to actually hold and watch rats you would get over this."

"Are you insane?" Rachel said.

"What she said," Nora added.

"Okay, Mommy, no, don't try to be cool," Rachel said. "It's so so sad when you do that."

The pieces of French bread hit the ruffled gray water and then were hidden beneath the flapping wings and snaking necks. A spring breeze was blowing Nora's hair around her face, and Rachel's hands were pushed deep into the pockets of the leather jacket she'd worn despite the fact that Nora had told her she would need a heavier coat. True spring came a little later right along the river. Two windsurfers in wet suits went by, waving at them. "Insane," Rachel said.

"Is that my jacket?" Nora said.

During high school Rachel had made criticizing her mother a hobby, especially in terms of appearance and apparel. Nora understood that what she wore fell into two categories as far as her daughter was concerned: things too lame to be allowed to pass without censure, and things that, in Rachel parlance, she could jack. Sometimes when Nora bought a blouse she could almost feel it slipping from her shopping bag directly into Rachel's duffel. But it usually happened before the tags were even off the garment, before Nora had had a chance to actually wear it and, she had assumed, pollute it with her lameness.

"Technically, yes."

"I've had that jacket forever," Nora said. "Jenny picked that jacket out for me years ago."

"See, and you never wear it anymore." Which was not really true, but Nora suspected she might never wear it again. It looked good on Rachel, which would not have escaped Rachel's notice. She wondered if Rachel had passed into her retro phase, in which she would take Nora's things if they had somehow been sanctified by the passage of time and the boomerang nature of fashion trends. She and Jenny had marveled over a magazine piece that said the leather bomber jacket was "back." "As if it ever went away," Jenny had said disdainfully.

"So you're really almost done with all your work?" Nora asked her daughter.

"It's amazing how little there is second semester senior year," Rachel said.

Nora remembered. It had given her endless hours to think about James and whether he would change his mind, which seemed pathetic to her now. Nora tucked her hair behind her ears.

"I'm glad you're not blond," Rachel said.

"What?"

"All my friends' mothers get blonder the older they get. Or at least all my friends in the city. It's like a gateway to gray, I guess. I saw Elizabeth's mom last night, and she is totally blond. It looks weird."

"Isn't she Brazilian?"

"She says she's from Venezuela. Is there a big difference?"

"In Brazil they speak Portuguese. In Venezuela I think they speak Spanish. I can't imagine her blond, but she did have that unfortunate surgery when you were juniors."

"Her face has kind of relaxed now," Rachel said. "That's another thing I'm glad you haven't done."

Bebe had once suggested that Nora's forehead could use a little bit of a lift, and that the lines around her mouth might be made to vanish, but she'd ignored her. She figured it was like her professional ambition; she simply didn't have that internal yearning for a smooth jawline or dewy skin that seemed to drive so many of the women she met. Part of it was Charlie. There were many uncertainties in her life, but Charlie's carnal response to her continued unabated. When he was uninterested in sex, it was more about how he felt about himself than how he felt about Nora. If he was having a bad week he would watch her strip for a shower and say somewhat sadly, "Your butt still looks like a million bucks."

"So, Mommy," Rachel said after a moment of silence. "This might be a good time to discuss my plans for after graduation." Oliver was already set with a job working as an assistant in the same lab where he had worked as a student. Nora had assumed Rachel would return to the city of her birth to pursue the kind of job that liberal arts graduates pursued, the kind that required their parents to pay their exorbitant rent for at least a year or two, even though they were living in tiny apartments designed for one person with two roommates and a temporary wall down the center of the bedroom.

"I've been offered a job by a great company in Seattle with excellent opportunities for advancement, and I've decided to take it," Rachel said, so fast that the words blurred together, which, again, meant that there was more to this than her daughter was saying. Nora was silent for a minute or two. Then she stopped and looked at Rachel, and the fact that she had to look up at her, that her daughter was three inches taller than she was, combined with the strengthening wind, brought tears to her eyes.

"Oh, my God, don't cry," Rachel said. "It's not that far. There are nonstop flights every day."

Nora laughed. "It's the wind," she said. "And the fact that you've left out the most important part of this announcement, which is that you're going to work for Christine, correct? And I just got off the phone with her and she didn't say a word."

"I wanted to tell you myself. Daddy's going to kill me, isn't he? Those nice people who used to live down the block from us, he used to say they were in the rag trade as though they were street peddlers or something, even though they were majorly rich."

"He'll be fine with it. It's a great opportunity. I know you know this, but I thought the business was ridiculous when my sister first told me about it, which shows how bad I am at putting my finger on the future. Little did I know that someday people would be wearing yoga pants to work. Which, by the way, I still think is a terrible idea."

"It's just, I don't know, all my friends from high school, most of my friends from college, they're all coming to the city. Which, by the way, is kind of obnoxious, isn't it, that we call it the city? There was a girl in my seminar from Paris, she said to me one day, 'You know, Rachel, there are other cities in the world.'"

"I suppose."

Rachel laughed. "I think that's exactly what I said. But anyhow, I realized everyone would wind up here, and we'd all go to the same bars, and the same parties, and it would be like a continuation of my childhood. And I don't want that. You didn't have that. When you came here it was a brand-new life for you."

"I'm not arguing, Bug. This is a really smart and mature decision. I'm gobsmacked and awestruck."

"SAT words," said Rachel.

"Right," said Nora.

"Are you mad at Christine?"

"Why? Because she treated you like a grown-up? Wow, you really underestimate me. When do you start?"

"Two weeks after commencement. I'm staying with her until I get an apartment. I'm hoping for an August first move-in."

Oliver's and Rachel's commencements were a week apart. "Oh, Jesus, talk about crazy," Charlie had said. "Two days of events with one, two days of events with the other. Like a triathlon for the parents."

"Three days of events," Nora had said. "But I talked to a woman once who had twins at different colleges whose commencements were on the same day. I'm just relieved we don't have to deal with that."

Nora and Rachel turned onto the museum block shoulder to shoulder, in the companionable silence of two people, one of whom had had something momentous to say, one of whom knew she was going to hear it, and both of whom had gotten it over with. Phil had thrown off his blanket and turned his face, with its stubbled chin, to the thin April sunshine.

"Beautiful day," he said to Nora.

"Phil, this is my daughter, Rachel. Rachel, this is Phil."

"Hi, Phil," said Rachel, shaking his hand, which made Nora proud.

"That's so you," Rachel said, when they'd moved down the block. "To know a homeless guy."

"He's not really homeless."

"That's even more you, to know a faux-homeless guy."

"Stop picking on me," Nora said.

"I'm not picking on you. I've decided not to pick on you anymore." Rachel put her arms around Nora. "My little Mommy," she said, standing on tiptoes so she could put her chin on the crown of Nora's head.

"Want to come up and meet my new assistant?"

"Richard?" Rachel said. "Love him. Love. We're phone friends. That girl you had before was just the worst. Tell Richard I'll meet him in person the next time. I'm late for brunch. I might go shopping after."

"Nice girl!" Phil shouted down the block when Rachel had disappeared.

"Yep," Nora said, and went inside, where one of their curators, a young woman they'd just poached from Tiffany's, was waiting. "We have a major problem," she said before Nora was even halfway across the lobby.

"We've got a major problem," Nora said when she finally got through to Bebe, who refused to carry a cellphone. "I didn't come this far to answer my own phone," she'd said when Nora asked why.

"Which is?" Bebe said. Nora could hear the clank of dishes and realized her assistant had probably tracked Bebe down at The Breakers in Palm Beach. She had told Nora the hotel had the best niçoise in the world, although Nora suspected there was probably someplace in the country of France that would argue with that.

"The star of Kashmir," Nora said. "Annabelle says she thought that it was sitting a little oddly on its stand when she looked this morning. She took it to the gemologist, who looked at it carefully, and says it's a copy. A very good copy, but a copy."

There was a long silence. Nora thought Bebe was thinking, then realized she was chewing.

"So?" Bebe said.

"So? Bebe, that necklace is one of the most valuable pieces in our collection. The insurance estimate was eight million dollars, and that was four years ago. Even then they thought it was low."

"It was low. Norman said it was worth at least ten, and that was when the market was depressed."

"So what I'm telling you is that it's gone, and there's a copy in its place, which is a major crime as well as a major disaster for the museum. We should call the police and the head of the security firm immediately. We also need to figure out how to handle this so the PR fallout won't be terrible. My understanding was that we had a fail-safe system here."

The greatest hazard of running a museum of jewelry, she had learned early on, was security. Unlike a significant Vermeer, say, or the skeleton of a T. rex, an important necklace was both portable and fungible. A thief might not be able to dispose of it as configured, but it could be turned into a handful of stones and still be valuable.

Nora had been happy that they had gotten publicity nearly everywhere for their innovative display cases, which were designed to deliver voltage sufficient to disable a two-hundred-pound man if they were broken or opened without a complicated computer authorization. One of the local TV reporters had even volunteered to be zapped by one of the cases, but the museum's insurance firm thought that was unwise. "You accidentally kill somebody on camera, it would be bad," the security chief said. "But trust me, we tested it on one of our guys, and it worked."

"It definitely worked," said a broad-shouldered man who Nora thought looked as though he'd played college football, and the way he said it made her think he was the person they'd tested it on.

Bebe had negotiated hard, demanding a clause that if anyone was electrocuted, the manufacturer would be responsible for damages. She was a shrewd negotiator, in part because she acted a little dim at the beginning of any discussion. The men on the other side of the table were always lulled into a false sense of supremacy until she pulled her real personality out of her pocket and laid it on the table. "I don't want some thief whose brain is fried suing me for a million bucks," she said of the liability clause, which the manufacturer had eventually agreed upon.

"They swore those cases were fail-safe," Nora said, tapping a pen on her desk and staring at a list of who had the computer codes.

"Hold on," Bebe said, and Nora heard her put the receiver down. "I want the berries, but no whipped cream. And no blackberries. Just the strawberries, raspberries, and blueberries. But no whipped cream. Last time I had to send it back." Nora heard her lift the phone again. The maître d' must have brought her the restaurant phone, the way they did in old Hollywood movies. "You there?" Bebe said. "Don't get your panties in a twist. That necklace is sitting in my home safe."

"What?"

"It has sentimental value. It's the last piece Norman ever gave me. I was going to that black-tie thing at The Pierre, and just for one night I wanted to wear the real thing. Not that any of those people would know. There was a woman there with a diamond as big as a Ping-Pong ball on her one hand, and I can tell you that it was no more a diamond than I'm Marilyn Monroe."

"That was months ago. All that time we've had a paste copy in that display case?"

"I told you years ago, no one uses paste anymore. And my copies are the best copies. I'm surprised anyone even noticed. When I'm home from Palm Beach I'll put the real one back."

"Bebe, we've been telling visitors that what they're seeing is the star of Kashmir."

"And they never even noticed the difference, right? So who cares? If nobody can tell the difference between real and fake, who cares if fake is what you're showing?"

PR NEWSWIRE: Attention Local Outlets

MUSEUM BEGINS SEARCH FOR PRESIDENT

The Museum of Jewelry will be searching for a new president with the resignation of its current leader.

Nora Nolan, who has overseen the museum since its opening five years ago, will leave at the end of the year, according to Bebe Pearl, the chair of the board.

"Nora has been the heart and soul of my fabulous brainchild," Mrs. Pearl said from her home in Palm Beach. "She's also become one of my closest friends. She will never stop being part of the Museum of Jewelry."

Mrs. Pearl endowed the museum and donated nearly all of her extensive collection of fine jewelry to it after the death of her husband, Norman, a real estate developer whose personal wealth was estimated by *Forbes* at slightly over $3 billion. There was skepticism in the museum community about what was often seen as a vanity project, but the museum has been unexpectedly successful under Ms. Nolan's leadership. No reason was given for her resignation.

Friends,

Andrew, Josh, and I are having a small private funeral for Jack. But we would welcome some time with all of you at our home, and will be receiving visitors from 6 to 9 P.M. this Tuesday. Please come by and share some stories about their father with the boys.

Fondly,

Sherry

Rumor had it that Jack Fisk had hanged himself. The funeral director had made the mistake of using the word *suddenly* in the paid obituary, which was technically accurate but in recent years had become a kind of covert shorthand for suicide. There was speculation that the remorse over what he'd done to Ricky, or anxiety over the outcome of the case against him, had broken him. But Nora knew that Jack had as little of remorse in what Sherry called his emotional tool kit as any man alive, and Linda Lessman had heard through the courthouse grapevine that there had been some deal made, that Jack would not be criminally prosecuted, that he could even continue practicing law. Ricky's account of what had happened now apparently dovetailed roughly with his.

"I wonder how much that cost?" Linda had said.

"I never even knew the guy had a bad heart," Charlie said.

"I didn't think he actually had a heart," said Nora.

"Enough," Charlie said.

Charlie believed that Jack had died of sorrow. Nora thought he died of bile. Maybe it was a chemical reaction of the two, like the baking-soda-and-vinegar volcanoes the kids had made in school. In any event, it was certainly natural causes. Whenever Nora imagined disaster, it was always dramatic: the plane on which they were flying to Bermuda plummeting into the cerulean sea, a cab rocketing around the corner and sending her flying while her children watched in horror. When the twins were small and she was carrying them she would always imagine stumbling; she endlessly rehearsed spinning, falling, cushioning them so that her own body took the full weight. But the crises were never what you thought, always more pedestrian: Ollie sliding down the banister and breaking his collarbone, Charlie complaining that she'd served bad shrimp and then having to have his appendix removed. Jack had apparently told Sherry he didn't feel well, took three Advil, lay down in the den, and died sometime between the evening news and the end of the Yankees game, with *The Wall Street Journal* open on his chest.

"I don't know that I'll ever make my peace with the idea that I was downstairs in the living room reading for all that time, and he was either dying or dead," Sherry said the next morning while Brutus pulled mulishly at his leash, his black eyes glittering as Homer sat patiently next to Nora.

Everyone on the block had salved themselves with the idea of Jack's as a good death, falling asleep in his recliner chair, without months of chemo or a long hospitalization or, what none of them said, the perpetual disgrace of being the guy who'd done that terrible thing to the poor handyman. But Sherry was not part of that hallelujah chorus. She had not seen her husband for hours, perhaps because it had become second nature to avoid him, and she tortured herself with the notion that he might have called for help and she not heard him, a classical station playing loudly while she read a British mystery novel down below. Her eyes darted up and down the block when she talked to Nora, ever suspicious that one of the tabloids might be casing her home. GOLF CLUB EXEC BEATEN BY BUM HEART. It hadn't happened. Jack might have once again become a page-five story, but the mayor's wife had recently left him for a woman—"who I know personally, and, believe me, she is a million times nicer and smarter than he is," Jenny had told Nora on the phone—and a photogenic twenty-five-year-old divinity student had been assaulted while she biked to class. Bebe had once told Nora that that was the best you could hope for when there was bad publicity—that something worse would come along. And she had been right.

Sherry had even decided against a memorial service. The memorial service had become the new funeral in New York City. No coffin, no body. The deceased was already long gone to the crematorium by the time some public venue hosted what was called a "remembrance" or a "celebration of life." Nora and Charlie knew the drill by now: slightly more than an hour of anecdotes, favorite readings, a little poetry, perhaps one of the more literary psalms. Slideshows were considered tacky, but classical music was de rigueur even if the person had hated the Philharmonic, WQXR, and Mozart. Sometimes Gershwin or very modern jazz was acceptable, and several people they knew had had "New York, New York" as the recessional. Occasionally a memorial would run close to two hours, and then you would see people sliding into the aisles and out the door early, grumbling in the sunlight about how important it was to be respectful of the time commitments of the living.

Afterward there was usually a light lunch.

The Fisk family—son, mother, son, brother whom no one knew—gathered on either side of the fireplace in the living room, food laid out in the dining room. Alma Fenstermacher had proffered her caterer, and Nora felt vaguely embarrassed by the passing thought that the food was very good. She looked around for George. This was exactly the sort of event he would enjoy, gladhanding his way through the mourners, telling the ones he'd never met before how close he and Jack had been, talking to the ones who lived on the block about how worried he'd been about Jack's health in the last couple of months, how ashen and haggard he'd been looking. Lowering his voice to a stage whisper to talk about "what happened—you know what I mean."

But he wasn't there. Instead, at the Danish-modern table she ran into Betsy, who was eating salad greens with her fingers, dipping each leaf delicately into a small pool of balsamic vinaigrette on the plate.

"It's nice that you could get away," Nora said.

"I had to be here. When George said he couldn't do it, just couldn't face it, I told him I would come and offer condolences."

"He's having a hard time?"

"Terrible. And he says he doesn't know what he'd do without Charlie. He says Charlie's friendship has been a godsend."

"Really," said Nora. Even to her it sounded like *"Really???"*

"He's been a rock for George." Betsy put down her plate and took a phone from the pocket of her black cardigan. Then she took another from the pocket on the other side. "Excuse me, Nora," she said.

Nora had to admit to herself afterward that she went looking for Charlie then only to be snide, to say, Wait until you hear this one. You're a rock. A godsend. In the den a clutch of men who looked like Jack's partners were watching a Mets game on the flat screen. It must be that they didn't know that that was the room in which Jack had died. One of them was even sitting in Jack's recliner, which Nora was pretty sure was precisely where it had happened. From inside the closed door of the master bedroom Nora heard voices, and she knocked softly. Alma and Sherry were sitting side by side on the love seat under the window, a box of tissues between them. "Oh, I'm so sorry," Nora said.

"No, come in," Sherry said. "I just had to get away for a few minutes. I feel as though I've been on a treadmill. I never appreciated how exhausting constant concern could be."

"Exhausting," said Alma, putting her hand over Sherry's.

"Some reporter finally knocked at the door this morning," Sherry said. "It must be a slow news day. I was so afraid Andrew would hit him. Think of how that story would have sounded."

"That's terrible," Nora said, putting her hand over the one of Sherry's that Alma wasn't holding. Sherry started to cry. Alma patted one hand, so Nora patted the other.

"Some young resident came out in the ER and told me he'd expired," Sherry sobbed. "Who uses that word? It made him sound as though he were a carton of milk past his sell-by date. *Expired*. Who says *expired*?" Her nose was running onto her upper lip.

"That's dreadful," Alma said.

"Passed away," Sherry said. "They could have said *passed away*." She wiped her face, then looked down at the pinkish streaks of foundation on the ragged tissue. "Oh, no," she said.

Nora squeezed her hand. "It could be worse. George could be here."

Sherry gave a harsh laugh that sounded as though it were stuck somewhere in her chest. "He wrote me a long letter," she said. "He talked about what a wonderful man Jack was and told some long story about how Jonathan had come here trick-or-treating one Halloween and Jack had invited him in and talked to him in a way that Jonathan would never forget."

"About what?" Nora said.

"I have no idea. I'm not even sure it's true. Every time Jack saw Jonathan, he called him 'that little weasel,' as far as I remember."

"That was Jack," said Alma.

"The other thing that's exhausting about all this is that these people insist on evoking some mythical Jack who bears no resemblance to my husband. His partners made him sound like Mother Teresa, until one of them mentioned his golf game, when they all shut up and the one man turned purple. And one of the work wives was telling a long story about how a friend of hers had gotten over being a widow through yoga. I hate yoga."

"Agreed," said Alma.

"I'm sorry, Nora," Sherry said. "I've been so mean to you the last few months, but I had no idea how to handle this situation. Which is ironic, given what I do for a living."

"I totally understood," said Nora. Sherry lay back on a stack of pillows. "Is it bad form to take a nap in the middle of something like this?" she said.

"Don't worry," said Alma, and she and Nora slipped out and closed the door. "I'm going to get all these people to go home," Alma said, looking at her watch, and Nora was certain she would make it happen.

"Has she taken something?" Nora said.

"In her place, you or I would certainly do so," Alma said, which Nora thought was true of her but not of Alma.

As they came down the stairs Nora said, "I keep thinking of this mother from the kids' school who was eaten up with guilt because she said she'd fantasized about her husband dying so often that when he did she felt as though she'd made it happen."

"Oh, goodness," Alma said. "If all the women who fantasized about their husbands' passings made them happen, there would be no men in the world. How were Rachel's and Oliver's graduations?"

"Oh, you know. Sad. Hectic. Lots of crying girls, hugging one another."

"We haven't yet reached the evolutionary point at which the boys cry?"

"I didn't see any," Nora said. "But Ollie's friends are all science and math guys. Maybe that explains it. I know Charlie told Jack's sons that if Oliver wasn't in Boston and Rachel wasn't in Seattle they would be here, but that isn't really true. They both really love Ricky. And they didn't much like Jack before, anyhow."

"Well, we're not here for Jack, are we?" Alma said. "We're here for Sherry. And it's after nine. I'm going to clear the room." Nora watched her approach the Fisk sons and then made her own escape out the front door.

"Where did you disappear to?" Nora asked Charlie when she got home. He was sitting in the living room in the dark and she began to turn on table lamps.

"I was sitting out in their backyard," he said. "I was out there last month with Jack. We had a cigar, talked a little about the case. I could tell he was feeling bad about what happened. I was sitting out there by myself tonight, thinking, One minute we were talking, and now it's not even a month later and he's gone. Just like that. He was really sorry about Ricky. I think that's what killed him. It wasn't the threat of a lawsuit. He just felt like a bad guy."

Nora sat on the couch, her knees nudging his. "I hate to say it," she said, "but in some ways he was a bad guy."

"I don't think so. He just got stuck in a situation and didn't know how to get out of it. And I was sitting there thinking, In ten years I'll be him. Circling the drain at work, so pissed off that someday I'll hit some poor bastard with a three iron."

"It's not true. You're not that guy. You'll never be that guy." Nora put her hand on his back and rubbed it, the way she had with the kids when they were babies, fretful, teething. Charlie turned his head and looked at her. "That's the nicest thing you've done to me in a long time," he said.

"Sorry, Charlie." She said it because she used to say that as a joke, when they first got together, like the tuna ad from when they both were kids. But it didn't seem funny now.

"Come to bed," she said.

"You go ahead. I'm going to sit here for a while. Just turn out the lights." Nora waited for a moment. "Go ahead," he said again.

As she started up the stairs she heard Charlie say, "Nora?" It was so odd, to hear him use her proper name. For years it had been Bunny or Bun, as though Nora were a name for other people and he had claimed a singular name just for himself. She tried to remember the last time he had called her Nora. It was usually when he was angry, but he wasn't angry now.

When she turned she could see his big pale hand raised in the darkness, caught for an instant in the streetlight coming through the curtains. He waved it in a circle that seemed to take in the room, the house, the city outside. "I can't do this anymore. I just can't."

He never came to bed. She never fell asleep. And so the day was done, and another dawned.

NORA NOLAN HAS MOVED.

HOME: 601 West 100th Street, apartment 15B

OFFICE: The Beverley Foundation, 60 West 125th

Street, suite 1010

She can be reached by email at

nora.b.nolan@nbnolan.net

or president@beverleyfoundation.org.

Nora and Charlie soldiered on for months after Jack Fisk died, but that night in the living room something had broken, and it became clear by inches that it could not be mended. When one of you wanted one life, and the other wanted something completely different, there was a technical term for that: *irreconcilable.*

Nora realized that she was familiar with three kinds of marriages: happy, miserable, and somewhere in between. Somehow the words Charlie spoke that June evening moved them from one column to another. They started to look around for middle ground and realized they'd been on parallel paths for so long that there wasn't any. One minute you were two people who loved each other despite your differences. And then one morning you realized—granola for him, oatmeal for her, skim milk for him, full-fat for her, coffee for him, tea for her—that you were nothing but.

"What do you think of couples' counseling?" Nora had asked Sherry, who was sitting in the Greek diner on Broadway while real estate agents wandered her house to decide which clients might buy it.

"I've never known anyone who stayed together because of

it," Sherry said. "Best case, it stops people from using tooth and claw on each other, which can mean it's really worth it. Do you know someone who needs a referral?" Nora didn't know what showed on her face, but Sherry put down a piece of rye toast and said, "Oh, no. Oh, goodness. Can I help?"

Expired, she thought to herself, looking at Sherry and remembering that evening at the Fisk house. We've expired. Charlie drank more and slept less. When he was home, the place somehow seemed even emptier. Jack's downfall and death had been like a dog whistle, sending Charlie a signal that only he could hear about his own existence.

It was a happy event that finally did them in, which she supposed came as no surprise. She remembered once telling Christine that at weddings people decided either to break up or to take it to the next level. They had been at the wedding of friends from high school, at a big country club overlooking the sound, boat horns drowning out the string quartet, and Christine turned to her and said, "I'm going to dump Bradley in the morning." Just like that. She remembered Charlie squeezing her hand during the vows. From this day forward, as long as you both shall live. Somehow when you're saying those words, you never realize what a long time "as long as you both shall live" will amount to.

Jenny had invited them to dinner at her apartment, although Jenny made it her business never to cook, early on saying it was a tool of the patriarchy and later insisting that with the takeout options in her neighborhood alone, it was simply foolish. "I think it's to admire her new kitchen," Nora told Charlie, the two of them sitting side by side in the back of a car like two strangers who left a party and realized at the curb that they had nearby destinations.

The cabinets were beauties, sleek to the ceiling, a pine with a showy grain that had been stained to a pale shadow of its usual gold, even prettier than the sample Jenny had shown her. And there was not a takeout container to be seen. Jasper had made a chicken stew with dried fruit and shallots, and a loaf of sourdough bread. Apparently he had a sourdough starter that he had been toting from place to place with him for years. "It's been his most enduring relationship," Jenny said, smiling at Jasper, dipping her bread into the stew, at which point Nora noticed the rigged silver band on her left hand. Nora looked at Jenny, then at Jasper, then pointedly back at the ring.

"I made an honest woman out of her," Jasper said, shrugging.

Jenny blushed. Nora had never, in all the years they were friends, seen Jenny blush.

"What?" Charlie said with his mouth full. "What am I missing here?"

The ring looked oddly familiar. "He made it out of a quarter," Jenny said.

"Doesn't that count as defacing currency?" Charlie said.

"Really, Charlie?" Nora said.

"That was a stupid thing to say. Let me see." Charlie put out his big hand, and Jenny dropped the ring into it. Charlie looked at Jasper and nodded. "That. Is. Cool," he said, handing it back to Jenny. He and Nora looked at each other, and he nodded again, and they had a moment of understanding: We had this once, but no more. It reminded Nora of that moment at the symphony when there is a silence and, instead of the end of a movement, it means the end of the piece. She was grateful that Jenny was looking down at her ring and hadn't seen.

When they had paired off over port—"the guy knows wine," Charlie said afterward—Jenny had said, ruefully, "He needed decent health insurance. You should have seen the premiums on his plan. And the deductible was a joke."

"Jen, it's fine," Nora said. "It's great. I'm thrilled for you. I'm just a little surprised, is all. Just please don't ever tell me he's your best friend."

"Excuse me, but you're my best friend. And does anybody actually say that except on television?" She looked down at the ring. "Who gets married for the first time at forty-eight? It's ridiculous. Whatever you do, don't give me a shower."

"I had a dream about a shower the other night, weirdly," Nora said. "We were here, at your place, and there weren't enough chairs, so we were all standing."

"That sounds right," Jenny said.

"And I realized I didn't have a gift and I was kind of panicked about that, and then I realized that the shower was for me, that I was pregnant again. Which would be some kind of miracle." And then, looking into her friend's face, she saw a deadness, a darkness in her eyes, and automatically reached out her hand. "Jenny, honey," Nora said. "You're not—"

"That *would* be a miracle, Nor," Jenny said.

"But is that . . . I'm sorry, I'm being ridiculously incoherent here . . . it's just that . . ."

"Calm down," Jenny said. "It's all fine. It's just one of those things that I realize now I'll never do. Never have, I guess."

"Like living in Paris."

"I could still live in Paris. But not that. I look at all of you and I don't know, after all those years of thinking it wasn't something I wanted, I wonder. But who has a baby at forty-eight? Movie stars. Besides, all this is way more than I thought I'd wind up with. No matter what, I really, really, really like being with him. That's what it comes down to."

And that was the thing, Nora thought as she lay in bed that night, listening to Charlie moving around upstairs in the guest room, letting his shoes drop to the floor, running the water in the bathroom. You had to really, really, really like being with someone. Yet somehow that was a decision they were all expected to make when they were too young to know very much. They were expected to make all the important decisions then: what to do, where to live, who to live with. But anyone could tell you, looking at the setup dispassionately, that most people would be incapable of making good choices if they had to make that many choices at the same time, at that particular time of their lives. Jenny had waited. They had judged her and joked about her and cautioned her and advised her. But maybe she had been right. A younger Nora would have been appalled that her friend the Theodore Pierce Foster Professor of Anthropology was marrying a cabinetmaker with a sourdough fetish. A younger Charlie had said, "Your sister went to Duke so she could design leggings?" But in the car on the way home, sitting with the estrangement well of the center console between them, they had agreed that Jasper was a pleasure to be with, that Jenny seemed happier than ever before, that Rachel was doing so well working for Christine. The only thing wrong was the two of them. Their hands had brushed in the backseat and they had both edged closer to the windows, bright with the red of brake lights.

They didn't rush it. From the outside they seemed much as before. They took things in stages, but after a while it became clear that all the stages led to a single end point. One evening, when Nora thought Charlie was napping on the couch, he said, without opening his eyes, "I ran into Dave Bryant on the street yesterday. He's doing a stint in London and he asked if I knew anyone who might want to sublet his place. I said I knew someone who would take it."

Charlie moved into the sublet on the East Side, partly furnished. Nora looked at places on the West Side but farther north, on the high floors of high-rise buildings. Ironically, one of the things Charlie had wanted so badly finally came to pass, although not as he had imagined. They agreed to sell the house, and as predicted, made a good deal of money. The windfall was less once divided in half, but a windfall it was. There was nothing else to argue about. The children were gainfully employed. The retirement accounts were already separate. Nora agreed to stay in the house until the new owners moved in. They each changed the beneficiaries on their life insurance to Oliver and Rachel. Someday, Jenny said, when Nora finally told her everything, Charlie's second wife would be infuriated by that, and Charlie might try to change it. But not yet.

It saddened Nora to realize that the one thing that might have precipitated real hand-to-hand combat between them had overnight ceased to be an issue. Nora had poured a bowlful of kibble one morning and Homer had refused to rise in Pavlovian response to the clatter. She carried the bowl to where he lay and put it right under his nose, but he lifted his head and then put it down again. Charlie pulled their car out of the indoor garage, and the two of them drove together to the vet, Homer's panting loud in the backseat. As she ran her fingers through his pied coat while he stood shivering on the stainless-steel examining table, Nora realized that there was no flesh between fur and bone. She kept telling herself that she was assuming the worst, but when the vet came in after the exams, the scans, she knew the news was terrible. She and Charlie held each other and cried, for Homer and for all the rest of it, as the vet gently pushed the plunger on the syringe and the dog's heart ceased to beat beneath their joined hands.

"He was always glad to see me when I came home from work," Charlie said in the car, and Nora started to say, "So was I," that way a wife was expected to do, and then she couldn't and she started to cry again. She was still crying when they ran into Linda Lessman on the pavement, Nora with the leash dangling at her side. "Homer?" Linda asked, and when they nodded wordlessly she threw her hands in the air and said, "Oh, Lord, everything is falling apart."

"We have to tell the kids," Nora said in the kitchen, pouring herself a glass of wine.

"Can we wait a couple of days?" Charlie said. "I'm pretty played out." And he trudged upstairs.

As far as Nora was concerned, they could wait forever. The afternoon they'd sat down together to talk to Oliver and Rachel would live inside her for the rest of her life. Both of them had been home for the wedding of a friend from high school, and Nora and Charlie had waited until Sunday afternoon so as not to poison the exchange of vows between Emily Sternberg and Jonathan Ward at the Metropolitan Club, dinner and dancing to follow, festive dress.

"Your mother and I have something to discuss with you," Charlie had said, choking up almost immediately.

"Please don't tell me you're getting a divorce," Oliver said.

"God, Ollie, of course they're not getting a divorce," Rachel said.

Afterward Nora replayed those two sentences over and over, wondering if anything either of them could have said would have been worse. Would it have been more terrible if they had both assumed that was the case? Or was it more punishing that somehow she and Charlie had allowed them to think that this would never happen to them, what had happened to so many of their friends? Nora had been in a bad car accident in high school; they'd been T-boned at a stop sign, the little car her friend Amanda had been given for her birthday rolling twice before it came to rest on its side on the shoulder. Nora could still feel that moment in her body, all these years later, the sound of collapsing metal, the hard thrust of the seatbelt along her hips, even a shiny smudge on the dash where one of them had spattered some soda. It was the same with this. She could see the grain of the wood on the dining room table, the faint shadow of a circle where someone had put down a wet glass, a spike of light through the upper panes of the French door and then one of the chairs falling sideways as Rachel stood suddenly and thudded up to her room.

"This sucks," Oliver said flatly. "This really sucks."

"It does, buddy," Charlie said.

It wasn't anyone's fault, and it was everyone's fault. Nora had been married to Charlie without seeing him for a long time. She realized that they all assumed that if their marriages ended, it would be with a big bang: the other woman, the hidden debts. Nora had had more reasons than most to imagine that, veteran of a grand passion built on a big lie. But now she thought that was an aberration. The truth was that some of their marriages were like balloons: a few went suddenly pop, but more often than not the air slowly leaked out until it was a sad, wrinkled little thing with no lift to it anymore.

Because the children changed, they required attention, drew the eye: the year Oliver's room started to smell like unwashed man, the year Rachel began to shut her door and frown when

Nora knocked on it. The strep throat, the failing course. But the sameness of husbands, of wives, too, meant that in some sense they might cease to exist on a daily basis. They were like drapes: you agonized over choosing them, measured and mulled, wanted them just right, and then you hung them and forgot about them, so that sometimes you couldn't even remember what color they were. Almost without noticing it, the young man who had kissed Nora on the forehead after walking her home from The Tattooed Lady had become a sad man who had seen the line of his life running off the reel like it was being dragged by a big fish in murky water. All the men, they feared loss of potency, of position, but what it all came down to was fear of death. Ricky's van might as well have been a hearse.

Charlie wasn't a bad man or even a bad husband. Like most men of his generation, he had grown up thinking that the basic maintenance of his life would be handled by women. And it was, by his assistant, the housekeeper, and, to a lesser and less solicitous and therefore less satisfactory extent, his wife. But arranging things for someone is not the same as loving him. It's work, not devotion.

Of course there had almost immediately been a woman after Charlie had moved out. Maybe she'd even been there during the months when he was sleeping upstairs and Nora was on the floor below. Why wouldn't that be so? Charlie was a nice man, freed from the accumulated weight of the petty grievances of ordinary married life. All her friends said women left because they were unhappy, and men left because they'd found someone new to be unhappy with. Nora realized how far they'd come when Charlie told her he was seeing someone and she realized she wasn't as upset as she'd always expected to be. The woman was the nurse in his doctor's office; they'd gotten to talking when he was waiting for the stress test during his physical. Nora could almost see it, the woman nodding her head sympathetically, Charlie confiding how hard the last months had been as she put a blood pressure cuff on his arm. She probably played golf, or at least was willing to learn. For her, a golf club would simply be a golf club.

"Transitional woman," Christine said. "The one who gets a guy from wife number one to wife number two."

"At least she's not younger than Rachel," Nora said.

"You sound pretty okay."

"I am pretty okay. I just worry about the kids. You know how you're supposed to tell them it's nobody's fault? We did, and maybe Oliver believes it—who can tell—but I think Rachel has decided it's definitely mine."

"Rachel is fine, Non. I see her every day. She's doing really good work, and she's made some nice friends."

"That's not how she makes it sound when she talks to me. She says all it does is rain there."

Christine laughed. "Nonnie, all it ever does is rain here. Calm down. She's just confused. And sad."

"She told me one night that she's in mourning for her life."

"That's Chekhov. *The Three Sisters,* I think, or it could be *The Seagull.*"

"She knows I was a history major."

Christine laughed. "I don't think she's trying to test your knowledge of Russian literature. She's just dramatic. She's always been dramatic, although I've got to tell you, she doesn't bring the drama to work, not one bit, or she wouldn't be doing as well as she is. Don't worry. You're a great mom. She has so much confidence. If I had a daughter and she felt like that, I'd feel like an enormous success."

Silence.

"Non?"

"Sorry, that was the sound of me crying."

Along with everything else, there was the inevitable split from Charity. Nora knew it was silly, the idea of having her stay on once the house was sold, the children scattered, Homer only a tin canister of ashes stuck in the back of a closet, behind the shoe boxes. Charity had not abandoned her. She had helped Nora pack Charlie's things up, sent the clothes Rachel wanted to Seattle, put boxes into storage, but then the tasks were done and it was time for her to move on. She'd taken a job with a family she'd met in the park the year before, before everything changed. Nora couldn't blame her. The family had two little girls, ages four and two, who were probably doomed to hear a fairy-tale rendering of the perfect manners and unquestioning obedience of Rachel and Oliver Nolan for years to come while they ate their after-school snack. Charity's sister Faith, who worked only as an evening and weekend nanny for a family in Chelsea, had agreed to clean and do laundry once a week for Nora. So at least there was that. Charity said Vance thought that was a good arrangement.

Selling the house was a relief, since every time she passed the Fisk house she couldn't help but think to herself, Ah, that is the place where the Nolans started to unravel. Of course it wasn't the Fisk house anymore. It had sold quickly, and Sherry had bought an apartment in the same building as her office. "They say you're not supposed to make any sudden decisions," she said as she and Nora had coffee in her new living room, with its view of the river, the same view that Nora had had during her morning walk for so many years. "Another thing they say that's ridiculous. Has your house sold?"

"It's under contract but still being shown," Nora said. "We had a full-price offer in ten days. It's insane."

"My sons keep talking about how great it is that I'm not in a place with stairs anymore," Sherry said. "They actually say that. Obviously they're already worried about the widow Fisk, and how she'll get around in her dotage."

"Oh, nonsense."

"No, it's true. I don't even mind. Thinking of me that way is good for them." She peered over the edge of her coffee cup. "I'm seeing a man who lives in my building."

"Seeing?"

"You know. He's an entomologist at the Museum of Natural History. He's very . . ." Sherry searched for the right word. "Sweet," she said finally. "I told him my husband was the man who'd beaten someone with a golf club. He'd never even heard or read the story. It was so nice. I met him in the elevator. It means he doesn't have to stay over. I've always preferred sleeping alone, and he doesn't mind. He just goes three floors down to his own apartment. The one time he fell asleep here, I woke up in the middle of the night and thought Jack was sitting by the closet, glaring at me, when it was only the extra blanket I'd thrown over a chair."

Nora scarcely knew what to say. She thought Jack Fisk was exactly the sort of man who would come back from the dead and glare at his wife.

"I don't think Charlie would do that," she said.

"Ah, but Charlie's not dead," Sherry said. "Are you seeing anyone?"

"Oh, God, no. I'm still trying to figure out exactly what happened." Nora lifted her cup. "I know it sounds stupid, but it's like we just ran out of steam."

"That doesn't sound stupid at all," Sherry said. "It's actually fairly typical. What's not typical is that while many marriages run out of steam, most of them keep on going. Or at least endure, steamless."

Nora lifted her hands and shrugged.

"It was what happened on the block," Sherry said, a statement, not a question, and Nora didn't even bother to disagree. "It changed everything."

"I don't know," Nora said. "It feels to me like everything changed but we're all still somehow the same. Does that make any sense?"

Sherry shook her head. "I have a friend who lives in San Francisco, in a beautiful new co-op building. Lovely, lovely apartment, so much space and light. Last year they found out the building is sinking. It's already gone down a couple of feet. The apartment doesn't look any different in any way, but she says when she lies in bed at night she has this feeling like she's falling. It's not rational, but it's real."

"Is she selling?"

"Who would buy it?" Sherry said. "I hear the Fenstermachers are selling."

"Oh, nonsense," Nora said.

Nora was not seeing anyone, although she was surprised at the attempts, most for what the twins had taught her to call hookups. Even Jim, whom she'd run into at a restaurant one afternoon, had asked her for a drink. "I hate to say it, but I always thought you and Charlie were a mismatch," he said, shaking his head. "No, we weren't," Nora said. She figured that would make Jim think the split had been Charlie's idea, that she was still pining, but she didn't care. She hated the way so many people acted as though part of divorce was a happy erasure of the past. Only Jenny, of all people, said, "You stayed together for almost twenty-five years, and you had two great kids. Your marriage was a huge success. Don't let anybody tell you different."

Bob Harris had called her the week she found her new apartment, as though from forty blocks south he could sense the sound of closing documents being prepared. "I hear you're getting a divorce and your dog died," he said. "I'm sorry about the dog. Good dog?"

"The best," Nora said.

He'd sighed. "That's a bitch," he said. "I had a springer spaniel that was worth ten of any person I ever met. Anyhow, now that you're getting unhitched, any chance you'd have dinner with me?"

"None," Nora said.

"You sure?"

"My husband works for you."

"I could ease him out. The fact is, I've been thinking about easing him out for a long time. He's a nice guy, but there's just something—I don't know. There's something missing."

"Please don't let him go. He loves his job." This wasn't really true, hadn't been true for ages. But as Sherry Fisk had said what seemed like years ago and was only last winter, without it Charlie would be nothing. He'd be like a vampire looking in the mirror: no reflection. In their world a man without a business card was a man who can't get out of bed in the morning. Even Ricky had had a business card.

Bob Harris had invited her in to talk that same afternoon,

although she had put him off for weeks, despite the fact that she didn't have a job anymore. His persistence was obviously one of the things that had enabled him to be a success in business. His patience, too. He had waited a long time for Nora to come around. He tapped his hand on his desk, thinking, then said, "What if I trade a couple of dinners for keeping Charlie on?"

"That is cheap and low," said Nora.

Bob Harris grinned.

"And you are married," she added.

"Ah. Now how do you know that?"

"I don't know. That way you know things. You're married to your college sweetheart and she lives most of the time at your horse farm in Virginia."

"Alpacas," Bob Harris said. "She raises alpacas. You know what alpacas are?"

"Pretty much like llamas?"

"Exactly, except people who raise alpacas don't like it when you say that. It's like, Stu Ventner. You know him? He tells me he's on the advisory board of the library. I say, What's the difference between being on the board and being on the advisory board. He says something, something, something, bull, bull, bull. Whatever. Leeanne says alpacas are friendlier and better-looking than llamas, and you can make things out of their wool, and llama wool is good for nothing. I have no clue whether any of that is true."

He kept on tapping his hand, looking down at it jumping around as though it belonged to someone else, finally saying, "The truth is that Leeanne and me haven't been what you'd call legally married for a long time now. But don't go spreading that around. I don't want to wind up in one of those stories about the eligible bachelors of New York, which always means the richest bachelors in New York. Then people who do what you used to do show up asking for money and women who are a lot of trouble suck up to you at parties. Sometimes literally. Hell, forget I said that. Why I asked you here in the first place, I've got all my ducks in a row on this foundation now, and I still want you to run it."

"How closely associated will it be with Parsons Ridge?"

"Not at all. Offices elsewhere. Whole different thing. No connection except the money, and me."

"The Bob Harris Foundation?"

He shook his head. "I already filed the papers for the Bever-ley Foundation. That's what it'll be called."

"Because?"

"After my mother. She was a second grade teacher."

Nora sat back. "Well, aren't you a boatload of surprises?"

"Not if you put on your 3-D glasses, honey."

"I don't know."

"This because your husband, or whatever he is, doesn't want you to take the job?" Bob Harris was studying her face. He was the kind of man who took a lot of pride in being able to read people, and it seemed he read her correctly. "Hmmph. If I were married to a woman like you I wouldn't sell her short."

"Yeah, you all think that. You all think you'll like it, but when it happens you don't like it at all."

"I didn't say I'd like it. But I'd like to think I'd take advantage of the opportunity."

At that moment it was clear to Nora that Bob Harris was thinking of making a play for her, and that Nora was thinking of finally giving in. But an expert on body language, like the ones who were always popping up on TV analyzing the presi-dent, could have told you by the rise and then the fall of their clavicles that almost simultaneously both of them thought, Nah. It was the beginning of what would be a wonderful professional relationship. In the years to come, they would feel that they might be the only man and woman in New York who had honest conversations.

"You should be with that guy," Jenny said when Nora described one of their interactions.

"Why ruin a good thing?" Nora had replied.

The city has informed residents that they will discontinue weekly baiting for rodent traps and will move to a monthly schedule. A firm has been retained to check traps and rebait when necessary to supplement the city plan. The cost will be divided among owners who agree to participate. NO TRAPS WILL BE CHECKED OR REBAITED IN THE AREA OF HOMES NOT PARTICIPATING.

George

Broom-clean, it said in the contract. The house was to be delivered broom-clean. Nora had smiled when she saw the words. Obviously the buyer's attorney was unfamiliar with the body of work of Charity Barrett, who had snaked a vacuum hose into the heating and dryer vents, who had actually scrubbed the grout in Ollie's bathroom with something just a bit bigger than a toothbrush, who had waxed the parquet so thoroughly that Nora was concerned the new owners would go flying if they walked quickly across the living room. In this operating-theater atmosphere, redolent of lemon, Lysol, and bleach, it was jarring to see a sheet of paper on the foyer floor. Her last George-o-Gram. Nora thought perhaps she should keep it as a memento, show it to the twins. Then she threw it in the last bag of trash waiting to go downstairs.

She was surprised that she was still on George's list. Perhaps he thought the newcomers were already in residence. The week before, Nora had solved the greatest problem she thought she was leaving the buyers of her house. She'd walked from her new apartment to the block just after dawn—she wasn't sleeping well, but it would take more than insomnia to make her hit the sidewalk before first light, when rats might still be foraging—and seen a woman putting a plastic bag on her front stoop.

"Wait just a minute," Nora shouted.

The woman froze for a moment, then pivoted with her hands on her hips. Nora couldn't help but notice that she was wearing a pair of Small Sayings workout pants, the Thoreau capri, with "I stand in awe of my body" inside the waistband. It was a sentence that smacked so flagrantly of yoga studio and empowerment jargon that Nora had insisted Christine double-check that Thoreau had actually said it.

"No, you wait just a minute. I am going to keep doing this until you stop letting your nasty little dogs go on the sidewalk in front of our building! I've stepped in it too many times to count, and I'm sick of it so I'm picking it up and putting it where it belongs, at your front door!"

"My dog's dead," Nora said, and to her surprise she found herself in tears, as though saying it aloud had made it suddenly true.

"What?"

"My dog died six months ago."

"All of them?"

"I only had one."

"Oh, come on. The doorman next door to my building said there were at least two, sometimes three. He said the man who lived in this house walked them in front of our building and never picked up after them."

"What kinds of dogs?"

"Some little dogs with bug eyes. I always forget the name, the ones who look like some kind of space alien." She raised her hands in the air. "I'm a cat person," she said.

Nora bent and gingerly picked up the bag. "You've been leaving these at the wrong house," she said. "The person you want lives right across the street. The doorman gave you the wrong address."

"Are you sure?" the woman said. And as though conjured by a magic trick, at that moment George came down the ramshackle steps of his house with three of his rescue pugs pulling on their leashes in front of him. The woman stared, then snatched the bag from Nora's hand. "Sorry," she cried as she sprinted across the street. "Sorry sorry sorry." Nora stepped inside and thought that George might never speak to her again, and hoped against hope that that would be the case, and then realized that it didn't matter, that she was unlikely to run into George for the rest of both their lives.

In that way that things sometimes happen, Nora was doing the last walk-through before the afternoon closing when she heard the doorbell ring. The house was completely empty. When she sneezed, it echoed. She had closed the door of Rachel's closet, which still had middle school graffiti: RN AND AB (which boy was that?), I HATE YOU (probably a message for her mother), various hearts and stars. She had refused to let Charity scrub it off. She'd also decided to let the area behind the kitchen door stand, the one in which they had measured the twins every year on their birthday. Pencil marks on paint: Oliver and Rachel, twelve, she taller by several inches; Rachel and Oliver, fourteen, after a growth spurt that had pushed his height up an inch and his voice down an octave. In college Rachel had insisted she was still growing when Ollie topped out at six feet and Rachel was four inches shorter. "Dream on," her brother had said, patting her on the head. Nora had taken a picture of the wall. Someday she would send it to her children, but not yet.

The bell rang again. A man with black hair, brown skin, and khaki clothes stood at the door. Two other men, similar enough that no one on the block would ever be able to tell them all apart, stood behind him. All three were wearing backpacks. "Hello, missus?" the man who was obviously in charge said, uptalking like a private-school girl in eighth grade. "My name is Joe? I do home repairs. My men will clean the sidewalks and shovel snow. Good prices for you."

"What's your real name, Joe?"

"Joe." He smiled, nodded. Nora noticed that he had no index finger on one hand, and as he saw her noticing, he curled his fingers into fists. "I work for Mr. George across the street? Also Mrs. Wooden?" Nora hadn't met the Woodens yet, and supposed now she never would. They had just acquired a house near the corner. As far as Nora could tell, they had no dogs.

"Do you have a card, Joe?" Nora said. "This isn't really my house but I'll pass it along."

That afternoon she had given the card to the couple at the closing. They'd paid five times what she and Charlie had. "You'll need a handyman," Nora said, as she signed paper after paper, first with her own name, then with Charlie's because he had not wanted to be there and had given her power of attorney. Nora didn't need a handyman, not anymore. She had a super instead. She lived now on the fifteenth floor of a new building, a white box with partial views of the river, along with an endless vista of wooden water towers and tarred roofs, that all-you-can-eat buffet of Manhattan aloft. Nora loved the light and the air. She loved not being known. She loved that there was no wainscoting, no molding, no charm, no history. She liked the nothingness of it, the blank slate. Wasn't this what living in New York was supposed to be like, the skyline, the anonymity, coexistence without intimacy?

"How did you sleep?" Nora asked when Rachel came to town and stayed in the guest room.

"Good," her daughter said. "It's like staying in a really nice hotel."

"Ouch," Nora said, making coffee in the tiny kitchen, which was just the right size for what she needed a kitchen for now.

Rachel stood next to her, hip to hip. The night before they had watched trash TV with their legs entwined on the couch. Now Nora leaned into her daughter, feeling small and sad. "I like nice hotels," Rachel said. She opened the refrigerator. "No plain yogurt?" she said as she took a banana from the bowl.

"First-world problem," Nora said.

"Mommy, I love you, but no one says that anymore," Rachel said. She hoisted herself until she was sitting on the counter, her legs dangling, the way she'd liked to do when she was in middle school. "So how are you, really?" Rachel said. "And that's not a rhetorical question."

"I take a lot of pleasure in having children who know what a rhetorical question is," Nora said, carrying coffee mugs to the dining table as her daughter followed. The table was new. The cups had been around for a long time. Charlie hadn't wanted much of the kitchen stuff. He actually hadn't wanted much at all.

She sat down and looked at Rachel and worked to keep her voice flat. "It depends on the day," Nora said. "Sometimes I'm sad and sometimes I'm okay and sometimes I'm even a little happy and sometimes I think we made the wrong decision but mostly I think we made the right one. I spend a lot of time worrying about you and your brother."

"And we both spend a lot of time worrying about you."

"And how are you? Also not a rhetorical question."

"Nice deflection, though," Rachel said, hugging her mug, biting her lower lip, shifting in her chair the way she did, all those little mannerisms that Nora knew so well. "I'm all right, in spite of everything. A year ago, not so much. I started feeling as though in my whole life I'd never really made a decision. Everything in my life just sort of happened. The guys I wound up with, my friends, they were just there. Like, even college, it was sort of, Okay, I've been here for reunions, it's beautiful, it's a great school, that's fine. But making the decision to leave New York, to do something so different from what anyone else I knew was doing—it just felt so good, to decide something all by myself. I know you think what I do is kind of lame and random—"

"I do not!"

"But I made a big decision and now I make small decisions every single day, and they may only be decisions about whether a onesie should have snaps or a zipper but I'm the one making them."

"I can say from experience that whether a onesie has snaps or a zipper is an important decision. I vote zipper, babe."

"So did I," Rachel said, and looked at her watch. "Oh, no, I'm going to be late for the Cotton Council meeting! And no judgment, please."

"You're talking to a woman who once sucked up to the Gemological Institute of America. No judgment."

At the door, as she was leaving in her grown-up suit, Rachel hugged her hard and said, "I'm glad you're here. It might be even harder if you were at the house without Daddy, or he was there without you. This is nice. It's a nice place."

"It's a nice place," Jenny had said, too, following the long hallway to the bedrooms, opening the glass-fronted kitchen cabinets, looking down on the buildings below. "Did Rachel approve?"

"She pretended to. There was a lot of pretending. I don't know what was worse, the pain last year or the pretending now."

"It's a dialectic. Wait for the synthesis."

"Thank you, professor."

"Really, I like this place. It's a new you."

"Is it? Or is it the old me with new furniture?"

"I like the new furniture. That white couch is great." Jenny leaned in toward the view until her forehead touched the window glass. "That roof garden must have cost a fortune," she said, looking down at the top of the brick building across the street.

"I've literally never seen anyone using it," Nora said, standing next to her.

Jenny put her arm around Nora's waist, and squeezed.

"Should I get a dog?" Nora said.

"It depends," Jenny said. "Do you really want a dog, or do you think you should get a dog because it will make it seem like nothing has changed?"

Nora sighed. "I've always wanted a white couch," she said.

"If you get a dog, get one who won't jump on the furniture," Jenny said.

It was funny, Nora sometimes thought, how, after the shock of becoming a separated person, of losing not only her home but her entire way of thinking about herself and her life, she had woken up one morning and realized that she would survive, that her former life was like a dress she had loved but that no tailor could take in after all the weight she'd lost. She wasn't stupid; she was working long hours at her new job, hiring staff, setting up systems, visiting schools, and instead of weekends only, she was running every morning through the park in the half-light. Keeping busy, that's what they called it. She knew there was a chance that someday she would sit down at the table at which she ate breakfast and feel loneliness like a flu, hot and achy and terrible and everywhere, the kind of feeling that made you want to stay in bed.

"Didn't that happen sometimes even when you were still married?" Jenny had asked.

Somehow she and Charlie had both wound up with what they hadn't known they'd always wanted. One evening they had gone to dinner with Lizzie's parents, along with Oliver and Lizzie, and it had been as though they were still together in some strange way, but better. Nothing had happened in the last day, or the last week, to make one annoyed with the other; there was no irritating subtext as they sat around the table, Nora talking about the foundation to Lizzie's mother, who headed a small private school, Charlie talking about the market to Lizzie's father, who was a hospital administrator. The only thing that made it odd was the end of the evening, standing on the pavement executing that dance of moving from saying good night to actually leaving.

"That was a nice evening," Charlie had said.

"Really nice," Nora said.

And then it was cheek kiss, cheek kiss, and turn away in opposite directions. Charlie had headed east while Nora went north. Nora had glimpsed something, just for a moment, on her son's face, and next morning, when the two of them had breakfast, she said, "Don't let what happened make you relationship-shy."

Oliver smiled a little sadly. "Mom, I draw conclusions based on all available data."

"And if the data is contradictory?" she said, thinking of Lizzie's parents, her mother's arm looped through her father's reflexively as they walked from the restaurant to the corner for a cab. Although who knew what that really meant? Charlie and Nora had looked like that to outsiders, so that when Nora had told her father they were separated he had said, "You're kidding."

"If the data is contradictory I continue to study the subject," Oliver said.

That first Thanksgiving Nora and Charlie had gone together, as usual, to her father and Carol in Connecticut. "Always welcome, always welcome," her father had said as he pumped Charlie's hand. The food had been the same, and the conversation, too, although Oliver had gone to Lizzie's and Rachel stayed in Seattle and had dinner with Christine. Nora assumed that next year Charlie would have Thanksgiving dinner with his woman friend, and the following year she might be his second wife, and so on and so forth. It was funny, how easy it was to predict the fine points of the future, and how the big things were incomprehensible until they were right there, on paper: Certificate of Dissolution of Marriage. Sometimes she thought about the block and wondered whether she'd wanted it because she knew it was what was wanted, whether life, at least in New York City, was an inchoate search for authenticity when imitation was always dangled before you like a great prize.

"Your new job sounds amazing," Suzanne said wistfully when their women's group met for lunch. "There are only so many swatches you can look at before you feel as though you're rearranging the deck chairs on the *Titanic*. Thank God I'm done with that house downtown. Although I do miss seeing James. That man is to die for."

"Have people finally stopped with the leopard carpeting?" said Jenny, giving Nora a look across the table.

Suzanne shook her head. "Ten years from now I will watch while every client decides to pull it out. If I'm even doing this ten years from now."

"One mistake I never made," said Jenny, leaning over her bowl of soup.

"You used to say that about marriage," Elena said, and Nora felt a movement under the table and realized that one of the other women had kicked Elena. "I mean that Jenny used to talk about how terrible marriage was, and now she's married." Kick. Kick. "What?" yelled Elena, and Nora started to laugh.

"First of all, Jenny wasn't the one who used to talk about how terrible marriage was," Nora said, looking around the table. "And second of all, I promise everyone, I will not fall apart if you mention marriage, weddings, husbands, or even boyfriends."

"Is there a boyfriend?" Cathleen said, her eyes enormous, and someone kicked her, too.

"She bought a white couch," Jenny said.

"You bought a new couch and didn't ask to use my designer discount?" Suzanne said. "I'm hurt."

"You're busy. I saw it in a showroom window and bought it on impulse. I'd forgotten how much I wanted one."

"It's every mother's fantasy piece of furniture," Suzanne said. "You can tell who won't let her kids in the living room by whether they order one. Some of them might as well have a velvet rope at the living room entrance."

"My kids are too old for jelly hands," Nora said.

"Have you lost weight?" Elena said. Kick. "What's wrong with asking if she lost weight?" Kick. "I'm going to be black and blue by the time this lunch is over!"

A block away from Nora's new apartment was a nice restaurant where she sometimes had business breakfasts, before she headed uptown to her new office, a restaurant where they now smiled and led her always to the same table in the corner. It was there one morning that she saw Alma Fenstermacher across the room, reading a thriller and eating an omelet with quiet concentration. The seat across from Alma was empty, and Nora threaded her way between the tables to stand behind it. Alma looked up and the delight in her eyes was immediate and unfeigned. She took a ballet class two mornings a week—of course, she did, Nora thought—and the studio was nearby.

Joe worked for the families on the block now, and Alma said she had heard he was good, although perhaps not quite as good as Ricky had been. The people who'd bought the Nolan house were lovely, although the younger boy was said to be a bit of a handful; the couple who had bought the Fisk house were doing a renovation and hadn't moved in yet. Nora told her that Oliver was preparing to apply to graduate school, and that Rachel had gotten a promotion and was helping to oversee Christine's new line of clothing. "It's called Smaller Sayings," Nora said. "It's the same thing she did with workout clothes, but for children."

"The future is now," said Alma.

"Oh, my goodness," Nora said. "That's their biggest seller. Apparently they can't keep up with the demand. That, and 'Sleep tight.' Both of those are Rachel's."

"I bought them both for a baby shower last month," Alma said. "Does Rachel like living there?"

"I think she's just happy to be away at the moment. If she says one more time that people are so real there, I'm going to scream."

"Ah, yes," said Alma Fenstermacher, who had children in St. Louis and Chicago. "The much vaunted western authenticity."

"Not like New York."

"Not a bit," Alma said, buttering her toast. "Perhaps they're right about that. I knew a woman here who talked ceaselessly about her years at Wellesley. How happy she'd been there, what a wonderful classical education she'd received, how beautiful the campus was. I was actually with her at a tea when she ran into two women from the same class at Wellesley. They both said they remembered her. One even said they'd been in a seminar on the Lake Poets together. I won't go into chapter and verse about how I came to know this, but the closest she'd ever been to Wellesley was a secretarial school on Twenty-third Street."

"Oh, that's so sad."

Alma smiled slightly. "I admired her when I found out. What a production, to create a life from whole cloth. Although maybe that's what we all do. Tell me about your work. From what I can gather, that horrid woman never deserved you."

The schools she visited, the projects she was thinking of funding, the kids who had so little and needed so much: Nora wouldn't have gone on so long if Alma hadn't seemed so interested and even ordered another cup of coffee. She told her about the first grant she'd made, creating a computer lab at a school that had been relying solely on a pair of aged desktops, and how the principal had started to cry when she'd seen the room finished, the students sitting at the new computers. Nora had started to cry, too, because after all those years of asking rich people for money she realized how much more pleasurable it was to give it away where it was really truly needed. The thing was, Bob Harris had come with her for this inaugural gift, and he'd wept, too. "Thank you," Nora had said to him when they came out of the school building onto a littered street with a cracked blacktop basketball court. "Let's get these people some decent playground equipment," Bob had said.

She didn't mention to Alma the day that she had realized she was in the neighborhood and had steeled herself to stop by Ricky's apartment. When she knocked at the door, a tiny girl in denim cutoffs with an infant on her shoulder and a toddler wrapped around her shin answered. "Oh, they're gone," she said. A young guy buying lunch in the corner bodega said, "Ricky? He won the lottery, man. He got so much money now, he can't spend it. He's got millions."

The old man outside by the hydrant in the folding chair said, "That fool inside don't know what he's talking about. Millions, millions—anytime anybody gets some money around here, they say it's millions. Ricky didn't win the lottery. He got money from some big lawsuit. A lot of money, but not millions. Maybe four, five hundred thousand. It's a nice piece of change, I will say that. The man limps, but come on. I'd limp for a couple hundred thousand dollars and a nice house. You want a Dr Pepper, miss? I got a whole cooler of them here."

"Where's the house?"

"The DR. The Dominican Republic. That's where Nita's

mom lives, her sisters, a couple of cousins. They opened a restaurant."

"That's a good way to lose a lot of money."

"That's okay. He's got a lot of money now. Not millions, though."

"I heard it was a million," said the young guy, coming outside with his sandwich and a can of Pabst Blue Ribbon. "He should have gotten that guy that hit him. He should have made him pay instead of letting him off."

"He made him pay, fool," said the older man, cracking a Dr Pepper with a hiss. "He made him pay with cash money. You got a choice between putting the guy away and taking his money, I'd take the money every time."

"Both," said the younger man.

"You're dreaming," said the other.

Alma Fenstermacher finally asked for the check. "I wish I could stay all day," she said, as though she meant it. "I miss you. I miss Sherry. You should visit." She saw the look on Nora's face and said, "No, I suppose not. That was unthinking. Has anyone told you that the lot is gone?"

"It's gone?"

"It's sold. Someone finally made an offer that was simply too large to turn aside."

"So Mr. Stoller agreed to sell?"

Alma leaned in and smiled kindly at Nora, the way someone smiles at a child who has been good about putting her napkin on her lap and using her fork. "I will tell you a secret," she said. "Sidney Stoller has been dead for years."

"Are you certain?"

Alma sat back. "Absolutely certain. I'm his daughter." Then she laughed, a throaty laugh. "Oh, Nora, the look on your face." Nora's mind was clicking like a Geiger counter, going over all the assumptions they'd made on the block: Greenwich, finishing school, one of the Seven Sisters colleges, even a debutante ball or at least a big society wedding. And she realized that, unlike the Wellesley woman, whose story had obviously been proffered publicly for her own reasons, Alma had never provided any of it. The decor of her home, the timbre of her voice, the cut of her clothes: all of them had assembled her biography from the way she was in the world.

"Someone is building a home there," Alma continued. "The Landmarks Commission has led them a pretty dance with their plans, and the end result is that they're obliged to build a kind of ersatz Victorian townhouse. I feel a bit sorry for them, actually."

"And what about the people who parked in the lot?"

"Oh, goodness, they'll find someplace else. I have to say, the greatest pleasure of the entire transaction, other than the size of the check involved, was listening to George complain. Although of course I didn't tell him that we were the ones who were selling. The bank sent him a letter about the sale. I didn't feel there was any point in shattering his illusions." Alma Fenstermacher kissed her on both cheeks. "I hope we run into each other again soon," she said to Nora.

"My apartment is right around the corner."

"Well, then," Alma said, shrugging into a navy-blue jacket. "You'll receive an invitation to the Christmas party, as always."

"That will be nice," Nora said, and the way she said it, and the way Alma smiled, told them both that Nora wouldn't go, that she would leave it to her successors, that leaving the block meant leaving the party, and the barbecue, and all the rest. A tiny dead end leading nowhere.

She felt it, felt the weight of all the goodbyes she'd been part of in the last year. "I brought you a farewell gift," Phil, the spurious homeless man, had said on her last day of work at the museum, and he'd handed her a battered Merriam-Webster's dictionary, the red cloth binding frayed and faded to a pinkish color. On the flyleaf was an inscription in beautiful handwriting: *For Arthur Billingham, on the occasion of his graduation, from his fond parents, June 1939.*

"I like reference books," he said. "No surprises in them—know what I mean?"

"I won't even ask where you got this," said Nora, letting the tissuey pages riffle through her fingers.

"Like I keep telling you, a lot of good stuff gets thrown away in this city."

"I'll cherish it," she said.

"I know the big boss wanted to get rid of me. I appreciate that you didn't let her. Maybe the new person will try. Maybe I'll move on. There's a side entrance to the Morgan Library I like."

"You could try the Met."

"Nah, the big showy places are bad," he said. "The cops are always moving you along. And there's a lot of competition. Those Good Humor guys, it's like, you want to buy a strawberry shortcake or you want to give a guy a buck for a sandwich. Most people go with the ice cream, the hot dog. It's hard to blame them. Some of the nice ones buy you food, you know, but I won't eat that stuff. I mean, street dogs? Come on."

"I'll stop by sometime and see you," Nora said.

"Nah," Phil said. "That's not how it works. Maybe sometime you'll see a guy on a corner and you'll think of me, and maybe sometime I'll talk to some lady on the street and I'll think of you. But we'll never see each other again, probably."

Nora laughed. "You're the only one who has been honest about that. The people here, the people on the block where I used to live, everyone says, Oh, we'll get together, we'll have dinner, we'll have coffee."

"Yeah, that seems like what you ought to say. But it doesn't happen, right?"

"I guess people say it because it's too sad to say what you said, that that's that."

Phil shrugged. "New York is a city of the mind," he said. "I'm in yours, you're in mine."

"Who are you, really?" Nora said. "A city of the mind? Come on. Are you doing a book on New York street life and this is all research? Am I going to show up in some college course about interactions between the homeless and the people who give them money?"

"You've never given me money."

Nora reached into her wallet and took out a twenty. "If I do, will you tell me who you really are?"

He grinned. "Nah, I wouldn't take your money. And I'm Phil. You know that. I'm Phil. Enjoy the dictionary. You'll remember me when you use it."

Nora kept it on her desk at work, with a plaster vase Rachel had made in second grade and a paperweight that was Oliver's handprint at age six. She didn't have anything that Charlie had given her; she'd put her wedding band in the bottom drawer of her jewelry box months ago, when she noticed that Charlie had stopped wearing his. That was the day she and Charlie had met to sign some papers and had started to talk and all of it had come pouring out, his feeling that he'd always been her second choice, that he'd taken the wrong turn in his work, that his life somehow felt like a rented house whose rooms were half empty. She thought back to that weekend in Asheville. "New York isn't the real world," he'd said. Someday soon he'd decide to move south, work as a financial adviser for some wealthy clients, play a lot of golf. They'd known people who'd done the same, and Nora had always discussed it with contempt, but Charlie had always just kept quiet, and she knew now that he had been thinking her contempt was not only for that life but for the life he wanted, the life he thought would make him happy, for him. He would marry the nurse and take her away from the daily grind. Nora would have to remind Rachel to be nice.

Everyone would move on in ways that would make it seem as though their lives were much the same, perhaps even better. Ricky and Nita had their restaurant in the Dominican Republic, George a new crop of residents to insinuate himself with and then to annoy. Before long everyone on the block would forget that anyone but Joe had ever snaked out their back drains or washed their windows. Even the story of how Jack Fisk had lit into someone with a golf club, sensational as it was, would begin to dim. Sherry, Linda, Oliver, Rachel, Charlie, Nora: they would all just go on, with resilience or denial or just the right combination of both. People go through life thinking they're making decisions, when they're really just making plans, which is not the same thing at all. And along the way, they get a little damaged, lots of tiny cracks, holding together but damaged still. Ricky would walk with a limp for the rest of his life. "Hell, I'd use a damn cane if there was enough money in it," the man in front of the bodega had said. Nora wondered if that's how Ricky felt.

Sometimes she would think of an alternate reality in which Charlie had worked for Legal Aid and she had gone to social-work school and their children had gone to public school and they'd had to turn the dining room into a bedroom because they'd only been able to afford to rent a smallish place. Would that have been so bad? Would that have been so good? The alternate reality she couldn't allow herself was the one in which she never went to The Tattooed Lady, never met Charlie Nolan and married him, although she knew that there were alternate realities without him that might suit the Nora she was today better. But once there were children, you couldn't zig where you had zagged. It was nothing but a parlor game, once you had children.

Sometimes Nora wondered, too, about that alternate universe in which Jack Fisk didn't need to get his car out that particular morning, in which Ricky went about his business as usual, Sherry Fisk didn't move, the Nolans stayed married, no one got a windfall and moved to the Dominican Republic. It was a little like watching a version of *It's a Wonderful Life* starring herself. But it also assumed that everything else remained in stasis. Was that what her life had consisted of, a game of statues in the center of a city that changed in ways big and small every single day, even Sundays and holidays, even Shavuot and Ascension Thursday?

Landed on her feet: that's what everyone would say of Nora. "Still young," her friends whispered, which meant still young enough to marry again. Running the foundation, furnishing her new place, starting fresh, except for Richard. He had followed her from the museum, gone from temporary to permanent. "That's more my speed," he'd said when she described the foundation, and it was. When they received applications for grants, he divided them into two piles: sketchy and not sketchy. Sometimes she took him on visits with her. She had rented office space on 125th Street, a part of the city she never knew before but which was growing more desirable every day, as every place seemed to have done. The areas of New York that were once shorthand for danger were changing one by one, until she heard her children's friends talk about renting in places she would never have dared to walk, places in which, if she had gotten off the subway accidentally, she would not have left the station. "You're saving me a ton of money in rent," Bob Harris had said, "but be careful. Even poor people figure you get what you pay for."

"In ten years there won't be any poor people in that neighborhood, trust me," Nora said. "I don't know if there will be any anywhere in the city."

"The Bible says they're always with us," Bob said.

"Yeah, pushed into places we don't want to live."

"Now, don't you go getting jaded on me," he said. "You were right for this job because you weren't, not a bit."

Nora's walk in the morning was different now, north instead of south, east instead of west. When she went downtown to visit another foundation, or to look at a charter school, she encountered new pieces of her past, her former self, her ancient history. The tired white-brick office building where she had once interviewed with a Princeton alum who had apparently been unimpressed; she had been rejected. The school where she had once been considered for a position as director of development; they had hired instead a very slick young man who later was indicted for writing checks for warm-weather vacations and bespoke suits. A restaurant where she and her sister had once had lunch and Christine had spelled out the plans for her new business; a Christmas party at another restaurant when she was pregnant with the twins and had thrown up shrimp puffs in a dark restroom that had an unpleasant smell. The beautiful building on Fifth Avenue, its paneled lobby seen only as a glossy sliver from the street, where she had spent a weekend with a college classmate who had briefly been a friend. Every time she passed it, two thoughts crossed her mind. She wondered how Missy was, and she recalled how, entering Missy's parents' duplex from an elevator that opened directly into it, she had seen the living room with its pale-yellow sofas and apple-green drapes, Central Park a decorative accent through the enormous windows, and thought, This is what it is like to live in New York. She'd laughed once, recalling it to Christine as they split a bottle of rosé in the living room, how she had thought life in the city would be so grand when it ended up quite different from how the Landis family had lived. But Christine had raised one brow and said, "If that's an invite to a pity party, I'm not going."

Phil was right: New York was a city of the mind. It was a ghost city, and one of the ghosts was Nora Nolan, young, not so young, single, pregnant, mother, married, not. Somewhere there was the apartment where she and Charlie began, the hospital room in which the twins were born, the office where she and Charlie had met with the mediator. Somewhere there was the goose woman, the juggler, the men playing dominoes, the cooler of Dr Pepper, the aluminum house, George walking his pugs past the place where there had once been a parking lot. New York City was all the strata of the earth. The old was covered over but it never disappeared. Somewhere in the bake shop (gluten-free) was a flyer for the old pizza parlor, and the shoe repair place that was there before that, and the kosher deli, and so on and so forth, down to the rocky remainders of the creek that once flowed through midtown before there was a midtown, before there was an America, that lay now beneath concrete and tar and earth. The price so many of them had paid for prosperity was amnesia. They'd forgotten where they'd come from, how they'd started out. They'd forgotten what the city really was, and how small a part of it they truly were.

Reinvention, newness was all, all built on the sturdy back of what was past. Somewhere a metal shard hammered by a Dutch worker centuries before oxidized in the ground beneath layers of street and road. And above it all the great city now, today, glittery new, just made, a monumental illusion.

Nora turned at the corner toward her office, her face raised to a glimmer of light between buildings. "You have a blessed day," said the man handing out free papers on the corner.

"You, too," she said.

ALTERNATE SIDE

ANNA QUINDLEN

A Reader's Guide

QUESTIONS AND TOPICS FOR DISCUSSION

1. *Alternate Side* begins with the epigraph "The secret of a happy marriage remains a secret."—Henny Youngman. Do you agree with this statement? Do you think Nora would agree with Youngman? Did the meaning of the epigraph change for you after you finished the book?

2. Among all the marriages in *Alternate Side,* do any of Nora's friends who live on her block have good ones? What do you think Nora would define as a good marriage?

3. New York City plays a very important role in *Alternate Side*—to Nora, the city is a large part of her identity, and it influences her marriage. Is there any place that has had a similarly strong effect on your life?

4. "It was crazy, but there was a small, secret part of Nora that was comfortable with trash on the street. It reminded her of her youth, when she'd first arrived in a nastier, scarier, dirtier New York City and moved into a shabby apartment with her best friend, Jenny. A better New York, she sometimes thought to herself now, but never, ever said, one of the many things none of them ever admitted to themselves, at least aloud: that it was better when it was worse." Do you agree or disagree that things are sometimes better when they are worse? Has this ever been true in your life?

5. Decades after they've broken up, Nora is still affected by her relationship with her college boyfriend James. Why do you think he is so

important to her? What is it about the relationships from our youth that make them have a lasting impact on our lives?

6. Although this is a novel about marriage, perhaps the most important relationships in Nora's life are those she has with women. Discuss Nora's relationship with the women in the novel—Rachel, Charity, Jenny, Bebe, and the women on her block.

7. The assault on Ricky is the catalyst for the change that happens in the lives of the residents who live on Nora's block. Discuss Nora, Charlie, and the other residents' reactions to the incident, and how it changed their lives. Did anything about the way they behave surprise you?

8. Race and class are important factors in the characters' reactions to Ricky's assault. Do you think the block's residents would have behaved differently in the aftermath if the person Jack Fisk hurt had been one of them instead?

9. After the incident, Charlie and Nora have different opinions of what happened. Charlie says, "I know what I saw, Nora. Just because you have a different version doesn't mean you're right," and Nora responds, "It's not a different version. It's the truth." Discuss the relationship between truth and perception in the aftermath of a traumatic incident.

10. About marriage, Quindlen writes: "In the beginning they all spent so much time trying to know the other person, asking questions, telling stories, wanting to burrow beneath the skin. But then you married and naturally were supposed to know one another down to the ground, and so stopped asking, answering, listening. It seemed foolish, fifteen years in, to lean across the breakfast table and say, By the way, are you happy? Do you like this life?" Discuss the influence of time on relationships, including romantic relationships, friendships, and relationships between family members.

ANNA QUINDLEN is a novelist and journalist whose work has appeared on fiction, nonfiction, and self-help bestseller lists. She is the author of nine novels: *Object Lessons, One True Thing, Black and Blue, Blessings, Rise and Shine, Every Last One, Still Life with Bread Crumbs, Miller's Valley,* and *Alternate Side.* Her memoir *Lots of Candles, Plenty of Cake,* published in 2012, was a number one *New York Times* bestseller. Her book *A Short Guide to a Happy Life* has sold more than a million copies. While a columnist at *The New York Times* she won the Pulitzer Prize and published two collections, *Living Out Loud* and *Thinking Out Loud.* Her *Newsweek* columns were collected in *Loud and Clear.*

AnnaQuindlen.net

Facebook.com/AnnaQuindlen